GAME OF LIES

#2 MESSENGER CHRONICLES

PIPPA DACOSTA

'Game of Lies'

2# Messenger Chronicles

Pippa DaCosta

Urban Fantasy & Science Fiction Author

Subscribe to Pippa's mailing list at pippadacosta.com & get free ebooks.

Copyright © 2018 Pippa DaCosta.

May 2018. US Edition. All rights reserved.

Edited in US English.

Version 1.

www.pippadacosta.com

CHAPTER 1

Huge moons there wax and wane
Again - again - again
Every moment of the night
Forever changing places
And they put out the star-light
With the breath from their pale faces.

— FAIRY-LAND, EDGAR ALLEN POE,
OLD EARTHEN

The fae have a saying: "Rain is the tears of the fallen"—those taken too soon by the Hunt. I used to stand in the rain, letting it soak me through, cool rivulets washing blood into pools at my feet until all the warmth had faded from my bones. Killing was easier when I felt nothing.

Now, crouched behind an abandoned home container, wet and cold, all I wanted was for the rain to let up so I could hear any Faerie soldiers attempting to outflank me.

It hadn't rained on Adelane, a moon colony, for as long as living memory served. But when the fae had returned to Halow just a month ago, they'd brought their storms with them. In the past, they had called their visits *cleansing*. A thousand years later, I suspected they no longer bother prettying it up. Rain washed the blood from their path, and that was all they cared about. What kind of self-respecting fae wanted worthless human blood on their boots?

"Where are you?" Kellee whispered through the small comms unit behind my ear.

"Right where I'm supposed to be, Marshal," I whispered back. He didn't like letting me out of my cage. Kellee thrived on control. Knowing his past as the fae's toy soldier, I couldn't blame him for needing control in his life, and I'd turned out to be uncontrollable—and also his enemy. That level of betrayal would make anyone anxious.

I scanned the abandoned street. Rainwater *had* cleaned the streets of blood. Crumbling walls and cracked roads shone, waiting for the population to return. But life would not return to Adelane. At least, not human life.

"Is the area clear?" I whispered, eyeing the blackness of vacant container windows. Hissing rain muffled all sound apart from the steady beat of my heart.

"All clear. We're ready."

I removed a crude transmitter device from my coat pocket. Kellee had only given me a few scraps of tek to work with. He didn't want me making something that could kill him in his sleep. We had trust issues.

I ran my thumb over the button and paused, holding my breath.

Three, two, one...

I pressed down. A flash of orange light washed through the sky, illuminating the hulking mass of a fae warcruiser hunched over Adelane's capital. For a second, the fae ship's illuminated beauty blinded me. Pearlescent colors rippled across its organic surface, and then the shockwave barreled down the streets, blasting everything in its path. I threw myself into the container and tucked my legs in. The roar thundered and the air turned hot, scorching the side of my face, and then it was gone, just as quickly as it had come. Debris clanged against the street, and fire crackled. I stole a glance. The raging fire engulfed the dark, and the warcruiser banked toward it.

I dashed from my hiding place. "Go, go, go!"

Kellee would have heard and seen the explosion and had probably already mobilized the refugee ships into action while the warcruiser was distracted.

With my coat casting an obscure-glamor as I ran, I splashed through puddles and vaulted over mangled wreckage. I ran so hard my boots beat like a drum. If Kellee had given me more tools, I could have created a transmitter with a longer range, but no, he had to be an asshole and keep my toys from me. At least he had returned my coat, although only after Talen had pointed out the chances of my running a few miles through fae-infested territory without being seen were remote.

Head down, I veered around abandoned vehicles and skidded into a narrow street. Tall container homes lined one side. On the other, a fifty-foot drop into a basin. The view had been spectacular, but now that view held the mass of a warcruiser thundering closer.

They believed they'd beaten the population of this little moon. The warcruiser was here to *cleanse* the area for fae habitation. The explosion shouldn't have happened. Was it an accident or sabotage? They were obligated to investigate.

I threw my shoulder against a container door and stumbled inside. Someone's abandoned living room spread before me. Trinkets had been left behind. Clothes lay discarded in the hurry to evacuate. I'd had a container just like it and the normal life to go with it. It had been a lie, but I'd liked it.

At the window, I ducked behind the wall and hit the button in my pocket a second time. Another blast rocked the abandoned city. The air, the ground, my bones—all trembled. I had to give it to Kellee: he knew how to make a bomb, even if he needed my tek to trigger it.

The cacophony rolled on. Kellee's voice crackled in my ear, but the external noise drowned it out. Hopefully, I'd distracted the fae enough for Kellee to get the refugees out of orbit and safely away from the warcruiser.

The massive ship rumbled over my position. Its engines vacuumed up air, creating a maelstrom beneath it. It growled like a world-ending beast would growl, so loud the air bent around it. Containers buckled beneath its onslaught. I clamped my hands over my ears, but it made no difference. The deafening noise shuddered inside my chest.

Something snagged my shoulder, yanking me off balance. I rocked and turned to face a fae scout.

She was a little thing, not much taller than me, but her size wouldn't lessen the impact of the crossbow aimed between my eyes.

Over the noise, I hadn't heard her approach or seen her nock the arrow that had skimmed my arm.

Shapely fae eyes widened in sudden recognition. She hadn't known who I was when she shot me, but she did now.

Her lips moved. I didn't hear her speak, but I recognized the shape of the word her mouth formed: *Wraithmaker*. She lowered her bow, mouthed a second name —*Oberon*—and thrust out her hand for me to take.

Few knew me on sight, and even fewer knew I belonged to Oberon. But she *knew* me. The real me. Not Kesh Lasota. Not the ghost-girl I'd created to live as a messenger and not the saru gladiator who had killed the fae queen. She held out her hand because Oberon—our king—had sent her, not to kill me, but to save me.

She beckoned with a wave and turned away, expecting me to follow.

This was my chance to escape Kellee's cage and finally go home, back to Faerie, where my king was waiting to reward me. My blackened heart fluttered. *I'm going home.*

I plucked the comms unit free, dropped it in the debris of a stranger's life, and raced after the fae.

The scout ran ahead, flitting easily between abandoned containers and around fallen hover vehicles. Rain hammered the ground, lending the walls and streets a shimmer, lit by the colored light reflected off the fae ship above.

I'm really going home.

An unmistakably male figure emerged from the shadows, abruptly blocking the scout's path. As the light caught him, silvery hair whipped around his face, and his violet eyes shone like the deep purple of Faerie's night skies. *Talen.*

His instructions had been to wait by a shuttle outside

the city. Realization dawned, accompanied by a sinking sense of inevitability. He had followed me.

"You should not be here," the scout told him, more right than she realized. Now that I could hear her clearly, her accent held the unwavering confidence of all Faerie born. "All flights were cleared from these streets hours ago."

Talen spared her a disinterested glance. When his attention slid to me, his eyes darkened with the sting of betrayal. His lips pressed into a tight, disapproving line.

I'm running for your own good! The sooner I was away from him and Kellee, the safer they would be. Why could they not see this?

A distant explosion rumbled. Loose gravel skipped around us on the road.

"Come, Wraithmaker," the scout urged, skirting Talen.

He looked down his nose at her. "Kesh will not be leaving with you." His tone left no room for negotiation. It was a fact. Kellee had told me Talen wasn't a fighter, but I had my doubts.

"Talen..." I started but trailed off. What could I say that I hadn't already?

The scout blinked at him and then at me as though she couldn't imagine how we knew each other, and then she laughed. The tinkling laughter sounded cruel and surreal in the war-torn streets. "I do not know whose *flight* you belong to, *Talen*, or who this *Kesh* is, but I do know this saru is none of your concern. My orders come directly from our king, Lord of Faerie, Oberon." She waited for Talen to react to the name, but it washed off him as easily as his dark attire snubbed light.

I inched my way toward the scout, my stare locked

with Talen's. "This must happen. I'm not going back to Kellee's cage. You of all people understand that."

The scout lifted her crossbow and lined up the sights on Talen. "There's no time for this." Her finger twitched, and for a single, terrible second, I saw a world without Talen in it. The curious fae who read antique human books, who had shared his magic with me, who had bowed before me as no fae ever should. He was *mine*.

I shot out a hand. "No—"

She fired. The bolt sprang free and carved through the air. My whip was suddenly in my hand, metal links lashing. I struck the bolt from its flight, but in those precious seconds, she fired again and again. A stab of pain hit me in the chest. I ignored it. Talen doubled over. His sweet lily-scented magic flooded the air and coated my tongue, and a fierce alien strength surged through my saru veins, setting my senses ablaze. The whip snapped in the air and coiled around the scout's neck. Choked, she dropped to her knees, clawing at the metal links digging and burning into her skin.

I reeled her in, pulled the loop around her neck tighter, and towered over her. Tears leaked from her beautiful eyes, and in their depths, she begged me to free her.

She would tell Oberon about this. This scout had done nothing wrong. She was following orders to bring me in. But my king couldn't hear of Talen's interference. He would take Talen from me. Take Kellee from me.

A dull ache thudded in my side, and more magic spritzed the air, more of Talen's strength pouring into me. It wouldn't take much to break her neck. Little more than a twitch. They had always been stronger, better, faster, but now, as I peered into the scout's eyes, I was in control. I

7

was stronger, faster. But better? No, a saru girl couldn't be better. Could she?

"Kesh..." Talen hissed, and I couldn't tell if he was pleading with me to stop or urging me on.

If I killed her, I would have to live with another death tangled with my spirit, and I wasn't sure my battered saru soul could survive it. I'd killed countless of my kind before, but only one fae—the Faerie Queen.

The scout slowly closed her eyes.

Oberon would know of this. My king was no fool. He would see a pattern. Kellee and Talen would be exposed. The fae and the vakaru. *Kill her and he doesn't have to know.* I'd already disobeyed my king by not crushing Eledan's heart. My orders had been to *kill* his brother. I'd gone against those orders to free the Calico refugees. One indiscretion I could manage. But two? I would lose Oberon's love, a love I'd worked my entire life to gain. My master's love.

He couldn't know.

Another thunderous boom shook the air.

Talen's strength filled me, surging through human muscle and enticing my senses. I loosened the whip, cupped the scout's face in my hands, and jerked her head to the side. Muscle and bone cracked, breaking her spine. The scout collapsed at my feet.

Rain pattered against her motionless body. It was done, and the coldness I'd carried inside for so long hardened to stone.

Accusations burned in Talen's eyes but not surprise. He knew who I was. No more lies. The urge to yell at him, to blame him, bubbled up inside, until I saw how he clutched the bolt's feathered edges sticking out of his chest. Blood streamed down the back of his hand. I touched my chest where the ghost of his wound throbbed, but there was nothing wrong with me. The pain throbbing deep in my chest—it was his. It had somehow transferred to me.

"You shouldn't be here," I said, echoing the dead scout's words. If he hadn't come, if he hadn't tried to stop me, she would be alive and I'd be on the fae ship, on my way home. Her death was *his* fault.

He swallowed with an audible click and stared back, defiant, stubborn, hurt—saying everything without saying a single word.

And I couldn't leave him bleeding out on a battle-torn moon.

I gripped his arm, and we hurried out of the streets, toward the unlit areas beyond the city. By the time we reached the shuttle concealed in a small rocky valley, we were soaked through and bloody. Inside the shuttle, Talen gingerly eased himself into the pilot's chair and fired up the engines.

"Are you up to this?" I asked, eyeing the bolt still wedged in place, oozing blood.

"There is no time. Once we're spacebound, I'll deal with it..." He winced.

I felt that pain as a second heated heartbeat throbbing in my chest. The fae healed fast. He would be fine, even if all the color had drained from his face and his hands trembled over the controls. He *would* be fine.

"You fool," I scolded. "You should have let me go."

If my words hurt him, he masked it behind a hard glare.

The shuttle lifted over the rocky cover. Sharp edges fell away, revealing a broken city in the distance and a flash of green light. The light rushed in, filling the screen and scorching my eyes as it blasted over the top of the shuttle. The warcruiser loomed, turning our way. An array of alarms and warning lights blasted across Talen's controls. The cruiser had us in its crosshairs.

CHAPTER 2

*T*alen banked the shuttle hard. As we turned, the monstrous warcruiser angled its nose after us. It was like watching something the size of a mountain notice us and realizing how pathetically tiny we were. Our entire plan to get the people off Adelane relied on stealth. I could only hope Kellee had already escaped.

My thoughts raced along. Our little shuttle may be able to outrun them in the next few seconds, but once the cruiser locked on, it could shoot us out of the sky from halfway around the moon. We wouldn't make this.

Another flash of green light sailed past. Warning shots in case we hadn't noticed the warcruiser squatting over a city.

"This is bad," I mumbled. Talen remained silent. "Can I do anything?" My piloting skills were limited, at best.

He worked the controls, hands deftly piloting us upward. "Hold on."

I gripped the chair arms and peered at the fae ship

filling the screen. It resembled a backward-facing claw, its back curved and edges sharp, but it wasn't a machine. The warcruisers were all living, thinking, breathing spacefaring animals bred for war.

Talen fired the shuttle's boosters, lurching us *toward* it. I fell back into the chair. The shuttle trembled, engines groaning.

Talen had a plan. He had to have a plan. We weren't giving up, were we? I glanced at his face, thrown into profile by the shuttle's glowing control panels. The firm set of his jaw and the steely look in his eyes suggested we weren't handing ourselves over. So, what in the three systems *were* we doing heading toward the planet-destroying warship?

"Trust me," he said, sensing my unease.

Trust him. A fae who had spent the last few hundred years behind bars because he was so dangerous. A fae who could turn an entire prison's staff against one another. A fae who could control human emotions with a single touch. A fae I was impossibly bonded with.

I faced ahead.

Green flares launched our way. Talen's hands swept over the controls, and our shuttle lurched upward, driving my guts down to my knees. Gravity tried to yank my consciousness through the floor, and then the shuttle leveled out, shoving my guts through my ribs and fooling me into thinking it was over. We dropped—dropped like a meteor out of the sky—and spiraled toward the ground. The world spun. Alarms barked and shrieked. The shuttle leveled out, and Talen sent us on a mind-warping spiral, weaving through empty city streets and container stacks. I squeezed my eyes shut and tried to keep my insides from finding their way to my outsides. A blast jerked the shuttle out of its rollercoaster ride and sparked something ablaze behind me. I smelled hot metal and burning plastic. Looking was impossible. Gravity was a boulder sitting on my chest. And then we stopped. My head spun, and sickness wet my mouth.

The shuttle ticked and hissed, metal cooling and contracting. I considered moving but thought better of it when a thumping headache tried to punch through my skull.

Talen's sigh of relief told me we'd survived. "We're safe —for now."

I blinked, trying to make sense of the landscape beyond the screen. We were sitting on a shiny, rippling surface, like the surface of an ocean but made of scales lapped over one another. Up was down and down was up. I tilted my head. The city I'd blasted to pieces hung *above* us.

"We're beneath the warcruiser," I muttered, completing the picture.

"Hiding among the cruiser's lower ailerons," Talen said from behind. He'd unlatched himself and was busy somewhere in the cabin behind me. *We're stuck to a warcruiser like a parasite on a whale.*

I leaned closer to the screen. "We're upside down?"

"The warship has us in its gravitational hold. It can be a little disconcerting."

A little?! My gut rolled. I quickly straightened.

"We'll ride them out of orbit and break off when she leaves the moon's atmosphere," he calmly added like all this was a day trip to a moon and back. "They won't see us among the ice she sheds."

We're upside down and stuck to a fae warcruiser. I am saru, and definitely not grown for this. The sickness rolled around my stomach. "Won't they wonder where we've gone?"

"For a little while. Which is why we have to stay here until they move off."

I turned the chair to face the rear of the cabin. Talen braced an arm against a side panel, his head bowed, silvery hair curtained in front of his face. "And that could be...?"

"A few hours?" His whisper lifted at the end, forming a question.

The fae offered answers as questions when they didn't *know*. Like all fae, he couldn't lie, for fear the Hunt would stalk him down, so a question was his next best option. A few hours stuck to a warcruiser, I could handle, but a few days?

Unlatching my belts, I eased from the flight chair on wobbly legs and headed into the rear section of the shuttle to dig out a med-kit.

The limited kit I found consisted of bandages, staunch pads, some tweezers, and a whole bunch of useless shit. I pulled down a stowed-away bunk and looked up to find Talen loitering in the cabin doorway, skin ashen. If we didn't remove that bolt, he wouldn't be standing much longer.

I patted the bunk. "Lie down. I've got this." I'd patched myself up enough times during my early arena battles. Nobody cared if the saru lived or died after the entertainment was over. In later battles, I'd learned how not to get hit.

14

Talen hesitated. "I can administer my own care," he said stiffly.

I arched an eyebrow and frowned at the big, strong fae who was afraid of a little saru female. "I'm an assassin, not a butcher."

I *had* just killed a fae scout right in front of him. What would he think had he seen me cut out Eledan's heart? Maybe I *was* a butcher. Hadn't I done worse to entertain them in the arena? Hadn't I carved up my own people to the sounds of their cheering?

Talen eased himself onto the edge of the bunk. I wiped a med-cloth over my hands, his gaze studying my every move. All the unspoken questions sizzled between us. Talen had a knack for making art out of long silences. This one was heavy with a dose of judgment, but it also tingled with anticipation. He could pretend all he liked, but he was fae, and there was little the fae liked more than a bloody victory. He had stopped me from leaving. It must have felt good. A few hundred years must have passed since he'd won a fight, even a small one.

"Unbuckle your jacket," I told him.

He focused on flicking open the four buckles on his jacket. Blood and dirt dashed his cheek. His silvery hair had a few bloodstained knots. All fae were naturally perfect, but Talen wasn't like all fae. Something about him was different in a way I couldn't figure out. It was the little things like his loud silences and his sharp, penetrating glances. Kellee had a beast inside him. Was there something lurking inside Talen too?

He pushed the jacket open and looked up, catching me staring.

"You're not alone anymore," I said. It was a foolish

thing to say, and the flicker of pain that crossed his face confirmed it. He had been alone for a very long time, and I *had* been about to abandon him on a human moon.

I grabbed the bolt and yanked it out before he could complain. Pain sparked across my chest—an echo of the trauma he rode out with his teeth gritted and eyes alight.

Working efficiently, I dumped the bloody bolt inside the med-kit, slipped my hands inside his jacket, and slid the garment off, over his broad shoulders.

"Kellee said you might defect during this mission." His words brushed my neck. Shudders tried to track their way down my spine. Good or bad shivers, I wasn't sure—maybe both, but I didn't dwell on it.

Kellee had been right. Again. The marshal was too clever for his own good.

Talen's hair tickled my cheek as I straightened, and the lingering scent of his magic made the part of me engineered to love the fae want to lick him all over. Made me want a whole lot of other things too.

I untied his shirt's fasteners and shoved that back the same way I had his jacket, up and over his shoulders, but this time, I deliberately brushed my hands over the smooth warmth of his skin. I was stealing a touch, something saru should never do, but damn if he didn't feel good. His cool breath brushed my cheek near my ear. He had turned his head. If I turned mine, we'd be close, so close.

I told myself the tightening way down low, that familiar coiling of need, was normal. The fae had designed all humans to love and admire them, had hardwired it into our DNA. With some engineered humans—such as the namu—the fae had crafted them to excel at song and dance and the art of lovemaking. Others, like the vakaru, they had designed to thrive in combat situations (and then they'd killed them all when that didn't work out too well). And the saru, they'd designed them to serve. The humans planted on Earth in Sol and left for so long they built tek armies that rivaled the fae's—I wasn't sure what their purpose was. But I knew Talen felt good because my engineered brain didn't have a choice.

Backing away, I grabbed a cloth and brought it up to the wound in his chest. And froze. Two things tripped my mind. One, the puckered wound had already stitched itself closed. It would be healed in minutes. And two, circular ink patterns marked Talen's skin. But these weren't the same thorned warfae markings I wore. His were tribal, made of sweeping arcs and concentric circles. They undulated with his abdominal muscles and stretched over his left pectoral, reaching upward toward his shoulder.

I lifted my hand, wanting to touch them, to trace their delicate outlines and discover where they might take me.

Magic, and warmth, tingled at my fingertips, urging me on. He radiated the kind of comforting heat I wanted to wrap myself in. His chest moved with every measured breath. I wanted to run my hands across his skin and soak him up, wanted to breathe the scent of his magic deep into my body, take all of him inside.

Talen's hand clamped around my wrist, breaking off the fantasy, and held me back or kept me from pulling away. He looked up, pupils wide with shock or indignation or something else I didn't understand, and then my past was crowding the little shuttle with us.

I was saru.

Old laws beat their way back into my thoughts. I was

17

not to touch the fae without their explicit permission. That was why Talen was wide-eyed. Shame poured in. Desire cooled. That little girl inside me wanted to curl inward.

I yanked my hand from his grip before he could chastise me and roughly swept the drying blood from his chest. Just a few scratches remained.

"Do you even need fixing?" I dumped the cloth aside, gritting my teeth at the bitterness in my voice.

"No, I'll be fine in a few moments."

"Good for you." Turning away, I drifted to the front of the shuttle and sank into the flight chair. Outside, the warcruiser landscape gently swelled and relaxed as though the beast was breathing. If I unfocused, I could pretend I was back on Faerie, watching the ocean swell. Although, I had never been this close to its waters. Such things were forbidden to saru. Much like Talen. My thoughts drifted back to his markings.

The light sweeps and stroking circles were unique. I had never seen anything like them before. They weren't rewards for killing. So, what were they for?

I knew so little about him. Kellee had found him scavenging ships in the debris zone on Halow's outer fringes. Beyond that, I didn't know what house he was from, what family line, whether he was courtly or humble. I had assumed he was a winterlands fae from the silvery hair, but he didn't have their quick-to-anger personality—not that I had seen so far. He was a mystery. One I kept falling into.

It didn't matter.

I didn't plan on staying with Talen and Kellee long enough for any of this to mean anything.

I watched pearlescent colors drift across the warcruiser's underbelly. The fae were so close, but I couldn't reach out without risking Talen's discovery. Oberon would not treat him kindly, and Kellee... Oberon would kill him without a second thought.

There would be other opportunities to slip away. Other missions Kellee would send me on. Other times I could protect them by leaving.

"He knows you love Oberon," Talen said, easing into the pilot's seat beside me. He had thrown his jacket back on, leaving it gaping open. "That's how he knew you would run."

I assumed we were talking about Kellee knowing everything.

"He thinks he knows me," I muttered, keeping my gaze glued ahead.

"But he doesn't understand you."

I looked up and found Talen gazing out of the window, trying *not* to see me. "And you do?"

"I understand how saru love their masters. It's perfectly normal." Still not looking at me.

Perfectly normal? Anger throbbed inside me like the beat of his now healed wound. "Did your household have saru?"

"Of course."

"What was yours called?" I asked.

He shrugged one shoulder in a very human gesture of indifference. "Over the years, I owned many."

"But there's always one. One or two special ones. Tell me about her."

His lips twitched around a thin smile. "It does not matter."

"Because saru don't matter?"

"No." His parody of a smile died. It hadn't been a smile at all, but a grimace. He turned his head and fixed me in his intense gaze. "Because she died, and I would prefer not to remember how."

His direct glare warned me to back off. I might have, once.

"You killed her," I said.

His jaw locked. He turned his head away.

The silence became a blank canvas for all the things waiting to be said.

I was probably right. I wondered if he had touched her and toyed with her emotions before she died, his poor saru girl. It would have been the fae thing to do. What was the life of one saru slave? Certainly worth a few moments of grand entertainment. And when one died, there were plenty more where that one came from. Was that why he had knelt to me? As recompense for murdering his slave? For all I knew, he might be a thousand years old. There could be a million and one reasons why Talen did anything. I could pretend I understood the fae, but I only knew what they'd shown me in my short life. The life of a saru, the life of a gladiator, and the life of an assassin. Those lives had taught me how to survive the fae, not how to live with them or get to know them and certainly not how to become friends with one like Talen.

I stared at the warcruiser's belly outside and fell into silence alongside him.

I was Oberon's slave. Kellee was right: I loved my prince—the king—but in my five years on Calicto, I had come to appreciate a small taste of freedom. A freedom Kellee and Talen enjoyed. I didn't have it or want it. But I could. Wasn't that what Kellee had been trying to show me?

Talen looked over after what felt like hours of simmering silence. "You're not alone anymore," he said.

I didn't reply. Didn't look. Didn't acknowledge his words. Not being alone was exactly what I was afraid of.

CHAPTER 3

*O*ur shuttle rode the warcruiser out of orbit a few hours later. Enormous pressure washed over our little vessel, bathing us in flame until the cruiser broke free of the atmosphere and plunged into the still blackness of space. We detached, falling away among the chunks of ice the warcruiser sloughed off. The beast of a ship drifted onward, disappearing against the black.

"Where did you learn to pilot like that?" I asked Talen once we were safely en route back to the prison.

"Faerie," he replied curtly, cutting off any opportunity for more questions.

Kellee greeted us at the prison dock, arms crossed, one dark eyebrow raised in judgment. He wore scuffed boots, faded pants, and a three-quarter length battered old coat. It all looked as though it had been left out in the summerlands too long. He still had the pretty-boy look that had caught my eye in the sinks, but the past few weeks had hardened it.

"I was about to launch a search party." He eyed the

silent Talen as the fae strode past him, jacket open, his bloody bare chest and markings on display. I watched the lawman for any sign of surprise and found none. Kellee then settled that disapproving stare on me as though I were to blame for Talen's frosty mood. Technically I was, but I wasn't telling him that.

I shrugged. He could see and smell the blood on us both. It didn't take a genius to figure out something had gone wrong. But we were back. Alive. Mostly unharmed. If Talen wanted to tell Kellee that I'd tried to run and that I'd killed a fae scout, that was up to him. I decided I did not need another dose of Kellee's disapproval on what was turning out to be a shitty day.

"That good, huh?" he remarked, falling into step behind me.

"Did you get the people off Adelane?"

"Safe and sound."

A warm glow thawed some of the cold inside me. A curious feeling. Saving people didn't make me good, not by a long shot, but it lightened the invisible weight I carried on my back. The weight of hundreds of lives I'd cut short.

Back in the central chamber where the glass and tek cage sat, I peeled off my coat and draped it over the couch. Talen wasn't anywhere in sight. He never hung around for this part.

The cage door hung open exactly the way I had left it.

Kellee stood on the fringes of my vision. The first time he had let me out, I'd tried to escape within hours, but there weren't many places I could hide from a vakaru on a prison rock. Acute senses meant Kellee could damn near track me anywhere. For that indiscretion, he had withheld the drug that kept the dreams at bay, plunging me back into the Dreamweaver's madness for two days. Bastard. After that, I didn't try to run again. And when he took me on a mission to help a group of refugees flee a stranded ship, I'd discovered it felt good to help people instead of hunting them down and killing them for praise.

I understood why the cage was necessary. I'd lied to him about everything. I was his enemy. I was the Faerie King's killer. I would cage me too—assuming I'd let me live.

"Are we going to have a problem?" he asked. I had dallied outside the cage too long.

"You know what a problem is, Kellee?" I planted a hand on my hip and faced him, mirroring his hard-ass stance. "A problem is running out of water, or losing a shuttle booster, or maybe getting shot... You know what a problem isn't?"

His eyebrow twitched, tugging the corner of his lips into a smirk. "You're clearly going to tell me."

"Locking someone up who has helped you save hundreds of people." I threw a gesture at the cage. "I could have abandoned you today."

He hid his surprise behind a soft laugh. "Why didn't you?"

"Talen got himself shot. And I..." I waved the rest of the story at him. I hadn't planned on telling him, and there it was, out there within minutes. He was a good listener. Too good. "I couldn't exactly leave him there."

Kellee's eyebrow arched higher. "You could have. A single shot wouldn't have killed him."

I realized that now. For all I knew, Talen had deliberately gotten himself shot to keep me from leaving. Come to think of it, he could have dodged that bolt.

25

Had that slippery fae plucked on my feelings for him? He was more than capable. But I wasn't sure it had all been fake. I'd seen the hurt on his face and felt it like my own. Maybe it had been my own? The bond meant we shared things. Things I didn't understand.

I didn't know what to think. Had Talen manipulated me? Did it matter, when I'd spent weeks doing the same to him?

Kellee snorted a laugh and shook his head. A stray curl escaped his ponytail and fell against his cheek. He swept it back. "I keep telling you to be careful around him. He's got you figured out, Kesh."

"Laugh it up, Marshal," I growled.

He reached for the door and held it open. "Get in the cage, Kesh." When he saw I wasn't moving, he added, "We're making progress. Don't undo everything you've worked for these last few weeks."

"I won't leave you." I'd killed a fae today for several reasons, and one of those reasons had been to keep Talen and Kellee safe from Oberon. I wouldn't hesitate to do the same again. I would leave them, but only when they were safe.

He flinched and lifted his chin. When he spoke, his voice was calm and controlled. Its measured tone was my last warning. "I would love to believe you, but you made sure I can't. So, get in the cage, Wraithmaker."

I marched into the cage and stopped dead center. The door rattled closed behind me. Kellee drove the lock over. It hurt. I deserved it, but that lock turning twisted inside me too.

I turned my head and saw him by the door, peering through the glass, his face so damn cold he might as well have been stone. "This won't be forever," he said, making it sound like an apology. Maybe one of these days I'd get a real one.

I wanted to tell him I respected him, that I always had. I wanted to believe in him and his belief that he could make a difference. A one-man army, the last of his people, against the fae. It was honorable and foolish, and brave, and stubborn, and all the things Marshal Kellee stood for. I wanted to tell him I was sorry. But it didn't matter what I said or how I felt, because he wouldn't believe a word of it. And how much did I really know any of him? The Dreamweaver spent months spinning me the illusion of Marshal Kellee. The Marshal Kellee outside my cage now. I wasn't sure if I knew him at all.

He turned away and headed for the door, but he stopped halfway and said, "This hurts me too."

I laughed, knowing it sounded wicked, and enjoyed watching his shoulders tense. "Talen would never cage me. A bloodthirsty fae who toyed with humans for sport would never lock me in here. What does that say about you, Kellee?"

"I never said I was good, Kesh." His hands curled into trembling fists. I wondered if he might turn around and show me that monster inside. I wanted to see it all, to see the truth of him, but he never fully let go.

"It tells me you don't know Talen," he added. "Never compare me to a fae again." Kellee left. The threat in his words echoed through the chamber long after he had gone.

THE CAGE HAD basic facilities hidden behind galvanized steel walls, but the main area, including the bolted-down bed, was exposed to anyone looking in. Talen had spent a few hundred years inside its walls, wrapped in glass and tek and observed by the occasional visitor, mostly Kellee. Fae were a social species. It would have been kinder to kill him. But whoever had signed off on his incarceration would have known that. Perhaps his punishment fit his crime? Whatever the reason, Kellee had caught Talen and then given the fae old books to read.

I wondered if the marshal got a kick out of watching his prisoners through glass. In his apartment—now destroyed—he had owned a goldfish in a bowl. I had thought it extravagant, but now I understood. Kellee had liked to watch that little fish in its tiny glass world that Kellee controlled. I was now that fish, and before me, it had been Talen. I should have hated the lawman, but I didn't. I was saru. Cages didn't frighten me. Only the ghosts inside my head did.

Talen had gifted me some of his paper books and was teaching me old Earthen so I'd have something to occupy my mind. I found new worlds within their pages and oddly simple worlds. Earthen humans—unlike saru today—had evolved with no idea they were a fae experiment, and so they'd foolishly believed they were masters of their own fates. They seemed equal parts ingenious and foolish. In a few decades, they'd created tek, and in the next, they'd warred, never knowing it was all supposed to be for the fae. Had they known their fate, I wondered if they would have been more like the saru, who matured knowing exactly who their masters were.

Humans had battled the fae before. They'd beaten

them back using monstrous tek machines, but it hadn't lasted, and now the fae were back. How many humans were left in Halow? Certainly the pockets of resistance that Kellee sought. Would the fae go farther? The original Sol system was still out there, and within it was Earth, an untouched museum and a symbol of humanity's beginnings and its greatest accomplishments. Had the fae encroached on Sol yet? Would they destroy everything their experiment had created?

I pondered many things inside my glass cage.

Dreams were an ever-present threat, like an itch I couldn't scratch. Eledan had delighted in pulling me into his mental machinations for months. Months in which I had been his toy. And the things I had seen and done at his whim haunted me like real memories.

I had stopped myself from killing him to save human lives, making me a traitor to the crown. But Oberon would understand. He had his brother's tek-caged heart. That would be enough. Maybe one day I'd get to kill the Dreamweaver for real. Those thoughts kept me warm at night.

My cage door rattled. I propped myself up on an elbow and watched Talen enter. He wore loose pants, a hooded top that hid his tipped ears, and a long, fae-style riding coat split up the back. His magic entered with him, spritzing the air with its unique flowery scent. He looked over his shoulder, checking the chamber.

"Are you all right?" I asked.

He stilled, surprised by the question, and lowered his hood. Shadows peeled back, revealing a partially smiling mouth and then those bright, intelligent eyes. "Why would you think anything was wrong?"

A hunch. I wasn't sure how to explain it. Maybe it was our bond? But something felt off. I swung my legs over the edge of the bed to stand, when Talen crouched down to my level. The intensity surrounding him kept me seated and my nerves tingling.

"Where's Kellee?" I asked.

Talen searched my eyes before answering. "How much do you know about the vakaru?"

Worry tightened my chest. What was going on here? "Hardly anything. Eledan told me some things. They were warriors. They turned on the fae and were all exterminated."

Talen swallowed and rolled his lips together, turning over his next words and searching for the right angle.

"Something has happened to Kellee?"

Talen's mouth tightened. I was right. "He asked me not to come to you."

"What is it? What can I do?" I shot up from the bunk, but the cage's closed door barred my way. "Let me out of here."

"It's not that simple."

"Talen." I whirled on the fae. "Let me out right now."

He approached, frowning as though this decision were difficult. It wasn't. "He told me not to tell you."

"Yes, I heard you the first time, but you told me, and that means you think I should know. So, whatever has happened or is happening, you believe I can help." I poked him in the chest and looked up, searching his eyes for the moment he gave in. "You know my feelings, right? You feel me through our bond. What am I feeling?"

"It's not as clear as it should be—"

"Talen," I warned. He was stalling. "Cut the karushit

30

and give it to me straight. Do you think I will betray you? Are you honestly getting that from me?"

"No."

"Then trust me." I placed my hand on his chest, soaking up his warmth. *See, it's simple. Just trust me. There's nothing to it.*

He blinked and caught my hand. "How can I possibly trust you?"

"I could have hurt you and Kellee a thousand different ways, and all of them would have been easier than what I'm doing now."

He stepped closer, shrinking the world around him. "What *are* you doing?"

"Protecting you." How did he not see it? How did he not feel it? I felt him, his anticipation, and his anxiety over whatever was happening outside my glass walls. The bond worked both ways, didn't it? "It's all I've been trying to do since you both saved me. It would have been easier for me to kill you both and remove you from my mission. I didn't. I did everything I could to keep you out of the way, to keep you from getting involved. I'm not your enemy. Kellee is too stubborn to see the truth, but you see me, Talen. You understand who I am." I spread my fingers wider, feeling the light *thud-thud* of his fae heart. "Let me help you help him."

He breathed in, expanding his chest under my hand. His heart beat strong and steady. What I was asking him was almost impossible. I'd lied to him more than I'd told him the truth. But he had always known I wasn't what I appeared to be. He had told me, the first time we met, that he *knew* me.

"You'll need this." Decision made, he handed me my

whip, stepped away, and waved his hand over the lock. The mechanism clunked, releasing the door, and he was striding away. "Follow me." Coat flapping, he disappeared down the corridors. I used to run circuits around the prison with him, but he had always held back. Now, I struggled to keep up. By the time I reached the area we used for sparring, I was out of breath, my heart racing, and there stood Kellee with his back to me in the center of the room, perfectly fine.

I tossed a frown at Talen, but he shot out an arm to stop me from going any farther.

The marshal turned. Something darker had devoured the cocky smiles and humorous glint in his eyes. The beast peered through, bleeding his pupils black. He tasted the air between viciously curved fangs. Even his body had changed. Claws had sprouted from his fingernails, each one capable of slicing through flesh with little resistance. He had torn through my battle-drone with those claws. They could rip through steel and easily through me.

"What happened?" I whispered.

"It's the vakaru. It needs the fight."

I couldn't take my eyes off Kellee. Somewhere inside that madness, the marshal still existed. Did he have any control?

"They were bred for battle," Talen murmured. "Without the fight, he will be lost to the hunger."

"You want me to... *fight* him?" *Why me? Why not Talen?* The fae healed quickly. I did not.

"He won't kill *you*," Talen said from the corner of his mouth, his stare locked on the dangerous creature in the room.

But Talen, a fae, Kellee would kill. I swallowed—*all*

32

right, then—and drawing in a breath, I lowered my hand to my whip. I had never fought a vakaru. Kellee was faster than the fae. I had seen him unleash something of his beast before. Those claws were lethal. Disable the claws—his main weapons—and I could subdue him. Maybe.

Kellee sprang, blurring forward too fast for me to track. I twisted the whip, flicked it into the air, and brought it down in a vicious crack between us, stalling Kellee's charge. He pulled back, indignation widening his eyes. I whirled the whip again, looping it over my head and cracking the air. The marshal's eyes followed the whip's tails, tracking that threat instead of me. I dug tek-flashers out of my pocket and tossed them into the air. Kellee had seen my tricks before and instantly twisted away. Light blazed, soaking the chamber in brilliance, and Kellee burst forward. His shoulder sank into my gut, lifting me clean off my feet. I rolled over his back and landed in a crouch in time to see Kellee's claws slash the air inches from my face.

"Talen!" I barked, skipping backward. Kellee stalked forward. "You said he wouldn't kill me!"

"He won't," the fae calmly replied from the sidelines.

Kellee whirled and threw a right hook that would have taken my head clean off if I hadn't ducked.

"He's sure trying!"

"It's unlikely."

Oh, it was unlikely now? Un-*fucking*-likely? Kellee spun up and kicked. I caught his ankle and twisted, expecting to flip him off his feet and plant him face down. Instead, he hopped, adjusting his balance on his back foot, yanked his leg free from my grip and, still balanced, kicked his heel into my jaw. Pain snapped through my neck. My head flew back. The marshal kicked my legs out from under me, slamming me ass-first into the mats, where I sat, jarred out of the frenzy.

I knew he had been holding back when we sparred, but I'd had no idea how much. He lunged, claws spread, murder in his eyes. I rolled onto my side and kicked. My foot connected at the right time, and my heel sunk into his gut, winding him. He staggered, giving me a second to launch an offensive.

I sprang off my grounded foot, launching away, and I *felt* Kellee chasing close behind. The wall raced closer. *Now or never.* Jumping, I kicked off the wall and twisted in the air, flicking the whip around *beneath me.* Its coils looped around Kellee's neck as he clawed at the air. When I landed, I yanked on the whip and pulled Kellee backward, jolting his balance out from under him. The marshal went down hard on his back, the whip locked around his throat.

He got his claws beneath the metal links. He would cut through them eventually. I pulled the whip tighter and placed a boot on either side of his hips.

"Yield."

The beast in his eyes blazed, his black pupils burning red at their edges. There was nothing human looking back at me. What kind of monster had the fae created in the vakaru?

I pulled on the whip, trapping his claws against his neck. Kellee growled, low and deadly, the sound more animal than man.

I bared my teeth and dropped a knee onto his chest, pinning him beneath me. "Yield, you stubborn, controlling piece of fae engineering."

His chest rose with each strangled breath, and he

glared as though he could burn me from the inside out. But he wasn't fighting. I shifted the whip, loosening its hold, and waited to see if he would retaliate. He dropped his hands to his sides. The claws retracted, and finally, something of Kellee's normal spark quenched the blackness in his eyes. His lashes fluttered, eyes softening.

"There you are..." I sighed, still wary. It took a few more minutes for his body to relax. I waited, keeping him pinned just in case his surrender was a ruse. "If I let you up, will you attack me again?"

He ran his tongue along his blunt teeth and regarded me, lips parted, the smaller tips of his canine teeth visible. "I might." He dragged those words up from somewhere deep inside so they came out rough.

"So, when does this end?"

I sensed Talen nearby, somewhere by the door, watching this all play out. At what point would the fae have stepped in? Never?

"When you remove the whip from around my neck." His smooth voice had broken into ragged fragments, like he'd spent a few rough nights in the sinks.

He wasn't looking away, and there was that challenge in his eyes, the one that had been there since I'd met him in the sinks. *Come play with me,* it said, *if you dare.*

An alarm chimed somewhere, and Talen left, apparently content Kellee wouldn't tear my throat out.

"So, this is a vakaru thing, huh?" I settled my other knee next to him and sat up, straddling his hips, keeping him pinned with the whip loosely looped around his neck.

"Part of it." He shifted his hips, and I wondered if he was maneuvering to buck me off, but I didn't feel any tension building in his muscles.

"If this is only part of it, what's the rest of you like?"

Kellee's hand brushed my knee, his fingers digging in with more than a little force. I let his touch linger, wondering if he was about to trick me into letting him go. I would have, in his position. I'd say all the right things to win a fight. But Kellee had a line he didn't cross. He didn't lie, and he didn't manipulate. When he attacked, he made sure his opponent saw it coming.

The heated look in his eyes turned sly, and the adrenaline rushing through my veins sought another reason to keep pumping. I tightened my thighs around him, trapping him under me, and leaned forward. My hair spilled over my shoulder and fell on either side of his face, hemming us in. In the dark, his eyes revealed their multifaceted greens and hazels. "Would you have killed me, Marshal Kellee?"

His hand brushed up my thigh, rough and deliberate. "I wanted to."

If he was anything like me, he wanted many things. I sank my fingers beneath the whip's coils to loosen them. Raw scuff marks peppered his neck. My knuckles brushed against his unshaven chin. "Do you still want to?" It was probably a bad idea to taunt the vakaru, but in that moment, he was penned in and mine. I likely wouldn't get another opportunity to tease him, and I was all about seizing opportunities when they presented themselves.

When he didn't answer, probably because it was a yes, I ran my hand up his neck, brushed my knuckles over his cheek, and sank my fingers into his ragged hair. Now that I had him and he was allowing me this much, how far could I go? The wildness in his eyes, left over from his beast, beckoned me.

I'd kissed him before, and we had shared a few

fumbling touches, but that was before he knew who I really was. Things had changed. Kesh Lasota would have been all over him, all over this, but the Wraithmaker couldn't afford to get close. This couldn't happen. I was a king's assassin and Kellee's enemy.

He brought his hand up. His fingers lightly brushed my cheek. "I want to hate you."

I fought not to lean into the touch. Eledan had been the last person to touch me like this, and that encounter had been all kinds of wrong. But Kellee wasn't Eledan. Kellee saved people. Kellee was good. He was all the things I was not. It would have been easier to fall for Kellee, to close that little distance between us and brush my lips over his, to go further and touch him where I knew he would gasp for more. I wanted to hear him breathe out my name and lose himself inside me. I wanted his mouth to taste me. I wanted the press of his body against mine. The hard press of his arousal nudging my inner thigh made his consent perfectly clear.

"But I can't," he whispered. His touch roughened, his thumb pressing into my cheek, and a snarl lifted his top lip.

I pulled back, just out of his reach, but kept control of him, clamped between my legs. His hand fell, and there we were, the two of us wanting something neither of us could have.

Talen cleared his throat. "There's a ship incoming."

Kellee growled. The sound reverberated through us, scattering delicious pulses of pleasure in all the right places. I climbed off Kellee and watched the marshal climb to his feet in the corner of my eye as I spooled my whip and clipped it to my belt.

A cold shudder rippled through me, and the ache of loss grew. I lifted my gaze to Talen, wanting something like compassion to show on his face, but it didn't. Talen's expression was as cold as I felt.

"It's the warcruiser," the fae said.

CHAPTER 4

The prison scanners highlighted the substantial mass of a ship approaching our prison rock. Its organic signature and size meant it could only be a warcruiser, and with nothing else out there, it had to be coming for us.

Kellee slammed his hands against the console, sending shudders through the entire panel. "How did they find us?" He straightened and laced his fingers behind his head, probably to keep his claws from showing. "You said you got away clean." The glare he threw Talen held a dangerous glint that had me reaching for my whip.

"We did," Talen replied. He stood to the marshal's left with his arms crossed, infuriatingly unfazed by both the marshal and the cruiser.

"Or that's what they let you believe so they could follow you right to us?" Kellee glowered.

Talen faced the marshal's accusation head-on and didn't give an inch. "Whether they followed us is not our greatest concern. They're here, and we must deal with it."

Kellee tilted his head, cracking his neck. He dropped his hands to his sides, and his fingers twitched.

"Is there an escape route?" I asked them.

Kellee growled in exasperation and turned to me. "It's a prison. It's designed so that all the vessels are funneled to the one dock. They're approaching from the only point we can escape from."

"So, we can't get by them?"

"Didn't I just say that?" he snarled.

I glared right back. "Then what are our options, Marshal?"

He looked again at the screens. Inch by inch, the ship grew larger from multiple angles. "Take as many of them down before they kill us."

I worked my jaw, carefully shoving my frustration with the marshal deeper inside. "That's *not* an option."

"We could evade them in the corridors?" Talen offered, watching the cruiser loom closer. Its scales shimmered, and looked like an enormous ocean creature about to devour us whole.

"To what end?" Kellee asked. "The prison is a trap. We can't run them in circles forever."

Were you planning on running forever? Only a lifetime. Eledan's voice whispered through my thoughts, unpicking my efforts to focus. I squeezed my eyes shut, rubbed my neck, and pushed the Mad Prince's intrusion away. There was a way out of this. There's always a way out. The fae's world was beautiful and monstrous and powerful and almost impossible to overcome, but for one weakness. And it was one of my strengths.

"Then we don't run." I opened my eyes to find them looking at me. "We can't escape in the shuttle, and we can't outrun them inside the prison. We can't fight a warcruiser's retinue of soldiers. So, there's only one thing we can do. We give up."

Kellee's brow wrinkled. "Seriously?" Even Talen frowned. Then the marshal laughed. "The Wraithmaker wants us to welcome the fae? Why am I not surprised?"

The marshal would find himself on the wrong end of my whip again if he didn't pull himself together. "Back on Adelane, Talen and I hid so close to them they couldn't see us. We can do the same here. We give them what they want."

Kellee folded his arms. "You want us to surrender?"

I nodded. "There's just three of us, and we can't fight *that*." I pointed at the screens, all filled with the shimmering warcruiser. "We either die fighting them or we give up, but under our terms."

"What terms?" Talen asked, curiously. He was catching on.

"To the fae, I'm the Wraithmaker. Kellee, you're the last vakaru and now my prisoner. And Talen, well... I don't know what you are to them, but I'll trust you like you asked and assume you can move among them without giving Kellee and me up?"

He bowed his head. "I can."

They looked at me as though I had lost my mind. "We lie," I said and then checked Talen, because he *couldn't* lie. The fae nodded, understanding what I was asking from him. Did I trust him enough to do this? I didn't have a choice. "We lie and play their game until we can regroup and find a way off the ship."

Kellee shook his head. "It won't work. You're wanted for murdering their queen."

"And now they have a new king. My king. If they're loyal to Oberon, they'll treat me well."

"And if they're not?"

I ignored Kellee's question. This was better than the alternative of dying while trying to fight them off, and no matter what they did, so long as I survived, I would find a way off the ship.

"Oberon's protection will extend through me to the both of you."

"You're still saru." Talen stiffened, his back and shoulders locked. He wasn't pleased. "Unless Oberon is on that ship, they'll treat you as such."

I rubbed at the ghosts of old scars around my neck. "They can't do anything I haven't endured before."

Worry knotted Kellee's brow. He didn't believe me. "We're a long way from Faerie. The rules you are used to at court may not apply out here."

How did he know what rules applied at court?

He touched his fingers to his forehead and frowned, thinking hard. "There's a better way."

The entire prison shuddered. The warcruiser had docked. The fae would be on us in minutes.

Talen looked up, and I felt the stab of his concern as though it were my own. "It's too neat. They won't accept the three of us if they find us waiting for them. We must stage it to reinforce the lie."

"What do you suggest?" Kellee asked, one eye on the door.

Talen's expression saddened. "You won't like it."

I PACED MY GLASS CELL, listening to doors clang and the percussions of fae weapons echoing down the prison corridors.

We had to make this convincing.

Now, standing at my cell door, I recalled Talen's sorry smile as he had locked the door on me. *"I'll find you,"* I had told him. He couldn't know I had said the same words as a threat to the Mad Prince. I'd meant those words then, but they had a different meaning now. Talen had smiled that same shallow little smile that said so much, and none of it had anything to do with happiness. As he'd left me, I'd admitted to myself how I cared for him. I cared for them both. Kellee's foolish righteousness and Talen's perplexing devotion.

Turning my head, I scanned the stacks of books the fae had given me. Could he truly care for me? How could a fae in any world truly care for a saru? They couldn't. And I was about to be reminded of the world I'd left behind five years ago.

Shouts sounded just outside the chamber.

I wondered if they'd caught Kellee and huffed a small laugh. Even the might of the Wild Hunt would struggle to bring down the last vakaru.

I breathed in and held the breath. I had to fall into the lies again, only this time, there was more than my life on the line.

The chamber door was flung open, and a line of fae soldiers poured in. They moved silently, branching off into two streams. Arrows gleamed, nocked on their compact crossbows. I counted fifteen, all similarly dressed in the dark, lightweight leathers of combat fae. Did any of them have warfae markings? Were any of them marked killers like I was?

I deliberately rolled up my sleeves and pulled my coat collar open so they saw the black tattoos circling my forearms. There was only one saru with warfae markings. I didn't have to tell anyone my name.

Silently, they circled my cage and locked into position, waiting for their superior. A flight like this, some sixteen warriors, they were an efficient weapon. Kellee would have killed a few, Talen too. But in the end, we wouldn't have survived them.

Tension threaded through the fae circling my cage, and in strode a female. Clad in blood-red leather, her flawless skin was the color of milk. Moss-green hair trailed in several braids down her back.

I dropped to one knee and bowed my head, grateful she wouldn't see the fear on my face. I knew her, though we had never spoken. Mab's closest allies would whisper of her: the ruthless female general who wore leathers soaked in the blood of those she had cut down with her longbow, currently strapped to her back. Sjora, the Harvester. She had been loyal to Mab, the queen I murdered. This was not the scenario I had been hoping for.

"Rise, Wraithmaker." Her voice was silk pulled through fingers, and already it crept around my defenses, fooling me into believing she meant me no harm.

I lifted my head and pushed to my feet. Outside the cage, she towered over me. Her lips held a permanent half-snarl, and her eyes were gray flint, brittle but sharp. She looked as though she would love to tear my heart from my chest and eat it in front of her troops as a message to all.

I would have preferred Eledan to be here instead of her.

"Free her from this offensive contraption." She flicked a pale wrist, and a soldier sprang into action. He planted a gel-like explosive around the seal. The charge blasted out the lock and sent cracks snapping through the glass.

Sjora beckoned for me to leave the cage. If Kellee had asked if one day I might prefer to stay inside his cage, I would have laughed. I wasn't laughing now. Sjora could kill me and claim I had attacked her. Oberon wouldn't likely reprimand one of his more powerful generals over a saru, even one as revered as me.

I approached the fae, aware that all the eyes in the room were on me.

She reached behind her shoulder and withdrew a long arrow from its quiver. The shaft was timber, but the magic spiraling around it more than made up for the fragile wood.

"Kneel, saru."

I immediately dropped into the position trained into me since before I could walk.

The arrow's tip pressed under my chin. She lifted my head, deliberately digging the point into my skin. Sjora's smile was alive on her lips. "Mm..." She flicked the tip of the arrow to my cheek and applied pressure to turn my face one way, and then flicked it to the other cheek, doing the same. "I thought you'd be more formidable up close." She stepped back and announced, "Bring in the prisoner."

Three fae escorted Kellee into the room. He ignored me on my knees, keeping up the appearance that we meant nothing to each other—or perhaps that was the truth. His gaze locked on Sjora, and all his murderous thoughts found their way to his face.

"This one wears a gold star as though it can protect him."

I didn't have the heart to tell her the star meant he protected others.

Sjora laughed at the snarl on his face, and the sound slithered through my soul. She looked down at me. "Rise and tell me what we should do with your jailor, Wraithmaker."

I rose slowly and turned toward Kellee. This hadn't been the plan. Anyone but the Harvester and we could have kept up the ruse. But she knew the Wraithmaker killed for sport. She knew the Wraithmaker butchered her own kind to the sound of cheering fae. Kellee had imprisoned me. And the Wraithmaker's wrath was no small thing. The answer was simple.

A muscle fluttered in Kellee's jaw. He knew what I had to do. We had to make them *believe* the lie.

I freed my whip. At the sight of the snake-like metal, Sjora's mouth stretched into a sickening grin. "Force him to his knees," she ordered, looking me in the eye.

Her soldiers struggled to drive Kellee down. One lost his grip, and Kellee swung at him, catching him with a sudden right hook. But another rushed in, and Kellee was soon on his knees, glaring up at me—his enemy—surrounded by the fae. The soldier to his right gripped Kellee's shirt and tore it open, exposing the man's chest. And in Kellee's black-eyed glare, hatred burned.

I can't do this.

I clenched my jaw so hard that pain throbbed through my skull.

I can't do this. I can't hurt him like this. But the Wraith-maker could.

I'm sorry.

I'm so sorry.

I dropped the end of the whip, loosening its tails, and approached Kellee. He bucked against the fae holding him. There was nowhere to go and no other way out of this.

Sickness crawled up my throat.

This was who I was. If it hadn't been now, Oberon would have had me do the same later. This was why I had tried to leave them. To protect them. Damn you, Kellee. *You should have let me go.*

"Do it!" he shouted, veins bulging in his forehead.

I threw my arm back, lifting the whip into the air—

"Stop."

Talen strode through the doorway, hood pooling on his shoulders. The hem of his split-backed riding cloak swept around his boots, and his braided hair fell in long plaited tails down his back, similar to Sjora's. He had never looked more fae. My whip's tails dropped to the floor between Kellee and me. A thread of intrigue tightened all the fae in the room. No one here would dare interrupt the Harvester, but Talen waltzed in like he had every right to do so.

The line of soldiers parted, letting him through without him having to say a word. He approached Sjora, his gaze firmly on her, his violet eyes alight with a foreign intensity I'd seen only once before—when we first met.

"The saru is mine. She answers to me."

His tone held the same factual weight as on the moon, but the Talen I recognized was gone. In his place stood a male fae who spoke with all the gravitas of the court. If I hadn't known him, I would have assumed much from the way he held Sjora's level gaze and the way he walked, as though his words were seldom disobeyed. He held a higher status than all the fae here, all but Sjora. He wore his power like a visible aura.

Kellee had warned me, hadn't he? Over and over. Talen was dangerous, and here he was, acting exactly like a fae who could crush human lives and scatter them to Faerie's winds. I tried to catch the marshal's eye, but he'd bowed his head, shoulders heaving.

Sjora lifted her chin and eyed the cloaked stranger warily. "Who are you?"

"We will talk more later, but for now, release my saru and the vakaru."

He hadn't looked at me, hadn't looked at anything or anyone else in the room. Only Sjora was worthy of his attention.

"You know who she is?" Sjora gestured to me with the tip of her arrow.

"Of course."

"She killed our queen." Sjora's voice trembled, leaving no doubt as to her impression of me. If Talen hadn't been here, she would have had me kill Kellee and then killed me herself.

Talen lowered his chin and peered through light lashes. "The queen is dead. Our king has risen from her shadow. It is his command we follow, the command of Faerie. Is it not?"

Sjora's eyes narrowed. "You do not need to remind me whose word I follow, stranger."

"Don't I?" Finally, Talen glanced my way, but his gaze

skipped across me and continued around the room at his audience, his witnesses. "Come now, you're no fool, Sjora. The Wraithmaker is Oberon's. She always was. But these things are not for public discussion."

Sjora's rigid stance relaxed. "Tell me how you came to be here with the Wraithmaker."

Talen visibly stilled, and his gaze fell to the cage before snapping back to Sjora. "I was imprisoned for many years. She and I came to an agreement. She..." He hesitated, searching for the right word that wasn't a lie. "She played a significant part in freeing me. She is *mine*."

A string tugged at my heart, a thread of truth tightening between us.

Sjora's smile was back, stalking her lips. "You are either a fool or more powerful than you appear. You're correct. The Wraithmaker is obviously Oberon's tool and a very efficient one. She lied her way to the queen's side..." She trailed off, blinked, and nodded at Talen. "You had better hope he is in a forgiving mood when our king discovers you have stolen his pet." Her attention turned to the rest of the room. "Kill the vakaru."

"Wait—" The word was out of me before I could stop it. Indignation flared in Sjora's eyes while Talen remained unmoved.

A growl rumbled up from Kellee. "You can try, you fae f—"

Sjora nodded. The nearest soldier pressed his crossbow to Kellee's temple, silencing the marshal.

Sjora's gaze burned into me. She knew—she *knew* there was something between Kellee and me. I couldn't meet her gaze, didn't want to see that knowledge in her eyes. She would use him against me, just like Eledan had.

"The last vakaru alive," Talen mused, the quality of his voice almost poetic. "A fine gift for a new king."

Sjora twitched as though Talen's suggestion had sunk its claws into her. "It seems this excursion was not a complete waste of time after all." She strode for the door. "Bring the Wraithmaker and her vakaru back to the ship. If I spend one more minute on this tek-riddled rock, I might slaughter the lot of you. And you." She turned and crooked her finger at Talen. "Stranger, you and I have much to discuss."

CHAPTER 5

*I*nside the ship, I was handed from flight to flight and escorted into the belly of the warcruiser. Few fae cared to meet my eyes, and I already knew none would deign to answer any questions, so I remained silent and soaked up my surroundings, wondering where they would take Kellee and if I'd known Talen at all.

The enormous warcruisers were *grown* and harvested from Faerie. During the few times they'd allow me outside the arena compound, I'd seen them drifting in the purplish Faerie skies, but I had never believed I would set foot inside one.

Where wires should trail, veins throbbed. And where girders would support the structure of a normal ship, bones arched like ribs. But it wasn't gory. The brightly colored surfaces shimmered like silk or the pearlescent sheen found inside shells, demanding to be touched and stroked and smoothed. I shouldn't have been surprised.

Everything on Faerie demanded admiration and love, even creatures bred for war.

The flight sealed me inside a small circular chamber barely four steps in diameter. I sat on the bench grown from the wall and leaned forward, threading my fingers through my hair. If I listened hard, I could hear the ship's two enormous hearts thudding in time far, far away. Mine beat out of time.

I smiled, but it sat bitterly on my lips. We were in the belly of the beast, just as I'd planned, and all I had to do was get Kellee and Talen out again.

If Talen hadn't arrived when he did, I would have whipped Kellee. I'd been whipped enough times to loathe the thought of it. If Kellee hadn't hated me before, he did now. And he had every right to.

No, *the Wraithmaker* would have hurt him.

As for me? I wasn't sure who I was anymore. On Calicto, it had been so easy to slip into Kesh Lasota's human life as a messenger. If I was truly that girl, then all of this was wrong. After Calicto, after falling into a human life, after seeing everything from outside the glass, I didn't want to be the Wraithmaker anymore. I didn't have to be, did I? Kellee had told me I had a choice to make. The bastard was always right.

I fell back against the wall and closed my eyes.

Years ago, the boy who had lived in the cell next to mine had dreamed of better worlds. I had thought his dreams were silly and told him so, but when we returned to our prisons, beaten and broken, he continued to tell his tales through the bars. Tales of how one day the saru would be free and stories of heroes that didn't exist. He dared to think of a place and time when the fae wouldn't exist either. I didn't believe him, but I enjoyed his stories. In the end, those dreams had killed him.

No—the Wraithmaker killed him.

Aeon had been right to dream. But if his tales had been true, the hero would have killed the villain. Aeon would have killed me. People like Aeon, like Kellee, saved others, but sometimes, they died too soon. I'd killed Aeon, and I would regret it forever. I would not lose my stubborn marshal too.

I drifted somewhere between sleep and wakefulness, where whispers beckoned and Eledan's dreams stirred, roused by the lack of Kellee's elixir. They would come and haunt me soon, just like my past.

Hours later, the fae led me through the ship's curving corridors. I mentally mapped the route and any quirks so I might find my way around alone and kept an eye out for any sign of Talen or Kellee. The warcruiser was the size of a small city and populated by an array of fae troops. The chances of catching sight of my pair were slim, but I hoped.

We passed a narrow window looking out into the blackness beyond. Stars drifted, or rather we did, gliding silently through the vacuum of space. Tiny flutters knotted in my chest. Were we going back to Faerie or pressing onward to conquer more human colonies? Either way, I had to get Talen and Kellee off the ship soon.

My guards escorted me into a long narrow chamber. The low ceiling curved around a table as if to protect its occupants. Five fae sat at one end, with Sjora at the head. The table, and likely the chairs too, appeared to have been carved or grown from the floor. As the guards left, I absently wondered if the ship felt us moving around inside it. Probably not. We were lice to it.

None of the fae acknowledged me. I stood at ease, watching, learning, letting their voices drone through my thoughts. They spoke of conquests and colonies I had been aware of but never visited and never would.

A saru girl appeared, jug in hand, to fill the waiting flute glasses with wine. Long dark hair trailed down her back to her thighs, and her slip of a dress gave her the impression of barely being there at all. *A ghost.*

You are a nothing girl.

Wraithmaker.

I reached up to rub at my neck, caught my hand halfway, and lowered it back to my side.

We had once looked the same, that girl and I. Same hair color, same waif-like limbs, same ability to blend into the background. That was until I had learned to stand out, until I had killed Aeon so Oberon would notice me. That girl across the table from me, she was my past.

"Saru," Sjora summoned.

The girl and I looked up. Sjora paused, admiring us with cold, hungry eyes. She wore a red gown made from several panels stitched together with thick green thread. The same green threads zigzagged through her hair, pinning it back from her angular face.

"Not you." She shooed the girl away and pointed at me. On her finger, she wore a translucent pointed thimble, likely crafted from glass. Fragile but sharp.

I approached the table and stood between her and the fae seated to her left. He dragged his less than impressed gaze over me. Each of them studied my appearance. My scuffed fae coat. My unkempt hair. The smell of metal dust and *human*. My marks were covered, not that it made any difference. They already believed me to be an animal.

Sjora arched an eyebrow, lifted her wine glass, and drank the contents down without stopping. She dabbed a finger to the corner of her mouth and lifted her glass for me to refill.

I didn't rise to the bait. I wasn't *her* slave. Apparently, I was Talen's, and he wasn't here.

"Well?"

As I was standing and the fae were seated, I looked down at her, a position that already had my skin crawling with the need to drop to my knees. I had earned the right to stand. I wasn't the nothing girl. I had risen among them. I was more than saru. I was the Wraithmaker.

A fae snorted a laugh. I didn't see which one. Laughing at me and my defiance.

"If you want wine," I said, "pour it yourself."

Murmurs bubbled.

Sjora's mouth twisted. She ran her gaze across those seated with her, reading their reactions. I kept my eyes on her. The others posed no threat.

"Wraithmaker." She tested the word on her lips. "Oberon's *pet*. He must have offered you fine rewards for killing the queen. What was it?"

Another snicker. They could laugh all they wanted. Only one fae's opinion mattered—or perhaps two, if I included Talen. Either way, this little group was nothing.

"Oberon had nothing to do with the queen's demise."

"Such sweet lies." Sjora's eyebrow twitched. "Oh, I

know. There's only two things saru want above all else: for their masters to be happy and to be adored by those they serve. Isn't that right, saru?" Sjora asked the girl hovering ghostlike in the shadows.

"Yes," she replied with typical saru conviction.

Sjora lifted her gaze to me. "I can't decide if I despise you or if I'm fascinated." She twisted in her chair, angling herself toward me. She appeared relaxed, but her grip on the glass whitened her fingers. "Your subjugation of the royal house was, some might say, artful. You blinded our queen to the poison creeping through her own household."

It wasn't worth arguing that Mab had asked me to kill her so that I might pass her magic on to her son. The idea had come from Oberon, and I'd seeded the thoughts into the queen's head over months. I had merely been the messenger. The fact remained, however, I had killed Sjora's queen, and whether Oberon had been behind the order didn't matter here and now.

"If it were my decision, I would flay your skin from your muscle and leave you to rot in the summerlands heat. You are not worthy of those marks you carry. You are saru. You will always be saru." Her eyelashes fluttered. "Alas, I cannot defy my king."

Her crowd made various sounds of agreement that briefly placated her. And then she summoned the saru girl over. The girl obliged, stopping beside Sjora, awaiting her command.

Sjora lifted her smile to me, snatched the girl's wrist, pulled her down, smashed her glass on the table, and plunged the jagged edges into the girl's arm. A terrible silence stretched for too long. The girl swallowed a scream, embraced the pain, and fell forward. The smell of her blood wet the air. I forgot the crowd and held Sjora's gray-eyed glare. The fae general waited for me to react, to do anything that she might construe as disobedient so she had an excuse to open my veins too.

"*Kneel*," she snapped.

The girl dropped to her knees, cradling her bleeding arm against her belly. Dark blood stained her dress.

This wasn't loyalty. This was brutality.

The fae guests did nothing. They looked on, bored, uncaring.

"You are better than this," I told Sjora.

She mock-gasped at my insolence. "Do you believe you are qualified to judge me?"

"Sjora, stop," a fae spoke up. His voice sounded distant, droll, like he cared but only enough to make his opinion known but not enough to truly argue. His words were lost beneath the thunderous beat of my heart. "Provoke her and you provoke Oberon's wrath," he added.

I flicked a glance at the speaker. His mahogany toned summerlands skin made his eyes gleam. Gem-studded earrings dangled from the highest point of his fae ears. But otherwise, he looked just like the rest.

"Oberon is a fool!" Sjora stood and lunged at me. I raised my arm, blocking her hand, but I knew this wouldn't end well and let her second strike get through my defenses. Her fingers clamped around my neck. "We are a long way from Faerie, Wraithmaker. Oberon isn't here to protect his pet. You will entertain us. You will bleed for us. And when we are done, you will return to the king having fulfilled your purpose." Her fingers dug in, and the pointed thimble broke my skin, stinging where it sank in. The pain was nothing compared to the agony the girl must be in. A warm dribble of blood ran down my neck. "Make no mistake. I have no love for liars and queenkillers. This is my ship, my world. I can make you disappear, saru. For our queen, it is all the justice you deserve." Sjora threw me away. "Get these wretched saru out of my sight."

I lifted my chin. I could have said more, could have driven her to kill me, but the faces around the table spoke for me. Her outburst hadn't won her any favors, and the sobbing saru said it all.

The summerlands fae who had spoken pushed from the bench and scooped up the saru girl, escorting her out.

Nobody stopped me from leaving, and no guards came to escort me back to a cell, so I put one foot in front of the other with no idea where I was supposed to go. I wanted to run, but I couldn't. I pressed a hand to my chest, feeling my rapid heartbeat, and wondered if Talen could feel it too. Was he close? Just around the next corner, perhaps?

Sjora was right. This was her ship, her world. And if we didn't escape, she'd kill us all.

I wandered in what felt like circles because everything looked the same and nothing ever changed. Eledan's laughter echoed in my head, memories of his basement illusion tripping me up.

"Wraithmaker." A hushed female voice pulled me up short.

I turned to find the saru girl Sjora had stabbed approaching me. Her skin was pale from blood-loss, but her wrist was healed. She waved me toward her. "How—"

"Come with me." She turned and was off, her fast slipper-silent feet breezing across the floor.

I jogged to keep up. We rounded a corner and came to

58

a set of descending steps and a door that automatically opened as she approached.

"Who do you belong to?" I asked. The door quietly closed behind me.

We were in a generous chamber, likely her master's. It was adorned in colored silks that sectioned off each living area.

"Lord Devere. He was there. He spoke up for you." Sonia stepped back and clasped her hands in front of her, adopting the neutral pose of a saru waiting for instructions. "He told me to find you."

"He did?" I ventured farther into the room, seeking any clues as to what this Devere might want from me. "Do you know why?"

"No."

She let me drift around the room, her big doe eyes on me.

"He fixed you up, huh?" I asked, gesturing at her wrist.

I caught her nod in the corner of my eye and watched how she rolled her lips together. How Devere had healed her so quickly, she wasn't about to tell me. Her clasped hands whitened as she squeezed tighter. She had fire in her, that one, buried beneath all the saru training. So many thoughts lay hidden behind her silence, none she would voice.

"Say what you're thinking," I prompted her.

"Defying her was a foolish act that won you nothing," the girl blurted.

I had moved around the room, putting her between me and the door. Of course she thought my defiance had been pointless. I had thought the same about Aeon often enough. His defiance had gotten him killed. Maybe mine would do too. It could have gotten her killed.

"I'm here with you, so it won me something." I tried to smile, but it must have looked predatory because she winced.

She shook her head. "You cannot stay here."

"But your lord wants—"

"He was wrong to bring you here."

"Wrong?" I smiled. "Now who's the defiant one?"

She blinked, caught out.

I clasped my hands in front of me, mirroring her stance. "Can you help me find someone? He was brought on board with me. Does this ship have cells, a brig, somewhere they keep prisoners?"

"Yes, but I don't have access to those levels."

"Who does?"

"You should go and find out." She glanced at the door and wrung her hands. She really didn't want me here. She wasn't about to kick me out, but she had followed Devere's orders and wanted me gone.

I had Oberon's distant protection. She did not. Sjora might kill her to prove a point. I had enough deaths on my conscience without adding hers.

I bowed my head and touched my fingers to the bridge of my nose. *"Nashey."*

She mirrored the saru gesture of thanks. "Now, please go."

I paused at the door. "Won't your lord wonder where I am?"

She pressed her lips together, pushing out the color. "My friends say you are cursed, that wherever you tread, death follows. After you killed the queen, some fae retaliated, killing their serving saru in your stead. Some young saru are afraid to say your name. They fear you might come to them at night and kill their cellmates."

I looked away. I hadn't known that. More saru had died in the name of the Wraithmaker. My name had become a curse among my own kind. Would it ever end?

"They say the Hunt will surely come for you."

Fear traced icy fingers down my spine. But we were a long way from Faerie. The Hunt couldn't find me in Halow. I hoped.

"But..." she added, fisting her hands into her dress.

"But what?"

"I'm not sure. I think... when I saw you at the table..." She bit her bottom lip, drawing a bright red dribble of blood. "I saw... me." Her voice dropped to a whisper. "I mean, what I could be. It's wrong. It's so wrong, isn't it?"

Something curiously warm unfurled inside me. I wasn't sure I'd ever felt it for someone else before. I had enough trouble feeling it for myself. Pride. "Did it feel wrong?"

A smile bloomed across her lips and set her brown eyes alight with glee. "It felt good."

"I think that's your answer." Bowing my head, I turned to leave through the opening door and jolted to a halt in front of a tall, dark fae. His summerlands skin contrasted with the multicolored panels of his coat, cropped unfashionably short. He cocked his head, and a flicker of curiosity expanded his dark pupils as though he were drinking me in.

"Sonia," he said, "the Wraithmaker is standing in my doorway."

I heard Sonia's papery dress rustle. "As requested." She had likely dropped to her knees.

I, on the other hand, peered into the fae's dark eyes. He was shorter than most fae, putting me in the rare position of being able to face a fae at eye level. I should have dropped to my knees too, like a good saru, but I'd stood up to Sjora and this one wasn't half as scary.

He stiffened, but not with indignation, more as though he had remembered the protocol. "Will you step aside, or must I linger all night in the hallway?"

He hadn't ordered me to move. Interesting. I stepped back, letting him glide in. Sonia rose to attend him, unbuckling his coat and sweeping it off his shoulders in one smooth, well-practiced motion. His long hair swished down his back. Dark, but not as dark as Eledan's midnight locks. Lord Devere, I assumed.

"You will have to forgive Sjora," Devere said. His fingers worked at his cuffs, unlooping the buttons so he could roll them up, exposing sunbaked skin. No marks. A social fae, perhaps. Someone who likely dealt in politics and whispers, not weapons play. He still had their effortlessly handsome genetics. Faerie was incapable of producing ugly fae, or at least now it was. It hadn't always been that way.

"Tek exposure makes her short-tempered," Devere explained.

"It's not I who needs to forgive her. She attacked your saru."

Devere stilled. Sonia flitted around him like a well-trained pixie. His gaze fell to her, and his eyes widened as he watched her move, and then they lifted to me, carrying with it understanding and a hint of something else. Intrigue? A small green gem glinted at the pointed top of his right ear. "You don't miss much, do you, Wraithmaker?"

"Mistakes kill where I come from."

"Ah, the arena. Yes, of course. I saw you fight once. You couldn't have been more than nine years old. Fiery little thing, you were. I placed a wager on the boy." Devere flicked his fingers. "We all know how that turned out."

I wouldn't be standing inside Devere's chamber if the boy had won. "What was his name?" I asked.

"You remember their names?" Devere asked, surprised.

Every. Single. One. I blinked, giving nothing away.

He studied me again, taking his time. Where his gaze lingered, heat spread like the kneading touch of warm hands. I'd known fae who could touch with their gaze. It was usually a private skill, one reserved for lovers, not saru they had just met.

"You should get cleaned up," he said suddenly. "Sonia, would you run a bath for..." He waved a hand at me, gems glinting on rowan rings slipped onto his fingers. "You have a real name, yes?"

"Kesh." I wasn't ready to give up that name just yet.

A bright smile lit his face. "Run Kesh a bath."

Sonia scurried off into an adjacent room. A moment later, I heard water flowing. Actual *water*. The ship must have reserves, probably sucked up from the various atmospheres of the colonies it plundered.

"So tell me ..." Devere strolled toward me but stopped beyond arm's reach. He *had* seen me fight and knew to keep his distance. "I do remember the boy... a feisty thing. You were a wonder to watch together. Now... what was his name...?" He gave his head a shake to try and stir up the memories. "Arren... Ah... Alen?"

The corners of my mouth turned down against my will, and trying to correct the error only made it more noticeable. I turned my face away, pretending to admire the silk-dressed chamber to distract myself from the hollowness threatening to swallow me up. "Aeon?" His name tasted like ash on my tongue. Usually, I was more careful to hide the truth, but this time—whether from tiredness or some strange talent of Devere's—I couldn't hide it.

Devere saw it all play out on my face, but instead of probing deeper, he sighed. "Aeon! Yes! He was a valiant little fighter. One of my favorites. He later attempted to kill one of the royals. So spirited for a saru." Devere laughed and turned away. He didn't see my mask crumble. "Let's face it, we all want to kill one of the royals at least once per cycle."

What he spoke of was treason. But he said it in jest, so... what was I supposed to make of him? "Let me be clear, Kesh." He paused, a thought occurring to him. "Your slave name?"

"No."

"Good. Some things are sacred."

His knowledge of the saru way was acute and impressive. Definitely a social fae, a courtly figure who liked to deal in favors. His gaze was on me again, working over my face, stroking down my neck.

"Are you deliberately attempting to unsettle me?" I asked.

"I may be." His eyes glittered. "Is it working?"

I almost laughed. Oh, this one was dangerous. I could feel myself falling into the trap of liking him. They did that, made you like them, love them, and then when they grew bored with their new toy, they used you up and tossed you away.

"So, tell me." He pointed a finger at me. "There is

something you want?" I opened my mouth, but he continued before I could get a word in edgewise. "Of course there is. Saru have nothing, and so they are forever wanting. I will help you, Kesh. But in exchange, you will help me. Now, tell me this thing you want?"

"A vakaru."

Devere frowned, his pretty face darkening. "You realize those are extinct?"

"One was brought onto this ship. He is my prisoner. I was returning to Faerie with him for my king."

"A real-life vakaru?"

"Yes. The last."

"My, my." Devere considered it and nodded. "If he's on this ship, I'll find him. Anything else?"

"A fae by the name of Talen."

"Sjora's esteemed guest. The ship is aflutter with his name. What about him?"

"I... I would like to see him."

Devere scratched his forehead. "You are an odd one, for a saru. Most would ask for simple pleasures, physical time with their masters, a little mental stimulation—"

"And that is why I'd like to see Talen. He is my master." Lies. Slippery things, they fell so freely from my lips.

"I can get you these things you wish for. But in exchange, I will ask something of you, and you will do it. No hesitation. Something only you can do."

Whatever it was, he would dress it up with pretty words and charm, but the fae were all the same. He knew who I was. He knew what I could do. There's only one reason any fae wanted the Wraithmaker on their side. Anything else, he had Sonia for. There were no misunderstandings here. He likely wanted me to hurt someone for him, perhaps even kill them. If he got me close to Kellee and Talen, I would help him.

The humor slipped, and something of the shrewd fae shone through. The gem in his ear sparkled. "Are we in agreement?"

"We are."

CHAPTER 6

*A*fter going without real water for five years, and sinking into its warm embrace now, I would have gladly killed to stay submerged forever. In Halow, water was a precious substance worth a fortune. To lie in it, to wash in it, was unheard of. Faerie had no such qualms. Water fell from the sky and filled rivers and mountain basins. Vast oceans covered half the Faerie lands. As a saru raised on Faerie, I had taken such luxuries as wet showers for granted. Water was among the things I had missed the most after fleeing Faerie to find Eledan.

And now, a guest-prisoner on Sjora's ship, I basked in a few glorious self-indulgent moments, letting the water lap at my body, washing away blood and dirt. It wouldn't last, which made it all the more exquisite.

Sonia arrived too soon, though the water had long ago gone cold. She lifted a towel beside the bath. "Sjora has summoned you."

I blinked lazily at the saru and watched her failed attempts to keep her eyes off me. The rippling surface distorted the heavy black marks inked into my body, turning them into writhing snakes. Her quickening breaths gave her fear away. Did she hate me? I had survived this long by climbing a mountain of dead saru. Chances were I'd killed relatives of hers in the arena. I'd slaughtered our kin so that I might thrive. The evidence painted every inch of my skin, and I would never sully their memories by denying it.

Eledan had asked me if my people despised me. But looking in Sonia's eyes, I saw no hate. Acceptance, perhaps. All saru did what they must to survive.

Gripping the sides of the bath, I lifted myself out and stepped into the offered towel. "Is your lord trustworthy?"

Sonia struggled with the answer. She could lie, but she didn't want to. "I owe him my life." Color touched her pale cheeks, and I wondered if Devere used his heated gaze on her. Probably. It would be unusual for a lord to sully himself publically with a saru, but it happened in private more often than the fae admitted, and it was the main reason for the saru population, besides breeders, being made barren. I'd lain with curious lords and spent nights lost in their thrall. Saru didn't have a choice but to love them. Neither did Sonia.

How easily I had forgotten our ways while pretending to be a human messenger.

I dried off and strapped myself up in my outfit once more, aware of Sonia's heavy silence.

"How many have you killed?" she finally asked.

"Hundreds." I buckled up my coat, focusing on that instead of the memories bubbling to the surface of my thoughts. "Ask me how many I killed of my own free will."

She fell quiet.

I turned and wondered if that was awe in her eyes or terror. "One."

"He must have wronged you."

"No." I smiled, because if I didn't, I might have sobbed. "He did everything he could to save me." I stepped closer, expecting her to step back, but she lifted her chin and looked me in the eye. "There is one thing you should understand, and it's something Aeon taught me before I cut his throat." She searched my face, her breathing faster, her caged heart fluttering. "The fae are dangerous, they are brutal and unforgiving, but a saru is all those things and more. We are their shadows." I touched her cheek, remembering the countless saru like her who had died at my hand. "We move unnoticed among them. They underestimate us. They forget us. And therein lies our power."

"I would never hurt my lord," she whispered.

"I'm not suggesting you do. Just that you *could* and he would never see it coming."

"Not all of us were raised to kill, Kesh. There are other ways." Her smile said more, and I wondered if I had underestimated her.

She escorted me from the bathing chamber and wordlessly handed me over to two guards. Devere was nowhere in sight, and when the guards led me into a vast high-ceilinged, bowl-shaped chamber that hosted several hundred muttering fae, I realized why. The elite were all here, their flights of guards too, and at the center, down at the bottom of the bowl-shaped room, sat a vacant flat area. Grooves channeled away from the center of the arena into shallow gullies around the edges. Those grooves created a multi-pointed star. It might have been beautiful if I hadn't known those grooves were in place to channel blood from the floor. This was an arena. Small by the standards I was used to, but designed for bloodletting entertainment.

As the guards maneuvered me through the seating stacks, I searched the crowd for Talen, but there were too many here and more arriving by the minute.

I heard sweet intoxicating laughter and turned my head, expecting to see Eledan among them, but the laughter drifted away, making me wonder if I'd heard it at all. He wasn't here. He couldn't be here.

The guards left me standing in the arena and took seats among their own kind. I didn't have to wait long before Sjora's presence stirred the crowd into silence. She didn't even have to lift a hand to demand respect. She entered the arena, her green cloak flowing around blood-red leathers, and tossed my whip at my feet.

I ignored the whip and studied Sjora's smirk. What game was this?

Sjora turned to the crowd. "We are honored to have the Wraithmaker among us."

Murmurs rippled through the air. *Honored* probably wasn't the word most fae would associate with me.

"A killer so esteemed she is marked as many of you are, deemed equal by Oberon. It would be remiss of me not to let our esteemed guest entertain you all."

The murmurs grew louder, turning to excited hoots of anticipation.

Sjora faced me, unlatched her cloak, and tossed it into the crowd. She strode back to the center of the arena, each lean stride a proclamation of strength. She didn't have any weapons on display and didn't carry her infamous bow, but

I'd never expected a fae to fight fair and that wouldn't change. She had magic—defensive or offensive, I wasn't sure which.

I couldn't win this. If I struck her, they'd condemn me for attacking a higher fae. Only Oberon could sanction this fight, and he wasn't here. She knew this. It was an act, theatre, like the wine glass. I wasn't supposed to win. I *couldn't* win.

Sjora's grin was a hook designed to slide right in and not let go. "Show me, Wraithmaker. Show me how you killed a queen." She waited, arms at her sides, fingers loose.

Did she mean to kill me?

Oberon would be furious, but with my being dead, there would be little he could do.

If I picked up the whip, I'd be taking up arms against a fae general. I didn't even need to attack for this to defy fae law. If she killed me, she would be right to do so. There was only one way I could win—the same way saru had been winning for centuries.

I knelt on one knee and bowed my head, presenting her with the back of my neck.

The crowd let out a wave of disgruntled jeers.

"Oh no, no, no, Wraithmaker." She clicked her tongue. "You do not bow to me. *We are equal.*"

She offered her hand, a trap. But if I didn't take it, she'd be within her right to be offended, resulting in the same outcome. This arena was her gauntlet, her game. And I had no choice but to play by her rules.

Her cool grip encircled my hand. She yanked, lifting me off my knee, and planted a fist into my gut. My lungs seized, breath whooshing out, robbing me of control. She lunged for my throat next—her teeth bright and sharp behind her pink-lipped sneer, and her eyes a storm-grey. I brought my arm up, blocked her reaching hand, and threw myself downward, enabling me to kick out her weight-bearing leg. It was fast and dirty, the kind of move I would have used on Kellee, and it worked. She fell, but instead of landing spectacularly on her ass, she fell into the motion, using her hands to spring back off the floor and come right back at me.

She moved fast, like a force of nature, her greens and reds blurring together. Magic bloomed, its burn almost painful on my lips. I brought both arms up and blocked her fist. It jolted me backward, and she struck again, pummeling me from both sides, driving me backward. My heels hit a seated fae. Hands shoved me forward as Sjora skipped backward.

She lifted her hands, dragging veils of sparking magic with them. The magic boosted her strength so that she looked like a willowy courtesan, but she hit like a muscled redcap.

I'd survived the first round. But she'd soon grow bored with the act, especially if I didn't hit back.

"Stop this, by Oberon's decree!" Talen's voice cracked like my whip through the sound of pounding boots.

Sjora's smile died, and impossible defeat sagged her shoulders. Talen outranked her?

I drifted forward, dabbing at my jaw where one of Sjora's punches had gotten through. Talen descended the terraces to the arena floor, the lines of fae parting for him without him having to jostle. He still wore his riding cloak, but beneath it, silver thread glistened through his newly acquired gray leathers. He'd look like a winterlands lord if not for the color of his eyes.

I looked into those eyes, and for a terrifying second, I saw a stranger looking back. He turned his cold face away, silver hair catching the light, and squared up to Sjora. "This game is over."

"By what right—"

"You know exactly by whose right this ends now. You cannot feign ignorance, Sjora." He straightened and turned his disapproval on the crowd. "None of you can. Oberon did not sanction this. You are all guilty of defying the king."

Who, by-cyn, was this fae, because he didn't sound like the Talen who had dropped to his knees and begged me to save him. He looked Winterborn, but he wasn't. He didn't dress courtly, but his body language, and that of Sjora's, said he outranked her. He was *something* for the entire fae contingent to fall silent. I tried to recall what Kellee had said about him. Something about rebellion and scavenging old ships. But there had to be more to it, more that Kellee didn't know. Whatever he was, I owed him for stopping this parody of a fight.

Talen extended his hand. I was his saru. I was supposed to bow to him and take his guidance, but for a few seconds, all I could do was stare at it.

"Kesh."

I slid my hand into his. Despite his tone, his touch was gentle. Dull aches vanished, and a thrilling flicker of his magic darted through my chest. Hundreds silently watched us stand in front of Sjora.

The general's glare burned. Talen had called her out. Her crowd wouldn't let this continue, not with Talen here.

Her eyes narrowed to slits. She stepped back.

Talen paused as we passed her. He bowed his head and

73

whispered something too softly for me to hear. The general's gray eyes widened in surprise. Her lips parted, then she quickly remembered she had an audience, and her guarded expression fell back into place. "I will hold you to that, Talen."

I let Talen lead me through the maze of corridors, glancing only once at the fae striding beside me. His eyes were cold and distant, nothing like Talen's curious glances.

"Talen?"

"Silence," he snapped.

I flinched at the growl of disgust in his voice. A new fear gripped me, one I hadn't considered. This fae who marched beside me, this fae who spoke to hundreds of his kind as though he stood over them in status, this fae who had faced Sjora and ordered her off her kill—what if he was the real Talen?

CHAPTER 7

By the time we entered a chamber I assumed was Talen's, the space between us sizzled with the unspoken. He shoved me through the doorway, and after the door closed behind us, he fell back against it as though he could hold back the ship and threw his glare toward the ceiling. His throat moved as he swallowed. I watched the tension drain from his body. He took a shuddering breath and sighed it out.

"You mean something to them," I said.

He swallowed again but didn't lower his gaze. Maybe he was thinking of all the ways he could lie without lying.

I waited, but he didn't reply. As I wouldn't get an explanation, I took a quick look around the room. The decor resembled Devere's chambers. Colored silks and furniture grown from the walls and floor. Warm light softly glowed from deep inside the walls. I bet Kellee wasn't enjoying such luxury.

Talen pushed off the door and strode across the room, his pace choppy. His fingers jerked at his coat buckles so roughly I expected the seams to tear. He tore the coat off and tossed it over the end of a bed. Behind him, I watched him plant his hands on his hips and his shoulders heave as he breathed out. I'd never seen him wound so tightly. "I know what this looks like," he said without turning.

"How does it look exactly?" My body buzzed, with adrenaline numbing the worst of the bruises. The rush from the fight pushed illogical thoughts into my head: Talen had planned this; he was home and had sway among his kind; he had *wanted* this all along. These thoughts were poisonous but potentially true.

"You'll have to pretend to be mine." He turned and pulled roughly at the hook and eye fasteners of his waistcoat, freeing himself from the layers of leather.

I laughed, but it sounded strained. "Will I?"

His glare locked on me so hard that I'd flinched before I could think to stop myself. "Do not for one moment believe I wanted this."

"What did you want?" I asked, ignoring the irritating flutter of fear shortening my breaths and readying me for another fight. "This was your idea."

"No." He shook his head and looked down. Taking time to clear his head or form the right words? "No, Kesh"—he tossed a wave at the room—"this was your idea. You asked me to do this."

"You modified my plan. You said they needed more convincing, that we should stage it. Well, you sure convinced them you're something special."

Why was he looking at me like this was my fault? I hadn't asked Sjora to provoke me. I was just trying to survive and keep them both alive. Although, he didn't need my help with that. I was a fool. I'd bonded myself to a fae to control him, but I could no more control him than I could the stars. I didn't know him at all.

I folded my arms and held his gaze, refusing to back down. While I had defended myself against Sjora, he had watched. Watching like always. He could have stopped it earlier. "How long were you there for?"

"Most of it. Devere found me and told me what was about to happen. She would have killed you."

"Oh, he did?" I arched an eyebrow. "And were you supping with your lordly peers when he found you?"

"Don't." He pointed a finger. "Do not judge me on a lie you asked me to tell. Does our bond mean so little that you'd let appearances sway your opinion?"

"I don't know what it means. I don't know what any of this means." I threw my hands up. "I'm just trying to survive them, and you're... you're one of them. So, how should I behave around you? Should I kneel?"

Anger raced across his face, but it quickly fell away, leaving a grimace behind. "Have you found Kellee?" He lowered himself onto the edge of a large bed and braced his hands either side of him, still tense.

"No, I haven't found Kellee. I've been fending off Sjora." I looked at him, really looked. The gray leathers, now torn loose and threaded with shimmering seams, combined with his waterfall of silver hair. He looked like the worst of them. "Must be nice, huh? To be home? To be among them again? This was what you wanted all along, ever since Kellee let you out. Were you biding your time, making me think you cared so you could hitch the next fae ride out of Halow—"

"Your ignorance is spectacular," he snarled, flashing white teeth.

"Ignorance?" I really was the fool here. He did have me pegged. Probably had since Kellee first introduced us. I marched across the space between us and stopped in front of him, close enough that he had to look up to meet my gaze. "Enlighten me, then, Talen."

"What would you have me do? Board the ship as your subordinate? A fae beneath a saru?" He laughed, a dark, dangerous sound. A shiver touched my spine. "That would have gotten us both incarcerated or worse. I am using them, exactly as you asked me. I have done nothing wrong, so do not treat me like your enemy. I have committed many dark things in my life, but nothing to earn your contempt."

My thoughts stalled. He looked up at me while I looked down, and knotted inside, I felt the racing beat of his heart and the strength of honesty that went with it. I stepped back. He was right. He was telling me the truth, but equally, he felt the simmering touch of hate inside me. It wasn't Talen I hated. I felt a whole lot of complicated, messy things toward him, but not hate.

"It's not you." I drifted away, needing to move to keep from falling into all the thoughts that had been chasing me since I'd boarded the ship. "I don't hate you. It's... I think it's them. I don't understand it, but I think I hate them. And love them." I laughed at the insanity of it. "I don't know what I'm doing here. I don't know who I am anymore. When I had Oberon's orders, I knew what I had to do. I followed those orders. But now I find I'm thinking things that a saru shouldn't think. And I... I look at them, at the fae, and I hate them, Talen." It was taboo to say it. I almost wanted to snatch the words back and choke on them. Once, I would have been beaten to death for uttering such blasphemy. But the words were the truth, and in a world of lies, that mattered. "I hate all of them."

He looked up, hiding nothing from his face. None of the confusion I also felt. None of the sorrow. It was all there in the tightness of his lips and the pinch of his brow. He was here, playing this game, but he didn't want to be.

"I'm a mess. All my life I've loved them, and since Eledan... since I let that sluaghbait go, since *you and Kellee* put the idea in my head about choices... I don't know what I'm supposed to do anymore. Before, it was easy. I was saru. Now, I don't know what to think."

He stood and approached, his strides deliberately slow. Tension crackled between us, emotions frayed and awry. "Then think for yourself."

I smiled at the innocence of the words. "I wish it were that easy."

He took my hand and placed it gently on his chest, over his heart. I looked at my fingers held safely in his hand and not at his face, afraid of what I might see there.

"Do you trust me?" he asked, and I wanted to tell him yes, but how could I?

"I want to."

"Then do."

I looked into the eyes of a fae I hardly knew. He defied everything I had learned raised among them. That alone should have been enough to trust him, but the saru inside me knew he and I were creatures apart. This game he played, it had to be a trap. It always was.

I wanted to touch his face—my mysterious fae—but if I did, I'd fall deeper into this game, and I was afraid. Afraid of falling too far, too deeply. Afraid of the illusion of him and what truth he hid behind it.

"I will keep Sjora's attention off you," he said, making it sound like a fact.

"How?"

"The how is unimportant. While you're around me, she will keep her distance. We'll find Kellee, find a vessel, and at the next Point, we'll escape."

He could have abandoned Kellee and me long before now. He could have let Sjora have her way in that makeshift arena. He could have made all of this so much worse. But he hadn't.

"I do trust you," I said, trying to believe it.

His lips curved into a soft smile. "This ship, our time here, it's temporary. We will emerge from this. And then you can decide what you want to do with the hate you carry." He released my hand, and reluctantly, I lifted it away from his chest, already missing the solid feel of him. "Stay here. I must resolve the situation with Sjora."

I nodded and watched him leave. When the door closed behind him, I pressed my hand over my chest, my fingers still warm. I could almost feel the beat of his heart inside my fist. The last fae whose heart I'd held I'd been trying to kill. I wasn't sure I trusted myself not to hurt Talen too. My feelings for my fae and vakaru, they were more dangerous than anything I had battled in the arena.

Eledan's laughter echoed through the room. A memory, a dream, it didn't matter. He laughed because I was falling, and falling hard.

"I'VE FOUND KELLEE."

I dragged myself from the clutches of a dream and

wondered why Eledan was talking about Kellee when we both knew Kellee was dead. We had killed him together, over and over and over and in vicious, bloody ways.

"Kesh?"

Fingers touched my wrist, brushing my racing pulse. Why did Eledan have silver hair? His hair had always been as dark as the nothing spaces between the stars. He leaned over, so close I could see the violet sparks in his eyes. That was wrong too, wasn't it? I snaked my hand around his neck and pulled him down, but he turned his head away before I could seal the poisonous kiss. A cool slither of rejection shuddered through the foundation of this dream, shaking out the truth.

"Talen..." I gasped, surprised it was him I was reaching for. I was even more surprised to feel the same need to pull him down and make him mine in ways that didn't require words.

"The dreams?" he asked, too close, too damn close to everything.

I dropped my hand from his neck and curled my fingers closed on the arm of the chair. A chair. I'd fallen asleep in a chair in Talen's room. Yes, that was real. If I could get a grip on reality and shake off this desire, I could then claw my way back. "Just..." I winced, hearing dark whispers. "Just give me a minute..."

"I don't have any of Kellee's elixir," Talen was saying from somewhere far away. I'd closed my eyes to shut him out, and he had moved away. That was for the best. I couldn't think straight with him so close.

"I'll... I'll be all right." I sounded far away too, like someone else was speaking. "Just... some time." The dream drifted around me, tangling itself in my thoughts to pull me under again.

"No. It will get worse."

I opened my eyes and waved him away or beckoned him forward. Which was it? He looked like a winter storm, all wrapped up and pinned down in fae finery.

"Let it..." I whispered.

"Kesh." Hands gripped my shoulders. His face filled my vision, all sharp lines and shadows. "I can't pull you out of this without him."

"S'okay," I slurred. The dream was warm and welcoming, and inside its embrace, I was Kesh Lasota again, the messenger girl, not a monster. I could fall there forever, and nobody would ever find me.

Something warm and soft brushed my mouth. Enticed, I parted my lips and chased the gentle touch, but it was gone, taken too soon from me. I wanted it back. I wanted more of that tease. I wanted to bite it and swallow it down. Opening my eyes, I found Talen still too close, his grip firm on my shoulders. Was it his kiss tingling on my lips?

He swallowed with a little click. "Are you here?"

I touched my lips with my fingertips, tasting the sweetness of Talen there, but before I could lift my gaze to question him, he let go and strode halfway across the room, putting cold distance between us. "I've found Kellee," he said.

"Kellee," I echoed, sitting up in the chair. Yes, this was real. I was back. Kellee. Find Kellee. Get off the ship. I stood and swayed. Talen tensed as though he might rush in, but if he did that, I'd lose myself again. I shook my head, poured strength into my dreary limbs, and tried to appear steady. "Is he okay?"

Talen delayed in answering, meaning the right words were eluding him again. "He's being detained, but he's unharmed. For now."

"Take me to him."

"Well, look at you two," Kellee drawled. His gaze lingered longer on Talen, weighed down by accusations.

Unfazed by the marshal as always, the fae blinked back at him, arms crossed and face blank. I doubted it had escaped anyone's attention that Kellee's two most recent prisoners were free and looking at him, the one now incarcerated through organic cage bars. Normally, I'd have pointed it out just to annoy him, but the situation was too grim for jokes, even ones at his expense.

His cell was roughly the size of the glass and tek one he had kept both Talen and me in. A soft orange light glowed through the back wall, illuminating the cell. Holes in the ceiling and floor inside Kellee's cage were likely for water, but they also made it drafty.

Fresh slash marks scored the inside of the bars. He'd been busy.

Kellee appeared to be faring well. He looked scruffy around the edges. Someone had thought to bring him a fresh shirt, but in a small act of defiance, he hadn't bothered to button it up.

"You can speak freely," Talen said. "There are no guards nearby."

"Kellee. I will get you out of here." I closed my hands

around the bars, testing their rigidity. Their construction was grown, like the rest of the ship. My whip wouldn't be enough to break him out, and I couldn't find a locking mechanism. Or, for that matter, a door.

He narrowed his eyes at me. "Don't go hurting yourself with all that effort you must be putting into it."

"Don't be an asshole," I said. "We're alive. That's good."

"Sjora will have you fight in the arena," Talen told Kellee.

Kellee didn't look surprised, but I was. "She is?" I asked. Why hadn't he told me?

Kellee chuckled. "I'll kill anything they throw in with me."

Talen arched an eyebrow. "That'll be Kesh."

"What?" I faced the fae and received the same flat look he'd given Kellee.

"I was going to tell you."

"When?!"

"Right now," he replied.

Kellee's chuckles darkened. "I'll refuse."

"Sjora will kill you," Talen said. "She's looking for a reason. Do as she says. Both of you. Entertain her and her troops. Buy time. She won't have you killed. My suggestion to hand you over as a gift to Oberon went down well."

Kellee leaned back, and stretching out his legs, he crossed them at the ankles. "You're giving the orders now, huh? It didn't take you long to fall back into your old ways, did it, fae?"

"Careful, Marshal," Talen warned, adding the highborn faeness to his tone—the one I hadn't heard from him until recently. "We're the only two friends you have this side of the bars."

"Friends?" Kellee tested the word and eyed Talen side-on. "Is that what we are?"

I smacked a hand against his bars, jolting them both to attention. Kellee's unimpressed glare landed on me. "Stop it. Stop this. This isn't you. You're better than this. Ever since Calicto, you've been a dick. Knock it off. We'll fight and give them a show if we have to. It's nothing we haven't done before, but this time, we'll have an audience. The more they think we're theirs, the more power we'll have over them. We're alive, and that means we still have a chance. We aren't weak. You're the last vakaru, Kellee. You survived. And Talen, damn it, you're an expert at lying without lying, and I'm pretty sure that's as good as it gets around here. And you both have me."

"The Wraithmaker." Kellee's lip curled. "Be still my vakaru heart."

"Not the Wraithmaker. Kesh Lasota. I'm not letting either of you go. Do you hear me? I don't care what it takes. I'm getting you out of here."

"Kesh Lasota is the dream of a killer who thinks she can pretend to be good, but you can't take the fae out of the saru and you can't take the lies out of the Wraithmaker."

I huffed at Kellee. "I'll prove you wrong, and then you'll apologize."

"I will, huh?" The corner of his mouth lifted.

"I'd like to see that," Talen muttered.

Kellee's sneaky smile grew. "You're on. Save me and his fae ass from the Harvester and her ship and I'll apologize any way you want, Kesh Lasota."

"Any way?"

"Any fuckin' way." He folded his arms, smug smile not going anywhere anytime soon. He didn't think I'd go through with this. Either he didn't believe me, or he believed I'd fail. He was about to discover how little he truly knew me.

CHAPTER 8

*T*he bowl-shaped arena had attracted several hundred fae—the most I had seen of the ship's retinue so far. They watched the guards lead me in, eyes as cold and shallow as forged steel. Some might have seen me fight on Faerie. All knew my name. I had a reputation to uphold. But so did the last vakaru.

Kellee stood across the arena floor from me, arms folded across his bare chest. The pretty marshal I'd met in the sinks had taken on a rough edge these last few weeks, and it was more pronounced now in his hard glare. A few renegade curls escaped his ponytail, and the shadow of short whiskers darkened his chin. His slanted smile sat loose and twitching on his lips. Behind his dark eyes, anger simmered. The fae had taken everything from him, but he still had his pride. He wouldn't make this easy.

My guards released me and backed to the edge of the arena floor. Just as I was thinking there was little to stop Kellee from leaping into the crowd and slicing through a dozen fae, a tremble rumbled through the room and bone-like rods shot up from the floor, bolted upward, and curved over, sealing themselves into a star above our heads. A cage of bone. Lovely.

Excitement shivered through the crowd and me.

I turned on the spot, scanning the faces of the fae at the front. Sjora was here, leisurely sprawled sideways in her chair and chatting animatedly with Devere seated beside her. The lord was equally animated, flashing smiles, his earrings glinting. On her opposite side, an empty seat waited to be filled.

I lowered my hands and spread my fingers. I hadn't been permitted my coat, but I had my whip coiled at my hip. Kellee had his claws.

"Welcome, everyone." Sjora moved to the arena floor. She walked around the outside of our dome, red split-coat flowing around her like blood in water.

The crowd fell quiet.

"We knew, when our king ordered us to take back Halow, that the worlds we encountered would be unforgiving. We knew"—she paused for impact and lifted her chin—"their tek-riddled existence would seek to expel us, but Halow is ours. It has always been ours, and no human tek can stop the might and justice of Faerie!"

A roar lifted from the crowd and rumbled through the air.

"Oberon was right, and I admit, I was not the first to kneel to him, nor was I the second or third." She smirked, and much of the fae grinned back at her, their smiles equally sharp. "But I cannot deny he succeeded where Mab failed. Halow has grown weak, its reliance on tek its undoing. From the very heart of Halow, Oberon guided his brother's hand at a great personal cost."

She spoke of Eledan, and that wasn't how I remembered any of it, but Oberon knew how to spin an opportunity in his favor, and I doubted Eledan—wherever he was —had the strength of mind to deny anything his brother said, if he was conscious at all.

"No resistance remains," Sjora continued. "And make no mistake, Halow is only the beginning. Sol awaits our return. And we will resurrect Valand from its slumber."

Kellee's snarl was subtle, but I heard it. Valand was a star system all but forgotten, much like the fae until recently. There was a connection there. Valand = vakaru?

Sjora stopped her parade around the dome and lifted a hand, spreading her fingers wide. The glass thimble twinkled. "Humans tremble before us, and behind us, the bones of our foes are buried beneath Faerie's touch." She closed her fingers into a fist.

The cheering grew so loud I felt it thunder against my chest. Halow. Sol. Valand. And the distant system Meda. The fae intended to take it all. They would wipe out the humans, exactly as they had the vakaru.

Kellee's gaze caught mine, and an understanding passed between us.

He had once told the Calicto survivors that he had a plan. He had never confirmed it, but that plan had likely been me. And while I had helped save Calicto's people, my betrayal afterward had crushed him. He had believed Kesh Lasota could be so much more, and now, as I locked gazes with the last vakaru inside a cage of bone, I believed he might be right.

"Today, I bring you a gift. Without you"—Sjora swept a hand at her congregation—"this conquest would have amounted to nothing. The strength of Faerie lies within her foundation, a foundation built upon timeless tradition. Each of us is Faerie brought to life." Sjora turned in a swirl of red. "And for Faerie, I present to you the Wraithmaker and the last vakaru." She gripped the bars, grinned, and said low so that only Kellee and I could hear, *"Entertain me."*

Kellee roared and burst forward in a blur. Instincts had me grabbing for the whip and flicking it high, combining the motion with an upward jump. The whip's tails looped around the star above us. I pulled and swung off my feet and around the swipe of claws cutting through the air where I'd stood a heartbeat before.

Kellee growled in frustration. He twisted so my inbound kick found his jaw instead of the back of his head. It would do. He grunted and took a step back to regain his balance, but in that time, I'd landed, ducked, and punched him in his gut. I wasn't the strongest of fighters, but I was fast. Kellee *oofed* over, snatched my arm, and yanked me into a messy left hook that found my ribs. The punch frazzled the nerves in my side, but bones didn't break. He was holding back.

I hooked my hand around the back of his neck and buried my face against his neck. "Just warming up?" I hissed.

Distant jeers and hoots filled the air. I didn't care about the audience. Only Kellee.

He pulled me off him, and with a dramatic snarl, he tossed me across the arena floor. I knew how to fall, how to relax my body so the impact didn't break anything vital. My hip and shoulder hit the dome bars. Pain bleated its usual alarm, and I fell to my hands and knees, shaking it off.

The throw had looked dramatic, but I was fine. I reached for my whip and groped at air.

It dangled from the center of the dome, directly between me and Kellee. He tilted his head, cracking his neck and spine back into alignment after the kick I'd dealt him.

At his side, his fingers twitched. Ten curved claws slowly descended. Those lethal weapons could suddenly appear on reflex. Their inch-by-inch appearance was all for show.

Cut out his heart... a sweet male voice crooned in my ear. An involuntary twitch tugged my focus away from the arena, away from Kellee, and down, down, down to where Eledan would whisper dark things and rouse even darker desires. I pulled my gaze away from Kellee and cast it somewhere outside the dome to banish the memory of my hands cutting him open time and time again. It had been one of Eledan's favorite dreams. The Dreamweaver... *He takes your mind, makes it his, takes your soul, makes you cruel...*

A hooded fae sat beside Sjora in the spot that had been vacant. With his face cast in shadow, only his violet eyes revealed his identity. Talen. I blinked, and those eyes darkened to a deep, swirling blue. The outline of his jaw squared-off, turning stubborn and proud, and I watched while horror closed my throat and turned my heart to ice. Thorned tattoos crawled across his changing face. *The Dreamweaver is here.*

Kellee slammed me against the bars, rattling my teeth. He pinned his forearm under my chin, holding me back. "What are you doing?" he hissed under his breath. "Wake up, Wraithmaker. We're meant to be putting on a show..." His reprimand trailed off as he saw the whites of my eyes.

He wedged his knee between my legs, his body pushing in, holding me firm. He breathed evenly, his chest calmly rising and falling. I snatched at breaths like they might be my last. To anyone outside, Kellee's stance looked aggressive, like he meant to smother me, but his eyes searched mine, all the while losing their fiery rage. He searched inside the fear I reeked of and saw the truth.

Kellee brushed his cheek against mine. His stubble grazed my skin. "He's not here. Fight or we'll lose." His lips tickled my ear, his whiskers scratching my cheek, and it all felt so real. This wasn't a dream. Kellee was here, with me.

I nodded, though he probably didn't see it. He shoved off and lifted his clawed hands to the crowd, making a show of returning to the center of the dome.

I couldn't look at Talen. Didn't want to see the lies my mind crafted around him. Never look outside the fight. Aeon had taught me that. *The audience means nothing. Your opponent is your world. Get distracted and you die. If you have to look somewhere, look inside yourself and find your strength. Find it and hold on to it. Nobody can take that from you. Not the fae. Not me. Like your saru name, your inner strength is yours and yours alone.*

Kellee grabbed my whip and flicked it free. Its length pooled at his boots. He lifted it by the handle, showed it to the crowd, and gave it an experimental flick. The metal links chinked together, broadening his smile, and the fae howled their approval.

Kellee whirled the whip around his head. He'd have to crack it faster if he meant to hurt me.

I dashed forward and dropped in low, skidding across the arena floor. My heels hit Kellee's boots, flinging his legs out from under him. He unceremoniously fell over, landing on his ass. I was already twisting onto my front, digging my boots in and rising. I snatched the whip from his hand and recalled its length, pulling it out of his reach.

It was a good move. I grinned at Kellee's startled frown.

He sprang back to his feet. We circled each other. My whip twitched. His black claws gleamed.

"Just getting warmed up," he said, eyes sparkling.

The world fell away until all I saw, all I lived and breathed, was the fight.

Kellee beckoned.

We clashed and danced in a macabre display until blood slicked the floor and my whip and his claws were painted red. Pain riddled my body, but all the ghosts in my head were gone.

After what felt like forever and no time at all, Kellee went down, feigning exhaustion, and I looped the whip around his neck, leaving enough room to avoid his claws.

"I submit," he grumbled.

The crowd was on their feet, baying for more bloodshed and carnage. I lifted my head, breathing hard through my nose, and found Talen and Sjora deep in conversation. Neither paid their main attraction any mind. I saw Talen nod at something Sjora said, and then he stood and left without glancing back.

Of all the wounds Kellee had inflicted, all the blood spilled in the name of entertainment, none hurt more than seeing Talen walk away.

Sjora got to her feet and approached the bars. She eyed Kellee on his knees and me standing over him, judging us.

She nodded and announced, "The Wraithmaker wins for Faerie!"

Wraithmaker.

Wraithmaker.

Wraithmaker.

They chanted. There was a time when I would have done anything to hear the fae cheer for me. Now, it turned my stomach. The name was not one I wore with pride. Not anymore.

The dome bars retracted into the floor, and Sjora's faithful soldiers spilled in, grabbing Kellee off his knees and dragging him out ahead of me. By the time I was escorted away, there was no sight of him.

"Take me to the vakaru," I told a guard. He blinked at me, marching on.

The after-fight adrenaline buzzed through my veins, sparking against nerve endings. I didn't want to go back to Talen's chamber. I would say or do something I couldn't take back. I needed to see Kellee. He would be okay; I'd barely hurt him and hadn't worn him down, despite how it had appeared. Had it all not been a lie, he would have won that fight.

Two guards flanked me, both bigger, faster, and armored up to their pretty chins with reinforced leathers. I tightened my fingers on my bloody whip that no one had thought to take away from me and listened to their in-time footfalls against the floor. Three, two, one... I freed my whip, ducked the oncoming spearhead, jabbed my elbow into the right guard's waist, and looped the whip around the left guard's ankles. Lefty stumbled to his knees. Righty spun his spear but found I'd knocked his balance out from under him. I blocked the spear's shaft and punched him in the nose. Blood exploded across his face. He snarled, unfazed by the sight of a little fae blood—until he realized I'd used the distraction to slide the crossbow at his back free.

I jabbed the pointed bolt under his chin. "Take me to the vakaru."

CHAPTER 9

*K*ellee took one look at my battered and bloodied guards and approached the bars. "Making friends, Kesh?"

"Let me in there." I jabbed Righty in the back with the bow.

"You don't give us orders, saru," Righty snarled, contempt alive in his eyes.

I let him go as though I believed he was right, then pulled the trigger on the crossbow. The bolt punched into his thigh, and he abruptly found himself on his knees, clutching at the wound and hissing like a pissed-off briggan.

Lefty was now the one to watch out for. Tension ran through his body, pulling him as tight as a coiled spring. He would lunge for me and soon.

"Don't," I warned, crossbow hot in my hands. "I'm just asking you to let me in with the vakaru. It's not worth losing your knees over."

The still-standing fae considered the risk and his

companion clutching his leg. Decision made, he jerked his chin at the bars. Three broke open, receding into the ceiling and floor, allowing me to step through. Kellee looked as though he might make a dash for it, but I shook my head. We had nowhere to go. Not yet.

"Sjora will hear of this," the fae snapped.

I waited until the pair had staggered out of sight and then turned to the marshal.

He raised a questioning eyebrow. "Got yourself a new crossbow?"

I shrugged and set the weapon down on the bench, aware I was trapped inside a cage with a creature who thrived on violence. "They'll only underestimate me once. That was it." We didn't have long. More guards would be here soon.

I assessed the marshal. He folded his arms and leaned a shoulder against the bars. Bloody slices crisscrossed his chest where my whip had caught him. Some gaped like hungry mouths. He should have been wincing in pain, but instead, he watched me appraise him, his expression almost bored.

I hadn't wanted to hurt him, had I? I couldn't deny the thrill I'd experienced in the arena. It still buzzed in my veins. "I tried to go easy."

I folded my arms, matching his posture, and leaned against the bars. Kellee made his nonchalance look effortless. I felt wooden. I wanted to move. To pace. To say I was sorry for everything. My heart raced, pumping blood hot and fast.

"I *did* go easy."

"I know." My mouth tilted upward. I dropped my

hands to my side and flexed my fingers. This was unexpectedly awkward. "I saw Talen."

"Next to Sjora. Yeah, I noticed." He reached up and tugged the leather band free from his hair, letting it fall around his face. He combed his fingers through his hair and drew the dark mop to one side. "You trust him?"

"I do." It came out confident, though I felt anything but. But Kellee didn't need to know that. He had enough to worry about without wondering if Talen was on our side.

The silence was back, and I eyed the doorway, wondering when the guards would return. I wasn't sure why I'd come. In the arena, we'd fought, and I'd loved it. Every second. Now, here, this... I wasn't sure what I was supposed to say or do.

He lifted his gaze. "Are you okay?" He nodded at the tears in my waistcoat, still keeping himself rooted to the other side of the cell.

"Just surface scratches."

"And in here?" He tapped his forehead.

The damage up there was a long way from surface scratches. I mustered up a smile. He didn't buy it.

"Here." He dug into his pants pocket and pulled out three little vials of clear liquid. "These were all I could grab before the fae came. They'll take longer to work if you drink them, but they should keep the dreams at bay for a few days." He crossed the small cell, took my hand, turned it over, and dropped the vials into my palm. "Eventually, you won't need it. But this is not the time to wean you off the Dreamweaver."

His touch sizzled, his hand warm against my chilled flesh.

99

Instincts said I should pull away, but I couldn't without tugging hard. He looked down at the vials, his touch and gaze lingering too long. He might have been about to say something, but whatever it was, he swallowed it and let go, retreating to his side of the cell. He rubbed his hand down the back of his neck and looked up at the ceiling. "I hate cages."

Oh, the irony. He hated being locked inside, but Marshal Kellee didn't have a problem using cages when it suited him.

I prodded the vials, more grateful than he could know. "Thank you."

He moved in my peripheral vision and sat on the bench, head bowed, fingers sinking into his hair and locking there. Part of me wanted to sit next to him. He was alone, but he didn't have to be. But he'd made it clear I wasn't in the friend zone. We'd just spent the last hour cutting strips off each other. He was Sjora's prisoner, and I was Oberon's assassin. What was I even doing here?

"You need to be careful around Talen."

I leaned back against the bars and rubbed a sudden weariness from my face. "I am."

Kellee looked up. Lines had gathered around the corners of his mouth, and some of the luster had vanished from his eyes. "This will be difficult for him."

I'd expected warnings from Kellee but not something like compassion for the fae. Perhaps I should have. The pair had always had an unusual relationship. Kellee had kept Talen behind tek and glass for centuries. They had formed a bond over that time. I was a prisoner and understood all too well how easy it was to sympathize with your jailor and befriend them. It was the saru way, but I had never seen a fae form that kind of connection. Probably because the fae were rarely held captive for long. "What do you know about Talen?"

He leaned back. "Only what I told you. Apparently the fae exiled him for rebelling. That's all I ever got out of him, and believe me, I tried everything to get him to talk. Even got him wasted once." He laughed softly, a good-natured chuckle. "That's worth seeing."

Talen *wasted?* I couldn't even imagine the reserved fae losing his inhibitions. "I'd pay good v to see that."

Kellee dwelled in his memories. "He said a lot, but none of it worth anything. He's careful with his words. I've known him for a few hundred years, and I'm still not sure who he really is."

"You've only known him through bars, right?" I asked. "Until recently, you didn't know him outside the cage?"

Kellee nodded.

"Then you're right to be concerned. Trust me, what you see through bars is nothing like the truth of a person."

He looked through me, into me, seeing my past in those words. Seeing the saru girl the fae had bred to serve them. Behind bars, I was a very different creature from the woman wielding a whip inside an arena. "Oberon pulled you out of that life."

"Yes."

"He will kill me."

I blinked. "Yes." A lie wouldn't do either of us any good.

"Will it be you?" His throat bobbed as he swallowed.

I had wondered the same thing during all the nights I'd spent alone in Kellee's glass cage. "It depends on how much he has told the court. If they openly know who I am, then yes, he'll have his Wraithmaker kill the last vakaru. If

I'm still something of a secret to the courts, then no, he'll keep our connection a secret."

"It's a crap secret. They know you killed the queen. They know he's now the king. It doesn't take a genius to draw the line between you and him."

"There's a big difference between whispers and the Faerie King admitting he killed the queen."

"Hard to deny an outright question when you can't lie."

"Who would be insane enough to ask him?"

Kellee's face darkened as he contemplated my words. "They didn't just kill the vakaru. They destroyed everything, our worlds, our heritage. Our system is dead."

"Valand?" I had never been. Nobody had for hundreds of years. The system had been abandoned long ago. Now I knew why.

He nodded. "If they kill me, they win. I'm not ready to die."

Hearing him say the words shook something loose at my core. A fragment of cold or the stalwart knowledge that he'd always be here. And I saw it now, the reason why he looked as though he had aged. This ship, this cage—he was surrounded by enemies. An enemy his people had fought and lost to. "You won't die."

"Will you save me?" His smile barely touched his lips.

Guards spilled into the room, one after another after another. My escorts had arrived, and I'd gained a few more in number.

I tossed a smile at Kellee and tucked the vials into a pocket. "I owe you that much."

CHAPTER 10

*A*fter cleaning myself up, I paced Talen's smartly dressed room with its flowing gossamer silks, waiting for the fae to return so we could discuss what he knew and how soon we could attempt an escape. The memory of seeing him talking with Sjora played over and over in my mind. Kellee's warnings also sailed around and around like water circling a drain. What was Talen doing? Where was he right now? Why wasn't he here? He had seen me fight and knew Kellee had hurt me. All right, not as badly as I could have been. But it would have been appropriate for him to acknowledge how Kellee and I had been forced to beat ten shades out of each other for *entertainment*. Instead, he'd upped and left before the end.

"This is ridiculous," I told the empty room. Talen didn't owe me anything. These thoughts were paranoia creeping in, dregs of doubt and anxiety left over from Eledan's damn touch on my mind.

I set Kellee's three vials down on a shelf and considered downing the first one. Kellee had said three would last me a few days, and then the dreams would find me again. Or I could *not* take them, ride this out, and be done with Eledan's influence once and for all.

The door opened behind me. I turned. "It's about time..."

Devere strode in, carrying the unconcious body of a silver-haired fae in his arms. It couldn't be Talen. Clothes draped off him in bloody tatters, and flashes of skin revealed the same vicious damage. Seconds passed too slowly, like the labored beat of my heart, like Devere's thudding footfalls as he approached the bed.

"Help me," Devere barked, but I only distantly heard him. He laid Talen down on the bed. A trail of blood led from the door to the bed, and it was already soaking into the sheets.

I moved, mind and body numb. "I don't..."

Blood ran red through Talen's hair. Mercifully, his eyes were closed. The lids twitched, lashes fluttering. His lips were so pale they were almost as silver as his hair.

"Warm towels. Go!" Devere snapped.

I sprang into motion, gathered towels from the bathroom area, tossed them into the bath and soaked them in hot water.

Who had done this to him? Why hadn't I felt anything? I should have felt something like when the scout had shot him on Adelane. If I'd known, I could have gone to him.

Someone did this to him.

Sjora.

I returned with the towels and silently helped Devere peel off the tattered remains of Talen's gray leathers. The cuts through his clothes and skin were clean, precise, surgical. Someone had taken their time. *Torture*.

Sjora's wrath on the battlefield was legendary, but why would she torture Talen?

I turned over possible scenarios instead of dwelling on the way the countless wounds wept too much blood. My fingers brushed his icy skin.

"He's not healing."

"He will," Devere replied, hitching Talen's boots off. "Keep the wounds clean. They'll seal soon."

"Who did this?"

"No one you can touch." Devere returned my glare with a level one of his own. He knew who had done this, but he wouldn't tell me because that knowledge was worth something. "Hush now. All we can do is make him comfortable."

I worked alongside Devere, dabbing at Talen's cuts, cleaning away the blood so the skin could stitch itself cleanly back together. I ran my hands down his arms, sweeping blood from his wrists and revealing the swirl of his unique markings. I did the same across his torso, gently feeling my way over every inch. Devere and I worked methodically, silently, until Talen lay naked and clean on the sheets. I stepped back from the bed and folded my arms to keep myself from shaking. He looked like a work of art carved from marble, his marks striking in their dark luminescence. His chest rose and fell, each breath strong, and his closed eyes darted. He was dreaming. That was good.

I tried to steady my breathing so it matched his and failed. Each precise cut had traced every one of his marks. Someone had carved up my fae like a piece of meat.

Useless tears blurred my vision, smudging Talen's dark markings.

"He will survive," Devere said. "Get some rest." He nodded at me to move away.

I wasn't going anywhere, and I certainly wasn't leaving Talen alone with Devere. Just because the lord had brought him back, it didn't mean he wasn't complicit in whatever had happened. "Is he stable?"

Devere wiped his forehead. His fingers trembled. "Yes. I think so."

I shot a hand out, locked my fingers around the fae lord's neck, and dragged him backward, away from the bed, away from my vulnerable Talen. Devere's magic blasted up my arm, fiery and sharp like raw electricity. Nerve endings screamed. I tightened my fingers through the pain and slammed him against the nearest wall. "Who. Did. This?" I didn't raise my voice. Didn't need to.

Devere barely struggled. Struggling would have made it worse. Clever male. He glared down his nose. "I do not know for certain."

"That's not the answer I want to hear."

"It's the truth."

Of course it was.

I dropped him. It was that or give in to the urge to strangle him, and he still had answers. I just hadn't asked the right question. Forcing myself away before I acted on the killing urges, I asked, "Sjora?"

He massaged his neck. "I don't know."

"What *do* you know?" I dropped my hand to my whip. "Start talking."

"I understand." He lifted a hand. "I do. He's your master—" The look I gave him cut off the rest of that sentence. "He *was* with Sjora, but I didn't see her do this. She summoned me. I found him as you saw him. She told me to bring him here."

I would kill her. And I'd do it slowly, making Eledan's butchery look like delicate origami compared to the mess I'd leave her in. "Why? Why did she do this?"

His other hand lifted so that he held out both, trying to placate me or hold me back. "Wraithmaker, you're not thinking clearly."

"Do not tell me what I'M THINKING!"

"Look at him," Devere suggested. He nodded, urging me on. "Look."

I looked and winced at the sight.

"He will be healed in a few hours. There is no need—"

"Get out," I snarled quietly. He didn't hear. "Get out, Devere, before I do something you'll regret."

"I can help you."

I turned the full force of the Wraithmaker's gaze on him, reminding him exactly how I had gotten my name. The fae lifted his chin and left. After the door closed, I sighed, feeling the rage fade away. Devere was right. Talen would survive. Once he woke, he would tell me who did this.

At the bed, I pulled up the sheet and folded it over him, covering him as best I could. I ended up on my knees beside him, peering down at his content face. "What did she do to you?"

His blue lips parted, but wherever he was mentally, it was far away from here.

"Damn you, fae." I angrily wiped tears from my face and shrugged off my coat, then I carefully laid myself down beside him. His limp hand fit surprisingly well in

107

mine. I locked my fingers with his so at least, wherever he was, he'd know he wasn't alone.

"This is only temporary," I told him, echoing his words back at him. "I'll tell you what I told a stubborn vakaru. You saved me, and so I'm saving you. I owe you that much." The fae and the vakaru would either be the death of me or, somehow, they would save me. We would soon discover which.

I CAME AROUND, aware that the bed was too big for one, yet there I was, sprawled on it alone, and with the sound of burbling water nearby. None of these things made much sense to my sleep-addled mind. I was missing something. Something important.

Talen.

I jolted upright, and the panic that it had all been a dream faded as I laid eyes on the exquisite male outline through the dark blue curtain separating the bed and bathing areas.

The urge to call out and ask if he was all right got lost as my mind snagged on what I was witnessing. I couldn't see *everything*, just the profile of his body behind the drape. He stretched his arms above his head, working out the stiffness from the physical trauma.

I ran my gaze down the length of the body I'd had my hands on a few hours ago. But that was different. I'd been helping him then. This was... an invasion of privacy.

I tore my gaze away and picked at my nails in my lap. It was wrong to look. Saru were not to admire their masters without their explicit permission to watch. But he wasn't my master. Technically, I was his. I peeked from the corner of my eye, taking my time to admire his stance, roaming my gaze up the outline of legs, thighs, around the tight curve of an ass I'd admired on several occasions without his knowing, and over narrow hips. He lowered his arms and leaned over the bath, spoiling my view, and then dramatically improving it as he twisted off the taps and straightened. What I couldn't see made the view worse—or better.

Men on Calicto often used tek stitched into their clothes to fake the physique Talen effortlessly exhibited behind that flimsy curtain. He lifted a leg. My breath caught. He climbed into the bath and sank up to his shoulders, ending the show.

I swallowed. Hard. I'd known a few women and men on Calicto who would have paid good v for the sight I'd just seen.

If Kellee had been in the bath, I could have gone over there and teased him. He may have risen to the bait if his overthinking didn't get in the way. But Talen liked his silences, his long looks, his distance. I wasn't even sure Talen noticed me as a female. Fae used saru, not the other way around. I wasn't namu either—the breed of saru the fae used in many ways, most of them sexual. I probably didn't register on Talen's radar as someone—some *thing* that could arouse him. And that was a damn shame because what I'd seen had both fascinated and stimulated me in all the right ways.

I pressed a hand to my chest and felt my heart racing. It had been a while since I'd willingly been intimate with a male. Eledan and his dreams didn't count. That had been...

wrong and wicked. But this wasn't a dream, and it didn't have to end just yet.

I lowered my hand from over my heart, skipped it across my stomach, and paused, heat rising in my face. Talen wouldn't know. The drapes whispered between us. He was still there, head resting back while his hands rested on the rolled edges of the bath. I pushed my hand inside my belt, slid my fingers inside my underwear, and brushed my index finger over the swollen sweet spot, careful to bite off the sharp intake of breath before his fae hearing could pick up on it. Pleasure spun through me. There was no way I could go all the way. He'd hear. But I was tempted. What if he heard? Would that be so bad a thing? This didn't have to have anything to do with Talen. This was all for me. I worked my finger gently, collecting the wetness in smooth strokes, and then I made the mistake of imagining Talen's face between my legs, his tongue replacing my finger. The gasp came unbidden. Delicious shudders tightened all my best parts. I snapped open my eyes, realizing I'd closed them, and stole a glance at the curtain. He hadn't moved. Though his hands had vanished from the tub's sides. I closed my eyes, turned my head, and explicitly imagined his tongue gently swirling, flicking. His violet eyes, bright and alive, watched me throw my head back. He felt my hips buck, with my hands twisted in his fine hair.

Oh, sweet cyn.

Talen cleared his throat.

I yanked my hand out and froze, trying to control my panting. My heart was another thumping telltale giveaway. He couldn't know what I'd been doing, could he? I snuck a look. He still rested in the tub. Good.

While Talen soaked, I set about cleaning away the torn clothes, bloody towels, and spoiled sheets.

"Thank you."

His words snapped all my attention back to him. The drape still hung between us. "Devere brought you back."

Water sloshed. I looked toward the drape, just in case he needed help stepping out of the bath. He had no idea— no fucking idea—what he did to me. A naked Talen was a challenge to ignore. A wet, naked Talen... I was only saru. I looked. He was fine. Damn it. And looked away, wondering why I tortured myself with goods I couldn't touch.

"Devere..." he repeated, sounding intrigued instead of angry.

"Are you going to tell me what happened?" I sounded cold. Hopefully, he read it as frustration for having his bleeding body dumped on me.

I heard buckles rattle and leather sigh. I'd lived through all kinds of torture. This was right up there. I couldn't stand it anymore and strode across the room. When I flung the curtain back, he straightened from doing up his boot and blinked innocent eyes at me. Then his lips did an odd little twitch, and a devilish smile stopped my heart for three solid beats. He *knew* exactly what I'd been doing earlier.

"Don't smile and think you can get away with not answering," I snapped.

His fingers tightened his jacket closed, locking all of him away. He brushed by me.

"Hey," I called. "You can't pull that shit and not tell me what's going on."

His damp hair swished down to his waist, leaving wet

111

trails down his back. He looked over his shoulder, and my ridiculous human heart practically swooned.

Stupid fae. Stupid human DNA. I ground my teeth. "Stop fucking with my emotions. I know exactly what you're doing."

"I'm not doing anything. It's all you."

I laughed, sharp and sudden, because he couldn't lie, and that meant this desire was all mine, and I was falling so damn deep and so damn hard that all I could do was laugh. "Fine. Fine! Don't tell me. I don't care what happens to you, anyway." He flinched. Good. "Have you at least discovered anything we can use? Anything about where we're going?"

"Yes. We're not returning to Faerie." He turned, his humor vanishing. "We're going back to Calicto."

Oh. That was unexpected. "Why?"

"Sjora has her own motives, and I'm not convinced they have anything to do with Oberon and his orders."

"You'd know." It was a low blow, but one that sailed right over his head.

He nodded. "This ship is a formidable force, as is Sjora's flight. But I have her confidence."

"You do, huh? Did *she* cut you up?"

He bowed his head. "No."

That couldn't be right. "Did she order someone to do it?"

"No, Kesh. Stop asking."

"No, I won't stop asking. When I saw you..." My voice cracked, betraying everything I wanted to hide from him, hide from myself. "Talen, I..." I wanted my whip, wanted to go into the arena and kick Kellee a few times, wanted to take Talen in my hands and shake him, and hit him, and kiss him. "You frightened me." That was all I would admit, and it was all the emotion he would get from me.

"I am sorry you had to see that. It didn't occur to me that you would be here, and it should have. It won't happen again."

"What won't happen *exactly*? You being cut to shreds or me seeing it?"

He kept his mouth shut. I laughed dryly. He wouldn't answer any of my questions because that was the fae all over.

"You know, I wish I didn't care. I wish I'd never met Kellee or you. You both just got in my way. Without you, I'd still be the Wraithmaker. Eledan would be dead. I'd be following orders and everything—*everything*—would be easier."

"Do you mean those things?" he asked, his tone level and detached. If anything I had said hurt him, he hid it perfectly behind indifference.

"Every word," I lied.

"Then Kellee was right." He was walking away again, and I had no idea how to stop him.

After he left, his words rang in my head. *Kellee was right.* Kellee was always right. Eventually, the trembling subsided, and my flighty heart slowed until all I was left with was my own foolish guilt for pushing him away when all I wanted to do was pull him close.

I huffed out a sigh. "Killing them would be so much easier than this."

CHAPTER 11

*K*ellee tracked me back and forth as I paced outside his cage. At the door, a sentry stood as silent as stone. Outside, there were more of them. I'd returned to Talen's chambers after the latest fight in the arena, found no sign of Talen, cleaned myself up, and came straight to Kellee—guards tailing my every step.

And here I was, tremors twitching through my fingers, boots clunking against the floor. Kellee's green eyes read every twitch, every trip. Like before, my heart thudded hard and fast, adrenaline stirring with anger, confusion, shame, regrets, and all the things I hadn't allowed myself to feel. I had always been the Wraithmaker. Ever since I'd stepped out of the delivery crate as a little saru girl, painted in the blood of her brothers and sisters. I'd had one mission then: to survive. And I had survived. I'd survived and thrived, and I'd made Oberon notice me and risen alongside him. Now he was my king and I, his shadow. I had always been the Wraithmaker. My life had always been simple. And now... now I wanted more. I wanted things the Wraithmaker could never have.

"Ah, Kesh." Devere shattered the beat of my angry pacing. His attention skipped over the silent Kellee before resting on me. "I was hoping to find you here." He smiled like we were old friends and clicked his fingers at the sentry.

The guard nodded curtly and left.

Devere waited for something, an acknowledgment perhaps. I lowered my head enough to show him I appreciated the gesture. His smile grew. "This one is for free." And with that, he turned and left the prison chamber. I waited for the guard to return, but after a few moments, it was clear Kellee and I were alone.

"Who's he?" Kellee grunted.

"Someone who wants something." I looked at the empty doorway, waiting and listening to the pounding inside my head.

"You okay?"

Kellee sat on his bench. Beside him lay a pile of soiled towels, and his hair was dripping wet. He'd cleaned up from our fight and thrown on a clean jacket, covering the worst of what I'd done to him. I hadn't been gentle. I felt guilty about that too.

"We're returning to Calicto."

He straightened out his legs and rubbed his chin. "Talen told you this?"

An ache throbbed up my jaw and around the back of my neck. Unclenching my teeth, I answered, "Yes."

"What did he do to piss you off?"

"Nothing."

"Nothing? You nearly took my head off in the arena. At one point, I wondered if we were even playing anymore."

I approached Kellee's cage and gripped the bars in my fists. "What did you see in me that made you think I could help you?"

He blinked, unbalanced by the sudden shift in conversation, but he knew exactly what I meant. He had told me once, after helping me back from the Dreamweaver's clutches, that he saw a spark in me. Told me, and others, I could help them. He had *asked* me to help him help the human survivors of Halow. That was before he learned who I really was. That was all Kesh Lasota, but the messenger girl *was* me. At least, I was realizing how much I wanted her to be. Kellee had seen something in me, something I couldn't see. Not yet, anyway. But I wanted to.

"I saw lies," he answered.

"No." Damn him. He wasn't getting away with that answer. "It was more than that."

"What I saw—the bravery, the hope—were lies. All of it. You're not the person I thought you were." His stare wavered like he wanted to look away, but he held on, glaring, challenging me to defy him.

I slammed a hand against a bar and swallowed all the knee-jerk accusations I wanted to throw at him. "You're wrong."

"No." He laughed cruelly. "I'm not."

It hurt. It hurt like him turning the key in my prison cell door. It wasn't supposed to hurt like this. It never had before. I let go of the bars and lowered my hands to my sides. "Help me, Kellee." He glared back, unmoved. "Help me find that spark. Help me be that person."

"You can't."

"I want to."

"She was a good person underneath. Underneath *you*"—he waved a hand at me—"there's a heart as dark as all Faerie's twisted creations."

"Says the man with a monster inside him."

"Yeah." He folded his arms. "But at least I know it."

Devere strode into the room, his footfalls deliberately heavy. He cleared his throat in a not-so-subtle attempt to catch my eye. When I finally broke away from Kellee's stare, Devere said, "Walk with me."

Kellee raised a single dark eyebrow. "See you in the arena, Messenger."

Outside the cell, Devere dismissed the guards with a simple gesture. I watched them file off down the curved corridors and wondered if Devere truly understood who he walked beside.

"We're just going to walk," he said and started forward, his stride leisurely. "We can do that without incident?"

I nodded and fell into step beside him, pushing all of Kellee's denials to the back of my thoughts alongside Talen's vague karushit and the mountain of doubts piling up around me. Instead, I studied Devere. His clothes were the elegant type often found at court. Flowing, thin, loose fabrics of greens, reds, and gold. They matched the gems that sparkled in his earrings. I hadn't seen him at Mab's court, and he appeared like the type who liked to be noticed, but I imagined Oberon's court was different. My king would have surrounded himself with trusted individuals. Was Devere among them? If he was, then he was on the wrong ship. Sjora was no fan of Oberon's.

"Things were getting tense back there," he noted. "How are you feeling now?"

"You were listening?"

"Yes. Why else would I dismiss the guards?" Mischief twinkled in his eyes and pulled at his lips.

I tried to recall everything I'd said to Kellee. None of it was too damaging. Just my pride was wounded.

"I'll admit, I find you and your partners fascinating."

"They're not my partners," I instantly denied. To imply I was anything more than a slave to Talen risked his life.

"No?"

"I serve Talen, and the vakaru is..."

"Yes?"

"A pain in my ass."

Devere laughed a deliciously deep, rumbling that sounded genuine to my lie-attuned ears.

"And Oberon?" he asked, straightening his face.

"What of the king?"

"Are you his?"

We had walked through twisting corridors and down gentle slopes. Now we came upon a doorway with a closed pod inside, similar to an elevator but entirely organic.

"We are all Oberon's," I replied, hesitating outside the pod.

"It's perfectly safe." Devere stepped inside and gestured for me to follow.

"Where are you taking me?"

"If I told you, that would ruin the surprise." As he said *surprise*, his white teeth flashed. He offered his hand. "Come, Kesh."

I looked down at his palm. His dark skin and glinting rings were all part of the fae seduction. I did need to see more of the ship to get a mental map of the layout for our escape. But a threat lurked behind this fae's bright smile. Devere was no different from all the fae. A predator. But this one had his own motives. So did I. I took his hand and stepped inside.

DEVERE SHOWED me enormous caverns littered with single-person spacefaring vessels. Like blind newborns, the vessels suckled on teats in their individual bays, waiting to be called upon by their fae pilots.

"The fae are highly attuned to their vessels," Devere explained as he noticed I'd stopped to admire the collection of ships. "From these small attack spawns to the ship herself. It takes great skill and presence of mind to pilot them."

The small offspring didn't have the warcruiser's foreboding appearance, but I had seen them darting through the skies during one of Kellee's rescue missions. They had enough firepower to cripple anything the human response could throw at them. Faerie effortlessly made beautiful things deadly.

We walked along catwalks, over shimmering streams of water, past enormous chambers that appeared empty. And then we came to one of the monstrous ship's two hearts. The chamber it hung suspended inside was locked behind three layers of organic doors, none of which opened for us. And inside, through a clear membrane window, I watched the huge organ thump vibrant green magic through arteries the size of oak trunks on Faerie. The same life magic Mab had given me to give Eledan, her son, in the hopes it might heal his tek heart. The same magic I'd used to bring my whip and Sota to life. I didn't have that magic anymore. Eledan had ripped it from me, and seeing rivers of it streaming through the ship's veins, I ached to have it back, to feel it rushing through my veins, to have something of Faerie to call my own.

I touched the membrane and spread my fingers. It was warm, soft, alive. This ship was a wonder of Faerie.

"Beautiful, isn't she?" Devere had been watching my reaction. He spoke softly, his voice heavy with reverence. "I might never have seen it had Oberon not insisted I join Sjora's flight."

At the mention of Oberon, I pulled my hand back and straightened. "The prince—our king suggested you board this ship?"

"He did." Devere smiled at the secret shared. Sjora didn't know or she would have refused Devere's presence. He was telling me because he believed I was Oberon's.

A shiver spilled down my spine. "Oberon ordered you to find me."

"Ordered..." Devere mulled over the word. "He asked. I accepted. How could I pass up an opportunity to meet the Wraithmaker, the infamous murderer of so many?"

I knew then by the ice hardening in my veins, that I didn't want to go back. I loved Oberon, I did, for everything he had done for me. But the last few months had changed me. If I went back, the things I had learned, the friends I had made, it would all be for nothing. I'd killed a fae scout to keep Talen and Kellee safe from Oberon, to keep my secrets as Kesh Lasota safe. I'd helped Kellee rescue people. I had made a difference to those who couldn't fight for themselves. I didn't want that to be lies.

"You will return with me, yes? As per our arrangement." He must have seen the doubt on my face. "I helped you in exchange for a favor. This is the favor I ask of you. Come back with me so we both might please the king."

I dragged a smile onto my lips and pinned it there. "Of course." The lie tasted bitter.

Devere beamed as he saw his chance to please his king fall into his lap. "Will you honor me with your company for dinner?"

I let him take my hand in his. "How could I refuse?"

CHAPTER 12

"We will be on Calicto in a day. There's plenty of time for a little respite." Devere lifted his goblet and tilted it in acknowledgment. "I believe you've earned it."

The spread of food and wine looked as though someone had spilled buckets of brightly colored decorations across the table. Vibrant fruits, bleeding red meats, plump grains—all Faerie harvested, which meant at least half of what was here was probably poisonous to a saru. Devere had offered me the feast without a price. I was to eat freely. Thankfully, I had spent enough time in the background at courtly feasts to know which offerings to avoid.

"Reports are that we've terraformed the human planet," Devere said. "Ah, what is it called... *Calicto*, yes." Devere spoke easily and gesticulated, making him appear animated and careless with his words. "The reservoir of magic found there made the process quite simple." He picked something small and bright pink off his plate and swallowed it in a single bite, white teeth flashing. "I imagine it will be quite different to how you remember it."

Calicto hadn't been perfect, but it had been human, with its tek cities and enormous environmental domes. Soon, it would be as though the human colonies had never existed.

Devere's saru, Sonia, drifted around our table, refilling our wine glasses and clearing plates with all the quiet grace of a well-trained saru. Devere ignored her and talked about his role as advisor to the new king. He told me of Oberon's elation upon discovering his brother's success in bringing down the Halow defense net and how he'd even boasted that his brother had endured centuries of tek exposure to support Oberon's claim to the throne. Of course, he lamented his brother's insanity and his mother's death. It was an *interesting* slant on events.

My thoughts fell to the new king and what he might be thinking. Oberon could have publically ordered for his mother's killer—me—to be hunted down. He hadn't, though most fae took it upon themselves to hunt me anyway. Devere spoke about rumors circulating, as they always did on Faerie, about my association with Oberon. None could say they were surprised. All this had been coming for a long time. Oberon was patient, to a point, but he'd had no intention of spending eternity as a Faerie prince when he could be Faerie's king.

I smiled through Devere's chatter, ate the food that wouldn't kill me, and drank the wine until the chamber took on a fuzzy hue and my battered body no longer ached. Exhaustion frayed the edges of my thoughts, plucking my concentration apart, and I relaxed. Devere was harmless, mostly. He wasn't a warrior, and he wasn't about to stab me in the back. He was still a courtly lord, but those I could handle.

Sonia refilled my goblet for the tenth—fifteenth time...? I'd lost count and didn't care.

"Your whip..." Devere came around to my side of the table. He had removed his flamboyant coat, revealing supple and loose dark pants and a surprisingly modest lace-up shirt. Its light color complemented his dark skin, which had a fine glittery sheen to it up close. Just like with the ship, I had to refrain from reaching out and touching.

He leaned back against the table, looking down at me in the chair. "May I see it?"

I'd been so lost in admiring him that I'd forgotten what he had asked.

Mischief played in his eyes. He knew I'd lost myself in thoughts of him. I was saru. I wasn't allowed to admire them for long. But I wasn't like the others. I looked up and held his gaze, a gaze that held power, daring him to chastise me.

His mouth curved into a smile. "The whip," he reminded.

I unclipped the whip and set it down on the table, rattling the few remaining plates and my goblet. Metal gleamed, cold and alien in this organic world. The magic it had once held was long gone, taken when Eledan ripped it from me.

Devere's eyes widened. He slid his fingers down one of the links, then quickly pulled back with a gasp as the cool metal burned his fingertips. "Delightful." He shuddered, thrilled.

Most fae despised the whip and what it represented. But not him. I found that... intriguing. "It was a gift," I said, unaccustomed to hearing the pride in my voice. "It used to be charged with magic and could think for itself. It was a delight to wield."

"A gift?

"From Oberon." It was the truth. I had told others Mab had gifted it to me, but that was a lie to protect my king. Nobody knew this whip's true origin but Oberon and me. And now Devere. I wasn't sure why I'd told him. Around him, my thoughts lost their edge.

I set my glass down and stood so I could run my hand along the train of metal links. "I used to make tek trinkets for the arena on Faerie."

"Oh, I remember." Devere laughed and shifted closer, pressing against my arm so he could whisper, "There was talk of it being banned."

"There was?"

His fae eyes widened, a glittering slyness playing there. "It wasn't the brutality you inflicted upon your competitors that concerned the arena council, more the fact you could find tek on Faerie at all." He chuckled darkly. "How did you?"

"I stole it," I admitted. "Me and... a friend would steal from the fae. Books, fabric, sometimes jewelry. But tek was difficult to find. There were stockpiles of rusted tek. I guess the fae tried to dissect it once. I don't really know... why they had it, just that it fascinated me." I stroked the whip, running my hand over its shining length. Devere's gaze turned heavy with desire, and I felt its touch run down my neck. Anticipation fluttered inside. "The day I stopped the assassination, Oberon noticed me."

"That infamous day," Devere echoed, so close we both knew where this had the potential to end up. "There are rumors, you know, that the boy's spirit haunts the arena still."

I hesitated, remembering Aeon's motionless hand cooling in mine. That memory above all others plunged like an arrow straight to my heart. I would never forget it and didn't want to. I faced Devere, faced a fae—a lord—who was looking at me as though I was worth something. "Oberon took me from the arena and trained me... personally." The more I spoke, the more Devere's eyes darkened, filling with want. "My affinity with tek... it disgusted him. I offered to stop, but instead of allowing his weakness to rule him, he turned it into his strength. He made it so human tek sensors wash off me. He *made* me a tek whisperer." I heard the awe in my voice, and Devere's gaze took on a mutual longing, perhaps even a mutual love for the king.

"Our king saw your use before the rest of us could imagine it." Respect lifted the edges of Devere's voice. His gaze dropped from my face to soak up the stroke of my hand on the metal. I swept my touch around the whip's loop. Static electricity danced across the back of my hand. His gaze followed, then flicked to my face.

He swept my hair back, pushing it over my shoulder, and the look in his eyes turned from fascination to hunger. The kind of hunger a fae lord was forbidden to share with saru.

Devere's warm hand moved to the back of my neck. His fingers gently closed, claiming me. "I'll take you back to him, where you belong," he whispered. "You have my word."

He was too close, filling my vision with his velvety summerlands skin with its subtle golden glitter. Elegant dark eyes pulled me in. I thought of Kellee's coldness and Talen's distance. Thought of all the things I couldn't have because of who I was and the terrible things I had done. But I didn't frighten Devere. He knew me, and he *wanted*. I could have Devere. Here and now. He had offered me everything, offered me more than food, and he was giving it freely. His lips parted, so close his minty breath brushed my mouth. I could cross the line and take what he offered so I could taste Faerie in him. It had been so long...

His fingers stroked my neck, sparking my body alive with a promise. I'd lain with the fae before, taken their gifts of pleasure, because it was always divine, even when to them it was a way to waste a few hours. Just forbidden entertainment. They had once driven humans mad with this same want and need and hunger because they were creatures of desire. I wanted to feel that with Devere, knowing it would mean nothing.

"You killed the scout," he whispered against my mouth.

I stilled. *How could he know that!?* Had Talen told him? No, he wouldn't.

His next words brushed my lips with a touch as delicate as pixie wings. "The nothing girl is lost in her dreams of another life."

Terror gripped my heart, crushing it tightly. I gasped, once, but his grip on my neck clamped closed and his mouth crashed into mine. His tongue thrust in, taking, owning. He tasted like I remembered, like sweetness and poison, like all the things that could destroy my heart and mind. He wasn't Devere, not anymore. Not to me. And to my horror, I kissed him back, open-mouthed and attacking, owning him as hate and ecstasy combined into a desperate, clawing need. The hand not clamped on my neck gripped my ass and yanked me against his hardness. We clashed, the feel of him too much, too soon. He pressed into me, shoving me against the table. I clasped his face in my hands and bit his lip, tasting sweet fae blood. He tore away, gasping, snarling. *Too fast.* Strong hands cupped my buttocks and jerked me up onto the table. I hooked my legs around his waist—the fae who wasn't here, who couldn't be here, the *Dreamweaver.*

I fisted a hand into his long black hair, fixing him in my grip. He laughed into my neck, his body rocking with mine, grinding between my legs, pushing his arousal close.

Insanity clawed at my thoughts, ripping them into nonsense pieces.

Something behind me fell from the table and shattered into pieces, and somewhere distant, a girl cried out. Her voice wasn't mine. *Not me. Not me. Not me.*

He's not here, I heard Kellee whisper. But when I opened my eyes, Eledan's severe face filled my vision, his heated mouth captured mine again, and his blue eyes blazed with lust and madness and *hate.* Everything was wrong, but his hands swept over my hips, jerking my pants down. The shock of the cold tabletop hit my thighs. His warm hands plunged between my legs and pulled my thighs apart. He pulled back and unlaced his pants, freeing his arousal. I throbbed, wet with need. Lost to insanity.

His hot mouth trailed down my chin, my neck, spilling pleasure in its wake. So fast. It was all happening too fast. The room spun, and his touch scorched. His serpentine laugh twisted around us.

I'm losing my mind.

He dropped to his knees and peered up the length of my body. His tongue touched my swollen, sensitive clit in one, long, lazy lick, and I exquisitely lost my saru mind. My fingers sank into his hair, threading it into knots, and the tip of his tongue swirled faster. Every flick lit me on fire and every tiny suck unraveled more of my control until there was nothing left but lust and need and a storm of his making.

Then, when my mind was about to break apart, he reared up, clamped one hand around my neck and the other on my lower back, and thrust in. I gasped at the sudden fullness, caught, pinned, drenched. He kissed my mouth, tasting of my own saltiness, pulled out so I snarled for more, and then thrust in so deep that pleasure stretched along the sharp edge of pain. Again, he thrust, hard, fast, grunting as his own control slipped. I watched his teeth flash behind a sneer and felt the coiled spring tighten harder and harder as he thrust again and again, pounding desperately. We rocked, locked in a unison of hate that had to be wrong but felt all kinds of right. Pleasure threatened to tear me apart, riding me higher and higher until I lost all sense of me, of him, of anything but where his hands held me down and his cock seated so deep. I threw my head back and cried out as the madness tore me open. He pumped, frantic and raw. Then his rhythm stuttered. He thrust again and spasmed, grinding out a pleasure-laden groan that wrung the dregs of tingling sparks from me. I looked him in his blue, Eledan eyes, felt all the disgust and fear drag their way back into reality, back to the forefront of my mind where the terrible truth lurked like a monster in the dark. And Eledan laughed. The same laughter that haunted me night after night. The same laughter I ran from in my nightmares.

I had the whip in my hand with no memory of

reaching for it and its metal links looped tightening around his neck, but the laughter wouldn't stop. Even as he clawed at the whip, tried to dig it away from where it burned into his flesh, even as he collapsed to his knees, choking, gasping, reaching, he still laughed.

Dread gathered like a storm cloud. A terrible, gut-churning knowledge that all this was wrong. What I was doing, it was wrong. This room, the sex, the feel of him. It was all so terribly wrong.

"*Die!*"

His neck snapped.

Eledan fell at my feet just like he had in Arcon, only this time he wouldn't be getting back up. My heart surged at the victory. His black hair fanned out and the gem in his earring glinted, mocking me with the truth.

Eledan didn't wear jewelry.

Reality barreled in, shattering all the lies my ruined mind had spun.

I dropped the whip and stumbled back, bumping against the table.

A sob broke free. I covered my mouth with one hand, then both to keep the pain inside.

He's not here, the Kellee in my memory whispered.

And the Dreamweaver wasn't.

He never had been.

Devere lay dead, half naked, unceremoniously sprawled across the floor, his head twisted at an odd angle.

My thoughts were tangled in a nightmare that was real. I looked around for the saru girl. Nobody was here. Just me. And what I'd done... I'd killed before. Many, many times. But not like this. Never like this.

Sickness burned the back of my throat.

I swallowed it down.

Another sob startled me. *No, don't fall apart here.*

I remembered—when I'd walked from the saru delivery crate all those years ago, stepping over the bodies of those I'd killed to earn my place among the fae—I remembered the fear eating me up inside, trying to drop me to my knees and force me to vomit up my terrible acts. It told me I could never survive this. But I remembered the strength too. The strength Aeon had known I had in me. The strength Kellee had seen. The strength that had kept me fighting. I had not come this far to be ruined by dreams parading as reality. Strength had driven that little saru girl to walk from that crate into a new life. I needed to find that strength now. The strength to survive no matter what.

The whip's links had dug into his skin. I plucked it free, leaving burnt triangles behind.

Encased in emotional ice, I walked from Devere's chamber through the ship's corridors. I walked down and down. Panic stalked my every step until I found the cells.

Kellee looked up through his bars. His eyes met mine and narrowed. He got to his feet, stirring the guard by the door. The guard that never saw my strike coming. I punched the guard in the throat, silencing any alarm he could bleat, and then grabbed him by the neck.

"Now is not the time to test me." I lifted my whip, letting this fae see the links and smell the burnt flesh. "LET HIM OUT."

The guard's trembling chipped away at my ice, but I needed that ice just a little while longer.

"Look into my eyes, fae, and understand me." I didn't sound like me, not anymore. Didn't even sound like the

Wraithmaker. "I was raised to kill. It's who I am. I've killed hundreds of my own people, killed a queen, killed fae just like you, and I will kill you if you do not open his cage."

The guard's eyes widened. "Sjora will kill *you*, saru," he sneered. But I heard the bars retract, glanced to check, saw Kellee step free, and slammed the guard's skull against the wall, knocking him unconscious. He would live, unlike so many who had met me.

Kellee straightened when I turned to him, his hands at his side, ready in case he needed to let loose his claws.

"I've done something," I told him, feeling more ice falling away, my walls crumbling. "Something bad." Why had I come here, to Kellee? He already knew what I was. He would judge me, hate me. But he was all I had.

"You'll have to narrow it down," he said it with the same typical lawman smirk that drove me crazy, but seeing it now shifted the ground beneath me.

"I killed a fae." I forced the terrible words out.

"And that's bad because...?"

"We were fucking," I said, cold, empty, and so close to screaming I wondered if I already was. "And I killed him."

"What?" Kellee blinked.

"He was Eledan. But he wasn't."

Kellee reached for me.

Fear cracked my ice. Fear that I might hurt Kellee too. Really hurt him. I stepped back.

"Kesh?" He moved closer, stalking me, fencing me in.

I looked at the whip in my hands and felt the wetness of Devere's seed between my legs and the ghostly grip of a dead lord's fingers on my thighs. "Devere was Oberon's, and he said he would take me back, but I don't want to go back. And then..." The ice was all gone and I couldn't get it back, and if I didn't say everything all at once, I might crumble with it and collapse right here in front of Kellee. This wasn't me. I was strong, cold, unyielding. But all that was lies, wasn't it. Because underneath, the truth revealed I was a nothing girl.

The marshal's hand found mine. I tugged to get free, but he pulled harder, and I let him, because if he let me go, I'd fall so far I might never find my way back up again. "With the wine and the Faerie food, it triggered Eledan's mindfuck, and... I er..." I flicked my fingers at my head and the knotted madness eating me up from the inside. "It er..."

Kellee's arm came around me so gently I was afraid it wasn't there at all. Was I imagining this? He pulled me close, so close I smelled the fae leathers he wore, but also the unmistakable earthy scent of Kellee. The stiffness thawed, and I melted into the marshal's touch, feeling small in his arms. Only Kellee could see me like this. Only Kellee could understand everything I'd told him and know what it meant. "I fucked Eledan," I hissed. "I killed him. But it was Devere, and his saru girl saw."

"She saw all of it?"

"Maybe. I have to stop her from talking. I have to—"

"No," he said, not loud, just firmly. His chin brushed the top of my head, and his arms tightened, holding me so close I could bury my head against his shoulder. He couldn't see me cry. "You can stop killing," he said. "Just stop. This isn't Faerie. You don't have to be the Wraith-maker anymore."

The room blurred. I squeezed my eyes closed, pushing out the tears. How did he know the right thing to say?

How did he understand my fears so explicitly when I didn't even understand them myself? I hadn't chosen to be the Wraithmaker. Faerie had made me her. And now... I didn't need to be that monster anymore.

Today, I had made my choice.

"Where's Talen?" he asked, and like a hook, it sank in and yanked me back into the moment.

I sniffed and pushed from his arms, quickly wiping the tears away with a trembling hand. "I don't know, but we have to hide. They'll find Devere, and they'll come for me. And you." I'd screwed up. We could have escaped, and now...

"*And* Talen," Kellee reminded.

Talen was at the center of it all, right beside Sjora, surrounded by a whole race of fae who would kill him if they knew he had willingly bonded with a saru that fucked and killed fae lords, but there was nothing I could do to protect him.

"*We* have to hide," I said again, firmer now. "Talen is on his own."

CHAPTER 13

We just had to make it to Calicto and get off the ship. It wasn't anything like the grand escape plan I had hoped to put into action, and I was missing Talen, but I hadn't planned on killing a prominent courtly fae either. That had been a mistake. I was making a lot of those.

I watched Kellee shove and drag a few crates around a storage deck, creating a secluded corner for us to shelter in. There were too many entrances, but our small fort of crates would suffice until we reached Calicto in a few hours. This was *only temporary*.

I tucked myself into the corner of our shelter and pulled my knees to my chest to fend off a bout of shivering.

Kellee propped himself against the opposite crate. When he stretched his leg out, his boot rested beside my thigh. The other leg he bent at the knee to rest an arm on. Considering we were on the run in the heart of a fae warcruiser, he appeared remarkably relaxed. In the short time I'd known him, I'd only seen him afraid once, when Eledan had cut his throat open. The Halow system was unraveling at the seams, and he had witnessed it all with barely a raised eyebrow. Probably because he'd seen it all before.

"What happened to the vials?" he asked, resting his head back against the crate.

After Talen's bloody appearance, I'd forgotten all about the vials. "I left them in Talen's chamber."

"You didn't drink any." Kellee gave me his *I told you so* look. "One day, you'll admit I'm right and listen to me."

I rested my chin on my knee. "Never." My teeth chattered. It wasn't cold inside the ship, so why couldn't I get warm?

"You're in shock."

"I'm fine."

He shuffled around and sat next to me. I expected an arm to come around me like it had outside his cell, but his hands lay in his lap. It didn't matter; it was enough just having him close. "Eledan's gone."

I didn't reply. The Mad Prince might have been as good as dead. Oberon undoubtedly had his brother locked away in a deep, dark hole somewhere, but he was still real in my head.

"You're human—saru, but still human. From what Talen told me, few humans survive the Dreamweaver. Devere's death was an accident. Don't blame yourself."

I closed my eyes and rested my head on his shoulder. "I killed a scout during our last mission. Devere said... he said he knew, but I think that was my mind mixing it all up.

Devere was going to take me back to Oberon and tell the king everything. He knew you and I, and Talen..." What were the three of us exactly? Friends? More? "He knew we're... close."

Kellee turned his head and looked down at me. I wondered if he was about to argue how close we were, but whatever he was thinking he didn't voice it. Something of it showed in his eyes though. Concern, perhaps. Confusion, maybe. But he wasn't judging me, and I was thankful for that.

"I'm worried," I said.

"That's reasonable." He let his head fall back again and closed his eyes, appearing to rest, but he was probably listening through the ship.

"Worried about Talen."

A low grumble rumbled in Kellee's chest. "Talen can look after himself."

He hadn't seen him ripped to shreds and bleeding all over the bed sheets. I'd thought Talen was invincible, but seeing him so broken made me realize how much I appreciated him. And Kellee. "How *did* you catch Talen?"

He drew in a deep breath and opened his eyes. "There were multiple sightings of activity in the debris zone. That place is a ship graveyard, littered with decaying warships and mangled human tek. Most folks just think it's a junkyard, but it's more than that. The debris is all that's left of the final battle in the first war. The radiation alone can kill a man in days." As he explained, his voice soothed my brittle thoughts. And I listened, like before, when I had asked Eledan's illusion of Kellee to tell me about his life. Only this time, Kellee was beside me, and real. "When the report landed on my desk, I thought it was a joke. Nobody stays in the debris zone. I almost tossed it, but I figured a trip to the edges of Halow on company time was a great way to earn some v. This was a few hundred years ago, mind. The fleet of marshal ships was slower back then. I took my time, did a little sightseeing around trading posts, and eventually drifted out there and poked around a few wrecks. I didn't find anything and was about to head back, when my ship picked up signs of life where there shouldn't have been any. I found Talen rattling around abandoned ships. He was weak and malnourished. Didn't put up much of a fight. I figured I'd caught a unicorn—"

"A what?"

"A mythical creature. Nobody believed the fae were even real anymore, and I had one. But the law intercepted my ship before I returned to HQ. They told me to keep my mouth shut or I'd lose my job and took Talen to a secure facility."

"That's not the story I was hoping for. Where's the vakaru-fae stand-off?"

Kellee snorted. "That's yet to happen... The first place the Law tried to hold him in, he escaped. Talen around humans..." The marshal rubbed his face. "He might as well have had a key to every lock. He convinced an entire prison population to riot. Nobody bothered to tell me how, but it must have been that touch of his." Kellee wiggled his fingers in a very un-Talen-like way. I fought off a smile. "He sparked *rage* in a bunch of grade-one criminals and walked out of the chaos untouched."

I had witnessed Talen's touch, and I wasn't surprised he had the potential to turn a crowd to his will. "How did you catch him?"

"He found me."

"He didn't run?"

Kellee shrugged. "He caught up with me on Point Juno. Just appeared at my airlock one night and told me to lock him up somewhere with better security."

"He *wanted* to be caught? That doesn't make sense. He told me his imprisonment wasn't voluntary."

Kellee glanced up. "He talks to you, huh?"

"Not really. Every time he tells me something, it leaves me with more questions."

"Exactly. He likely meant he had no choice. Like the rebellion information I got out of him. He's never explained it, just said he made a mistake. When the Law locked him up this time, they managed to hold him for a few decades. Then he turned a guard into a paranoid wreck—turned them all paranoid. He walked out of that prison too."

"And found you again?"

"No. After the first time, I was assigned to monitor him. That time I got there before he could escape. After that, his next prison was the glass box. No visitors except me. And there he stayed until you showed up and things got interesting."

There was only one reason a fae would expose himself to tek. The same reason Eledan hadn't gone home. "He was hiding from Faerie."

Kellee nodded. "That's what I reckon. I figure he's upset some powerful families back home and the prison here kept him hidden and alive."

But the tek in Halow tortured him every hour of every day. It chipped away at his magic, at everything that made Talen fae. What waited for him back home had to be worse than that. I could only think of one thing that would cause a fae to run and keep on running.

Gooseflesh scattered across my bare arms. If I was right, Talen was running from an immortal's worst fate: Death. I'd never seen the Hunt. But I'd heard it once, even deep within my cell. Heard the thunderous hooves and the baying hounds come to turn the light of the living into darkness.

"When did you stop hating him?" I asked, rubbing my arms to brush off the fear.

Kellee smiled, but it was his thin, ironic smile. "Halow changed, people grew old and died, villages became towns became cities. I stopped belonging. But Talen stayed the same. Halow is a mortal system. Life decays and lives again, over and over. Valand—my home—wasn't like that. Time flowed differently there. Talen reminded me of that, of home... I think." His brow knotted, memories surfacing. Then he noticed me watching, and the frown vanished behind a widening smile. "You ask a lot of questions."

"It's refreshing to have them answered." And it kept my mind off the dead fae and the swarms of guards hunting us down.

Kellee shifted, angling himself toward me. He studied me in that unblinking way of his. "Do you know what the first thing Talen said when I let him out?"

I blinked back at Kellee, assuming it wasn't "thank you."

"He asked where to find you. Three hundred years in a cage and he asks for the messenger with a tek-whip. And that was before I told him exactly what he'd agreed to. Turns out we wanted the same thing: to get you away from the Dreamweaver."

142

I could understand why Kellee had come back. I'd saved him, and his sense of honor demanded he save me. But Talen's motives were as gray as ever. "Why me?"

"I don't know." And the look on Kellee's face told me not knowing bothered him. "You had Mab's magic when you met him. Maybe he wanted that."

"Maybe." I didn't think it was that, but I didn't have any alternatives. Talen was on the run and alone. He had been running for a long time. Maybe he saw me and saw a piece of Faerie like Eledan had. A fae alone was a broken thing. Did he think he was alone right now?

I had to find him and tell him the truth, that Kellee and I hadn't abandoned him, that Devere had been an accident, that I didn't mean those things I'd said to him. "He's not safe here."

"No one is." Kellee looked up at the curved organic ceiling. "You think this beast of a ship wants us inside it? It only does as the fae say because it doesn't have any other option. It's a prisoner, same as us."

I chewed on the inside of my cheek. The shakes were subsiding. I'd be all right in a few hours. We'd get away from Sjora, leave the ship, and find somewhere safe to hole up on Calicto. After that, I had a new path ahead of me, one I'd been ignoring. "I want to help you, Kellee." *Help you and Talen, just like you asked me to all those months ago.* "Help you save people."

He looked at me side-on, but he wasn't smiling. "If you mean that, I'll help you. Screw me over again, Kesh, and there won't be any second chances." His teeth flashed as he spoke, their points sharp.

"No second chances," I agreed, my damaged heart fluttering with hope. I could do this. I *wanted* to do this.

"For the record, your rescue plan sucks."

It was hard to argue with him when we were hiding behind storage crates inside the bowels of a Fae warcruiser. "It's not over yet."

"Just sayin'..." He stretched out a leg and folded his arms. "You've got a long way to go to get that apology."

"THEY'VE FOUND US." Kellee's words snapped me from the dreamlike state I'd been drifting in. He had his hand on my shoulder and his face close to mine. He pressed a finger to his lips and lifted his head, listening. I froze, soaking up the background *thwomp thwomp* of the ship's twin hearts and listened for anything out of place. I didn't hear anything, but Kellee's senses were vastly superior to mine.

His hand slipped down my arm and rested gently on the back of my hand.

I slowly hooked my fingers around my whip's handle. There, I heard it, the deliberately soft placement of a boot, then another. We were being stalked.

Kellee flicked a finger at the opposite side of the crates, indicating I go that way. He leaned toward the edge of the crates in front of us, readying to take a look. Claws silently stretched from his fingers.

I inched to the right and stole a peek over the top. Eight fae guards had entered the storage bay and were silently moving toward our corner. More were coming through the doorways. All of them had their crossbows up and loaded. They knew we were here.

There were too many of them.

Kellee would fight them and probably get himself killed.

I opened my mouth to stop him, but in a blur, he sprang from behind the crate and slammed into the first guard, knocking the fae clean off his feet into his comrade. The third didn't see the claws coming. Confusion crossed his face as he dropped to his knees, clutching handfuls of his slippery insides. The fourth fired off a bolt, for all the good it did him. Kellee's claws opened his throat. Kellee had taken out four guards in the space of a single heartbeat. Shouts went up. Their crossbows swung in. I vaulted over my crate, flicked my whip, and snatched a bow from the hand of a guard. He dropped to a knee, making himself smaller, and flung something thin and sharp my way. Poison dart. I skipped to the right, and his dart sailed through my hair. *Too close.* The whip recoiled, snapping above us like lightning, then sliced downward, catching the fae across the face, zipping his cheek open. Another charged in. Hovering behind, brilliant bulbs of light flashed in my eyes— pixies. I batted one out of the air, but the others tangled in my hair. Fiery pain bloomed in my ear. Tiny claws tore at my neck. I whirled, circling the whip around me and using it as a shield. Somewhere, Kellee roared, but a guard barreled into me before I could see where the marshal was. I wrestled free and sprang backward, straight into another. Steely arms locked around my chest, pinning me against him. I kicked and bucked. The guard grunted as my heels scraped his shins. I cracked my head back, felt something crack like fragile crockery, and tore free.

Too many.

A dozen, maybe more, started forward. I couldn't fight them and survive. I lifted my hands to surrender.

A hiss of air blasted from above, drenching the chaos and me in white clouds. The guards were gone or a few steps in front of me, I couldn't see to know.

Muffled grunts sounded to my left and right. Someone cried out. Their cries abruptly ended, and a body thumped to the floor.

I can't see.

I backed up, feeling my way with my heels.

Even the pixies knotted in my hair untangled themselves and darted away, creating swirls in the fog.

My boot treads slid on blood. I looked down, and out of the rolling fog I saw the hand, then the arm it belonged to, and finally the unconscious body of the guard.

Kellee was taking them out—one by one.

A bolt shot out of the mist. I lunged aside, but it kissed my cheek and sliced through my ear. And then the guard strode out of the clouds, crossbow aimed between my eyes. One twitch of his finger and the bolt would punch through my skull.

"Vakaru!" he called, panting hard. "Stand down." The smoke swallowed his voice and rolled it around us. I heard only the pounding of my heart that matched the ship's. *Where are you, Kellee?*

The guard's eyes showed too much white, and he breathed too fast. Kellee already knew where he was. He had seconds to live.

"I have the Wraithmaker. Stand down." His words quivered. His eyes darted. His aim shook, but the finger on the trigger was steady.

A soft, dangerous smile lifted the corner of my mouth,

even as I lifted both hands. "You hear that?" I asked. "The silence?" It surrounded us, this one guard and me. A hair's breadth away, lurking somewhere in the smoke, stood one of Faerie's deadliest creations.

The fae swallowed. Sweat glistened on his brow.

A growl rumbled behind me, or was it behind him? The smoke toyed with sound.

"I'll kill her—" The guard never finished his threat. His body jerked and back arched, jolting the crossbow high. The bolt sprang free, harmlessly sailing over my head. Blood bloomed on the front of his jacket, and his eyes bugged. He dropped, and in his place stood a beast straight out of Faerie's darkest corners. His eyes were red, his fangs gleamed, and his chin was drenched in fae blood. There was no light in Kellee, only darkness. The beast looked at me, its glare salacious, hungry. Wild. It wasn't a man, wasn't of the light, but it was part of Faerie. Or had been, once. Its claws twitched. It sucked in air through its teeth, tasting it, tasting me.

I lowered my whip. The beast growled, low and deadly.

"It's okay..." I set the whip down on the floor, ignoring the bodies sprawled around us now that the smoke was clearing, and straightened. "See..." I showed him my empty hands. "I won't hurt you." Recognition softened his gaze. *Yes, here I am. You know me.* "We're friends, remember? I don't want to hurt you, Kellee."

Tension darted through him. His claws extended, and snarls bubbled from his lips. He whirled, his attention yanked in the direction of the doorway.

Sjora came in, a vision of blood red and luminous green. She held her longbow aloft, the arrow alight with fae power. Kellee lunged, and the Harvester loosed the arrow. The two met in mid-air. Kellee jolted as though he'd been snagged from behind and then crumbled to the floor.

No, no, no...

Sjora nocked a second arrow.

I snatched for my whip, and then the world plunged into darkness.

CHAPTER 14

I squinted into the light as the guards led me from the shuttle.

Calicto, but not as I'd known it.

Gone were the towering containers, glittering tek-made buildings, hover trams, and huge environmental domes. Lush jungle-like vegetation had devoured almost all traces of human habitation. Enormous trees reached for the shimmering sky where containers had once been stacked high. Now, roots clamped around the metal homes like enormous hands, slowly crushing any trace of the humans. Birdlike whistles and calls filled the air, joined by the singsong clicks from darting pixies. They flocked above in sweeping clouds, their wings cutting at the light, scattering color into the darkest corners.

I stomped onward between my escorts, wincing as thorned vines cut tighter and tighter into my wrists. I'd tried to break the vines during the flight down to Calicto's surface, but they'd dug their thorns in until pins and needles raced through my numb hands. Saru had lost limbs

149

trying to writhe free of similar bindings. I'd stopped fighting.

Blood had glued my hair to the right side of my face. It itched and served as a reminder that it could have been worse. Sjora could have killed me. Had she killed Kellee? I had tried asking the guards, but none would look at me, let alone answer. If he was alive, the chances were he was caged and bound in much the same way I was. He had to be alive. Sjora wouldn't waste the last vakaru.

I could only hope that Talen was working somewhere to help us.

So much for my escape plan.

Light glinted off a human-made structure in the distance, between the trees. I peered into the light and spotted the pointed tip of an enormous glass pyramid. Faerie's lush life magic had almost swallowed Arcon whole. That was probably for the best.

"Seems I just can't stay away."

The guards from the ship handed me over to a flight of ground troops. Each of them brandished startle-prods—the kind used to discipline feisty saru gladiators back on Faerie. My whip was gone. My coat too. Sjora probably had both. All I had were the clothes I wore and my name. I wouldn't be fighting my way out of this.

I breathed in, tasting magic on my tongue. A slither of acute pleasure sailed all the way down, tingling through my battered and bruised body. It wouldn't be long before Calicto was exactly like Faerie.

"Nice weather you've manufactured here," I chatted, sounding absurdly happy.

Nobody replied. I'd gained another two guards, raising my retinue to five. Ahead, down a straight stone path, three more waited, stares glued ahead like I didn't exist. "All we need is an insane prince and it'll be like I'm royalty."

I didn't see the blow coming, but I sure felt it when the spear snapped across my jaw. I spat blood onto the mossy earth. Seemed I'd hit a nerve. The butt of the spear jabbed me in the back. I stumbled on, but I threw a glare over my shoulder at the guard getting frisky with his weapon. "I ripped the heart out of the last male fae who hit me. What do you think I'll do to you?"

"Keep walking, Wraithmaker. Your bites are toothless here."

I walked on. The fae were everywhere, their touch on everything. Polished stone shone, and too-bright flowers bloomed, spilling dreamy toxins into the air. I'd once found Calicto's recycled air sickening, but at least the fake perfume didn't drug its inhabitants. I could already feel my resistance waning, my human DNA wilting under the onslaught of all things bright and beautiful.

The resident fae stopped and stared, done up in their flowing finery. And there I was, wrapped in dirty leathers and smeared in blood, my teeth chattering like the animal they thought I was. They watched with their almond eyes, their pink bow-shaped lips so quick to smile or sneer, and with their elegant gestures, they swept the passing Wraith-maker from their minds.

I'd forgotten what it was like to be among them.

Forgotten how, with every breath, their pheromones whispered sweet desires to lure me into their deadly embrace. I'd lived with it for so long I hadn't realized how passively lethal it was, until I'd left, until Calicto, until I'd lived a real life somewhere buried deep below this pretty little world they'd built on top of the ugly human one.

By the time they dumped me in yet another cell, this one carved from white rock, my gut kept trying to heave up the poisons, but Faerie wasn't something you could vomit up and be rid of. Faerie got under the skin, got into the blood, and took root in your soul and fed on your humanity. Like Eledan's story of how the fae had taken humans and made them dance for them, made them love them until they died, Faerie couldn't be resisted. There was no escaping it.

I paced, listening to the sound of my boots instead of the tinkling voices finding their way through the high arrow slit of a window in the room outside my cell. Back and forth, back and forth. Laughter threatened, but I couldn't voice it because I wasn't sure it was mine. Eledan's words haunted me, skirting the fringes of my thoughts and darting away every time I tried to get a grip on them.

Was this madness? It felt like it might be the beginning of it. It didn't matter. I was alive, and that meant there would be an opportunity to escape. Escape, find Kellee, find Talen, kill Sjora. Not necessarily in that order. So, there were a hundred fae soldiers watching my cell and thousands of fae already on Calicto. I didn't care. I hadn't come this far and survived Faerie this long to let them beat me now.

No more killing.

Kellee was one to talk. He had killed those fae as though they posed no more threat than felling wheat.

The door to the room outside my cell opened, and Talen entered. He looked... fine. I gripped my cell bars. "You're okay."

A muscle twitched in his jaw. It was the only outward sign he'd heard me. His fine silvery hair was braided into multiple tails and bound together to create one long plait that trailed over one shoulder. The pale blue panels of his high-collared frock coat were stitched together with fine gold silk. Blue was a courtly color. He wouldn't have looked out of place at Mab's table.

"It was a mistake—" he began but didn't get to finish.

Sjora breezed in, her long crimson cloak swishing around her boots. She placed her hand on Talen's shoulder and stroked downward. For a second, I thought he would ignore her too, but then he tilted his head and smiled a friendly, almost comforting smile at the Harvester, slayer of thousands.

Something sharp and bitter twisted inside. I let go of the bars and stepped back. It was a lie. It had to be. Talen would never side with Sjora. He was bound to me. He was mine. He had practically begged me to save him. We had some*thing*. Didn't we?

Sjora's catlike eyes flicked to me. Her dark lashes fluttered, revealing her delight at my reaction. "I believe the Wraithmaker is infatuated with you, Talen. You can see it in the poor thing's eyes. All saru fall the same way eventually. They simply can't help themselves."

His smile stayed, stuck like glue, but as he faced me, his beautiful eyes filled with sorrow and pity—for me or for the doomed saru who had no choice but to love their masters? "Their feeble minds cannot resist," he said.

I felt each word like a punch. The knot inside tightened, making my heart ache.

So, this was what betrayal felt like. I pressed a hand to my chest and tried hard—so damn hard—not to let the pain show, but the two fae silently laughed with their eyes.

I wondered if, all those years ago, Aeon had felt this terrible sickness when I'd drawn the blade across his throat.

Oh, Talen. I'm sorry I hurt you. I understand why you're doing this. I understand... I had told him he meant nothing to me, and he'd believed every word. Of course he had. I was the Queen of Lies, wasn't I?

"What do you want from me?" I tore my gaze from Talen and fixed it on Sjora's smug face. I didn't blame Talen, but her... "Why am I here?"

She slid her hand off Talen's and approached the bars. "I've had a wonderful idea that you will simply adore." The glass thimble twinkled on her finger.

The only thing I'd *simply adore* was punching her perfect teeth down her perfect throat.

"You're clearly unstable," she announced. "If the crime of killing our queen wasn't enough, the poor diplomat Devere did not deserve your callous affections."

So, Sonia, Devere's saru, had witnessed it all and told Sjora. I'd held on to some thin thread of hope that I wouldn't be blamed. Still, what was another death? I couldn't argue I was innocent. That was a lie nobody would believe.

I clenched my jaw. My fists too. I wouldn't explain how Devere's murder had been an accident. She hadn't earned the right to the truth. But I ached to tell Talen, if only so he didn't listen to Sjora twisting the truth.

"Oberon cannot deny his Wraithmaker is a loose end," Sjora continued. "He can't be seen to help you, not publically. To do so would confirm he had a hand in the queen's demise. And so I've requested he sanction a trial here, on Calicto." She grinned. "What is it the humans say? Kills two birds with one stone? The spectacle will rally the troops and remove you, a thorn in the side of his rule."

A trial? But that was absurd. No fae court would find me innocent. I *wasn't* innocent. Oberon knew that.

"He won't sanction it." My king would protect me.

"Darling." She chuckled. "He already has."

Shock, combined with the heartache, washed numbness over me, and for the first time, I realized I wasn't escaping this. I would die soon. "You might as well kill me now."

She laughed her brilliant, tinkling laughter. "Where's the entertainment in that? No, you will fight as you always have, and you will die for our entertainment. It will be the first grand spectacle in Halow. A celebration, if you will. Don't look so surprised. Surely you knew the Wraithmaker would always meet her end in the arena?"

A trial by combat.

She had planned this from the beginning. That's what the fights had been for on the ship. Practice. And this had nothing to do with justice. She wanted revenge for Mab. Public. Bloody. Revenge.

My thoughts raced, piecing the past few days together. "You want me to kill Kellee?"

She beamed. "It will be glorious."

"I refuse."

"If you survive, you walk free."

She would never let me walk free. If I survived, I'd meet with a fatal accident right after. And I didn't care. I wasn't killing Kellee just so I could live. I wasn't that person anymore.

I stepped closer to the bars, closer to her. "I won't fight him, or anyone, for you."

She turned her head and moved to Talen's side. "Oh, I think you will." Her arm looped through his. Their hands locked, and he gently squeezed. "The celebration commences in one week. Be ready for the fight of your life, Wraithmaker."

CHAPTER 15

*E*xhaustion eventually dragged me into the depths of sleep where even Eledan's dreams abandoned me. Guards came early the next morning and escorted me to a bathing house where two saru silently stripped me down and cleaned me up. If the guards or the saru took umbrage at my warfae ink, they didn't say a word. Strictly professional, all of them. They gave me food and water, and I knew refusing either would hurt only me. With no whip and no magic, I was vastly outnumbered. And even if I escaped, where would I go? Calicto was theirs.

I woke the next day to find a book sitting outside my cell. I hadn't heard anyone enter, but there it was, sitting innocently on the floor as though someone had sat down to read and forgotten it. I snatched it through the bars before a guard entered and noticed. Paper pages with a hard cover. The pages fluttered as I ran my thumb over them, scanning the text inside. It appeared to be a ledger, written in fae, each page populated with lists of supplies.

I bent the spine, fanning the pages, and heard a

metallic *plink*. A tiny gray tile had fallen from inside the pages. It winked at me from the dusty stone floor. I scooped it up and popped it into my palm. Thin silvery veins crisscrossed its surface: human Tek. It wasn't much, but it was something. Talen must have tucked it inside the book's pages for me.

I flicked through the pages again but nothing else fell out. The tek went into my jacket pocket. I sat down on the bench and considered what tek trinket I could make.

The next morning, a second book waited outside my bars. Inside, Talen had tucked a few loops of wire and some additional tek-tiles, enough to start constructing something. But what? I had four days left. Smuggling tiny pieces of tek to me inside books wouldn't provide me with enough materials to make anything substantial. I would wait and see what the next delivery brought.

The next day: a tiny lens, no larger than my smallest fingernail, and an equally small skin-thin UV power source. I knew what to build.

WITH FOUR DAYS left to the "celebration," fae guards removed me from my cell and walked me through open-air pathways into an adjacent building that appeared to have been carved from Calicto's native rock and smothered by dangling floral vines. Pollen tickled my nose and clung to my hair, claiming me as Faerie's. Inside the building, in the lower saru quarters, the guards led me to a small dressing room and left me in the hands of the same two saru who had bathed me.

"We have instructions to dress you in this," the female

said, lifting a heavy green all-in-one coat and vest. It shimmered with the unmistakable touch of magic. I knew that coat, or one just like it. Could it be the same coat, but *altered?* This new version had unnecessary silver swirls and flourishes running along each seam like fine lace. The silver almost looked like... tek.

"By whose instructions?" I asked.

"Lord Talen," the saru bowed her head, eyes averted. She came forward with the coat ensemble held out in front of her like a shield. Was it Talen's name she feared or me?

Lord Talen. I gripped the coat and met her startled look. "I can dress myself. I don't need your help."

She cringed and let go, scurrying back to the edge of the room. I'd insulted her and wished I could find the compassion to apologize. "You can leave."

She lifted her doe eyes to her male partner. He stared ahead, face blank, like the perfect invisible saru the fae had trained him to be. I turned away from them and stripped down. I wasn't angry with them. I barely knew them. The anger was mine, for the girl I'd been, for Sonia who'd had no choice but to sell Sjora everything, for all the saru moving silently and unnoticed in the fae's shadow. For the little liar girl from my past and the boy in the cell next to hers who had dreamed of a better time. What would Aeon make of me today?

A gasp from one of the saru tugged on my nerves. The pair had seen the thorned warfae marks running down my back. They knew they were attending the Wraithmaker. A killer of their kind. Shame crawled across my skin. Would they stab me in the back? Did they ha—

"Lord Talen," the girl said.

I clutched the coat to my chest and turned. There he was, looking every bit the fae at home surrounded by saru servants and needless fae finery. Even the way he moved was different from what I remembered. He swept a hand at the two saru, dismissing them without looking.

The dressing room, swollen with countless clothing racks and heavy drapes, felt too small for the both of us.

"I'll be missed if I stay too long." A curious hint of regret softened his words.

I didn't move. Barely breathed. Was he mine or Sjora's? I should use the time to get answers out of him, but all I could think about was how it hurt, even now, to see him so fae-like. So distant, so alien. So not the Talen who had dropped to his knee and surrendered himself to me, the Talen who had raced me around the prison circuit, the Talen who had stopped me from leaving. He had stood next to Sjora and looked down on me as though I were just another saru. Was that what I was to him?

He stood there, proud and lofty. "You told me to do this." He took a single step closer.

I backed up. "Don't. Don't..." I clutched the coat, hiding behind it. "You can't lie, you can't, and those things you said to Sjora, about me, about Kellee—"

Another step. "All careful truths." He reached out but hesitated when I lifted my chin and held his gaze. He dropped his hand to his side and muttered, "I feared this would happen."

He looked like them, sounded like them. Of course he did. I was a fool to think him anything else. I'd known he was dangerous. I'd known how he could twist the truth around him. I'd only bound him to me to keep him tame, keep him controlled. If I thought back through everything that had happened since he'd stopped me from running on that moon, I could trace it all back to him. Kellee had feared as much when he'd accused Talen of leading the fae straight to us. He had thought it an accident, but I wasn't so sure. Talen had Sjora's confidence. He walked among them. He wore their clothes and spoke their words. They looked to him in respect. He could easily have orchestrated it all.

"Please tell me you didn't plan this. Please tell me this isn't you." I sounded pathetic, like a begging saru girl infatuated with her master. And I didn't care. I needed to know the truth, even if it crushed me.

He lifted his gaze and regarded me coolly, his expression expertly carved from stone. "I have done only as you asked."

"No!" My cry made him flinch. "This is *not* on me. I didn't ask you to betray me and Kellee. I did not ask you to do that, Talen!"

He moved—one second standing across the room, the next so close his magic coiled around me, licking naked skin, touching my warfae marks. His hands gripped my arms. Warm. Solid. He peered down as though he might, in the next breath, say something that would crush my heart. I couldn't read him. Did he mean to hurt me? I felt his touch too keenly, felt his magic move like a curious third person stalking around us, felt his violet-eyed gaze burn through me. I'd thought Kellee was dangerous, but Kellee's threat was brash and obvious, while Talen's cut like the flash of a precision scalpel—so cleanly you didn't know you were bleeding until it was too late. Nerves overloaded, I trembled like some poor creature at his mercy.

"Who are you, really?" I whispered, pinned beneath the weight of his fixation.

He breathed too fast, and shades of violet shone in his eyes, bleeding into the darkness of his dilating pupils. A battle raged inside him, one I had no hope of understanding.

"I'm going to die in four days," I whispered the words, barely giving them voice. "Tell me the truth."

He bowed his head. "I'm yours." His words brushed my lips, and then his mouth followed, just a light touch, but enough to ignite desire and stoke it into a raging need.

I gently, so gently, tasted his mouth, knowing if I took too much, too soon, he'd turn to ice and withdraw. His lips were velvety soft and warm and tasted too good to be real. I opened wider, teasing with my tongue, gently taking more. The coat slipped from my fingers, and I stood naked and exposed in his grip. A shudder tracked through him, his breath coming short and sharp. I still didn't know if he desired me or meant to hurt me. I pressed my hands to his vest, holding them there instead of wrapping around him and yanking him close like I ached to. He could hurt me, could crush me. Beneath my reputation, my shields, my whip and tek, my quick words and sharp threats, I was just a saru. He was stronger, faster, and he had magic. Magic to make me feel anything he wanted. Had his last saru girl felt like this before he killed her?

His fingers skipped down my arm and delicately skimmed over the rise of my breasts to my collarbone. His mouth sought the corner of mine, asking for permission. And I would give it. I'd give it all. And take more. Take everything he offered and drown in the feel of Talen.

His other hand spread across my lower back, pulling

162

me in. His kiss settled, butterfly soft, like I was glass in his hands, and then quickened, turning hungrier. Need throbbed hot and heavy. My hard nipples brushed the leather of his vest, reminding me of my stark nakedness. I should have felt vulnerable, but all I thought of was how there were too many of his layers between us. Too many thoughts too.

I felt the wall at my back. Didn't remember moving and didn't care. He rocked into me, the kiss breaking down, becoming nothing as clean as a kiss and more of a statement of need. He broke first, freeing my mouth to snatch at air. I desperately needed him closer. I dug my nails into his back. His mouth found my neck. His breath fluttered over my pulse, so damn carefully. He paused, and his hands stilled, one on my hip, the other in my hair. The taste of him lured me in, pulling me deeper. His magic was inside me, his heart pounding with mine. I wanted *him* pounding inside me. All of him.

"I—" he began, voice ragged and torn. "The bond. This is... You should hate me."

No, don't talk. Don't spoil it.

"I am everything you fear, everything wrong that's ever been done to you. I can wreck you with a touch..." His fingers brushed so lightly against my chin that I wondered if this was real, if he was real. "...with a kiss."

I made a noise, like a groan, but it was more of a protest at the fact he had stopped moving, stopped touching, and I wanted more. I knew what he was capable of. His hands scorched my skin and I knew he could turn my emotions inside out, but I also felt the soul-wrenching ache inside him, that matched my own. This wasn't manipulation. It was truth, naked and exposed.

"No..." I wrapped his hair around my hand like a rope of silk and ran it through my fingers. It felt as though I was sweeping my hand through warm water. Fierce eyes studied me, waiting for me to pull away. "No, Talen. I don't hate you."

"I am telling you this because I cannot lie and you need to know..." He licked his lower lip. "Knowing this, you must trust me. *I am not who I once was.*" Those last words were cracked, raw whispers, as though to speak them might summon the depths of Faerie down on us. He sounded broken, like I'd dragged him down to my level and ruined him. I wanted to ruin him some more. This wasn't enough. It would never be enough. But he was pulling away, shutting down. There was so much more to him that I didn't understand, but none of it mattered, unless we made it matter.

I plunged my hand down his back, cupped his ass, and yanked him against me, feeling exactly how much he truly wanted this. A possessive growl rumbled up from deep inside him, and his magic flared, pulsing bright and hot through us both. He smelled of spices and warm leather, of the wildness of Faerie and her mind-numbing magic. He tilted his hips, grinding the hard bulge inside his pants against my hip. It was all I could do not to drop my hand and feel him buck against my palm.

His smooth fingers caught my jaw and forced my head away. Blunt teeth nipped at my neck. I gasped, trapped under his weight. It was then I knew the gentleness was necessary, because Talen unleashed would be a force of Faerie.

"You won't die in four days." He growled the words, making them sound like a threat. Delicious shudders emptied out my thoughts. All but one. I wanted him. I wanted him to take me here, roughly, now. And then I'd turn around and take him—every damn inch of him—and make him mine.

He stepped back. The cold rushed in, leaving me stunned and trembling. I hissed air through my teeth and pressed my hands against the wall, holding myself still. Desire swam in his eyes. And to see it there, to know he wanted me too... He was right, he could wreck me. He had been right to pull away. Because if he hadn't, I couldn't have stopped.

"Wear the coat," he rasped and took another step back. His eyes flashed a warning. After realigning his cloak, he almost looked presentable, although it would take some time to soften the erection straining against his pants. I had a sudden, startling mental image of him sprawled in the bath, his hands no longer on the rolled edges because he was stroking himself, pleasuring himself in secret. I rolled my lips together and swallowed.

His gaze roamed my warfae markings, tingling each one alive. "Get to the arena," he growled. "I'll do the rest."

"And the tek?" Remarkably, my voice was crisp and clear.

He frowned. "Tek?"

"The books?"

"I haven't—"

"Lord Talen..." Guards charged into the dressing room. They saw my naked, flushed body and Talen some distance across the room, drew their conclusions—a fae lord fucking with a saru female—and thought little of it. "Apologies for the interruption."

Desire snuffed out of Talen's eyes as easily as he might

pinch a wisp between his fingers. He neatly buttoned his coat closed, hiding his arousal, and faced the guard. "Yes?" All the ice and hardness of his fae lineage was back, reminding me of the dangerous game of lies he played.

"Your presence is requested in the Great Hall."

He left among them—and didn't look back. I was learning that about him. He never looked back. In the silence that followed, with the heat of desire rapidly cooling, I threw on the clothes and buckled up my new coat with its metallic edges. By the time the saru returned, I wore my own mask and let them lead me from the room, wondering if Talen hadn't sent the books and the hidden tek, who had?

CHAPTER 16

*N*o more books arrived, but I'd crafted my little spy. The tiny camera sat on the tip of my finger, no larger than a fly, complete with delicate paper wings. But without life magic or a lot more tek, I couldn't get the ocular signal to work. The signal would allow me to see what it saw. Pretty vital for a spy.

Thanks to Talen, I had a coat with unknown abilities, and I had two days left to figure out a way to escape.

He had said to make it to the arena, but that left little room for mistakes, and lately, mistakes had been plaguing me. I needed a plan too.

An arena was just another prison cell, that prisoners were expected to dance in or die. They weren't designed to allow gladiators to escape. I had no idea what Talen planned, and I doubted I'd see him again before the fight. Trust him, he had said. And he'd told me exactly the kind of fae he was, told me the ugly truth of him. Those words had cost him.

Trust.

I had never trusted easily. Trust opened a door to the unknown, and sometimes an open door invited the monsters inside. I knew because I was one. Was Talen one too?

I tucked the spy-bot into my pocket and called out to the guards outside my room. "Hey!" One eventually entered. "Take me to Sjora."

"No." Stern-faced and as cold as ice, he was the same guard who had gotten frisky with his spear right after I stepped off the shuttle.

"I'll be dead soon, and then she'll never know what I have to say."

His thin mouth ticked. "Tell me and I'll tell her."

He couldn't lie. He would tell her. After I was dead. I draped my arms through the bars and slowly, methodically, checked him out from head to toe. Pale skin, eyes the lightest shade of blue, white hair, thin and fine, as delicate as moth wings. His natural beauty had turned cruel some time ago. He was winterlands, for sure. Quick to anger, quick to judge, and curious to a fault. I could use that. "How long have you served Sjora?"

"I'm not permitted to talk with you." He whirled on his heels and headed for the door.

"Well," I drawled, "you already broke that rule, so you might as well break it some more. Aren't you curious?"

He stopped.

"In two days, I'll be gone. No more Wraithmaker." His back straightened. I had hooked him. Now all I had to do was reel him in. "Ask me anything."

"Did Oberon order you to kill the queen?" He didn't even turn around.

Ah, I hadn't expected that. That was the golden question, wasn't it? The one they all wanted an answer to but were afraid to ask for fear Oberon would surely have them killed in their beds for treason. But this guard and I were a long way from Faerie, and I had all the answers on the tip of my tongue.

"Come here and I'll tell you," I told his stiff back.

He exhaled a short laugh and turned around whip-fast. "Do you think me a fool?"

"It depends. How much do you want to know the answer?"

"You'll lie." His sneer was so dismissive. He didn't know what it was to lie, and even that intrigued him. I saw the twinkle of intrigue in his eyes.

"Maybe," I drawled. "Or maybe I want to meet the Hunt with a clear conscience."

He faced my cage, eyes slitted as he tried to figure me out and weigh up his chances. "The Hunt does not waste time with worthless saru."

It was an insult worthy of any true immortal. Time and its passage were worthless to them, and so to waste something worthless on a saru made that saru virtually nothing. *Nothing girl.*

I'd heard all the insults before and fluttered my lashes. "Are you afraid of the Wraithmaker?" I crooned in a singsong voice. *He takes your mind, makes it his, takes your soul, makes you cruel...* I tilted my head and cracked my neck, using the small dart of pain to banish the Dreamweaver's song. *"She'll take your heart,"* I sang. *"She makes you hate her. Dare you get close to the Wraithmaker?"* Madness laughed inside my head. I let it.

"You're insane," he sneered, but macabre curiosity had him taking a step closer.

169

I smiled. He was probably right. Hadn't the Mad Prince lost his mind to the voices in his head? *"Come, little fae, come closer. Dare you tempt the Wraithmaker?"* I sang.

He lifted his chin, gripped his spear tighter, and approached the bars to show he wasn't afraid.

That's right, you curious thing. These words I kept to myself. *Come for the proof, stay for the truth.*

"Closer..." I drawled.

"You can say it—"

I shot an arm out, grabbing for his spear. He snatched the weapon back, grinning in victory, until I kicked between the bars, my boot connecting with the sensitive parts between his legs. His light armor shielded much of the impact, but unbalanced, he reached for the bars to steady himself. Big mistake. His hand found mine instead. I locked his fingers in mine and pulled, throwing all my weight into yanking him forward. His face smacked into the bars, splitting skin and cracking a tooth.

"I'll take that." I snatched his spear and jabbed the point under his chin, trapping him awkwardly against the outside of the bars and me.

Fury burned in his eyes. I leaned in, close enough to kiss his pale lips. *"She killed a queen, made a king, but they say she thinks it's all a dream."* I planted a messy kiss on his locked lips, knowing it would haunt him for the rest of his long fae life, and patted him on the cheek. "Take me to Sjora, sweetheart."

"IT SEEMS those you do not kill, you traumatize." Sjora stood at the edge of a balcony with her back to me. A breeze played with a few loose strands of her moss-green hair, those not braided into one long sideways braid that rested over her shoulder. "Perhaps I've given Oberon too much credit and you really are the architect of all this madness." She laughed, and it echoed on and on into the vast, empty space she looked upon. "What a surprise that would be. A saru so dangerous she toppled her fae masters." She laughed harder. "Goodness, if that were to escape, we'd have a rebellion on our hands." She braced her hands on the balustrade and peered down into what I assumed was a huge natural chasm. "A good thing, then, that your kind and mine believe you to be insane."

While she listened to the sound of her own voice, I wondered if I could shove her off the balcony and escape. Behind us, a line of eight guards blocked all the exits. If I killed her, I'd die seconds afterward. There were better causes to die for.

In my pocket, I teased the little tek spy between my fingers and thumb. If I got close enough, I could fix it to her coat. It still wouldn't work without life magic, but she was more likely to encounter a surge of life magic than I was.

Finally, Sjora looked over her shoulder, seeing me for the first time since the guard had marched me all the way up here. One of her thin eyebrows arched at the sight of Talen's coat. "You have a benefactor, I see. I'd take it off you, but there's little point. An illusion won't save you if that's what that garment offers. The vakaru senses pierce simple illusion."

Mention of Kellee tripped my heart a beat. "Is he all right?"

"He's vakaru."

171

"That's not what I asked."

Her eyes narrowed at my insolence. "You'll discover soon enough." She dragged her slate-gray gaze from my head to my toes and then gestured at the nothing space beyond the balcony. "Come. See the view for yourself."

I stepped to the edge and the world fell away beneath the balcony. Vertigo took hold, washing me in a flush of heat and sickness. I closed my hands around the balustrade rail and gripped tightly. The wind brought with it the hollowness of empty spaces. The balcony jutted over an enormous concave bowl. At first glance, the depression in the earth looked like a bomb crater, but then I saw the terraces snaking up the sides. An arena that could potentially host hundreds of thousands. There was nothing like it in Halow. Only Faerie's arena matched it. The fae here had been busy.

"What makes you different?" Sjora asked. "Gladiators come and go. Few survive longer than a season. Most are felled by their own failings. Human minds cannot withstand the arena for long. What drove you to kill so many of your own kind night after night?"

I didn't answer. I wasn't sure I even knew the answer. I'd killed to live.

"Do you hate your own so much?"

Hate the saru? No, I... My knuckles whitened.

She laughed softly. "Do you think you can survive this? Survive Faerie? Do you know how much tek we had to cleanse from Halow to make it ours again? And through it all, nothing stood in our way."

"Because Eledan infiltrated Arcon. It wasn't your superiority that won you this war. It was a single fae in the right place, at the right time. It was luck."

"Luck? The Mad Prince's sacrifice was... glorious."

I shuddered at the reverence in her voice and side-eyed her. Her lashes fluttered. She lifted her head and looked at the pink-tinted filtered sky. She had admired and served Mab for thousands of years, and with the queen gone, her loyalties fell *not* to Oberon, but to his brother, to Mab's beloved son, to the hero who had let Faerie back into Halow. Eledan had won this war before it even began. I knew that look on her face. Love. Eledan was her hero. And probably a hero to the entire fae race. Wherever he was, his prison of madness was likely a good thing. If the prince had been coherent, he would have returned Oberon's gift with a dagger to his brother's heart and taken Faerie for himself.

What if the Mad Prince ruled Faerie?

It would never happen. Oberon was no fool. He'd keep his brother in a deep, dark hole where nobody could get to him.

"The coward will not come," Sjora whispered.

She wasn't referring to Eledan.

Her hand on the rail closed into a fist. "His rule is weak, built on a throne of lies. He should be here, at his own victory celebration."

She was right, but Oberon wasn't foolish enough to leave his throne a few months after taking it. He knew there would be dissent, likely knew Sjora was a part of that. If he came, he'd be walking into a trap.

I swallowed and faced ahead, eyes closed to block out the sense of emptiness yawning in front of me.

"Why did you kill Devere?"

I opened my eyes and peered down into the pit. *Because Eledan still owns parts of me...* It was a truth I couldn't speak, light a nightmare better left alone. To voice it would make it too real.

"He was Oberon's envoy." A tremor undermined Sjora's words. "You killed him. The saru girl refused to talk and lost her tongue, but the burns on his neck matched your whip."

Still, I looked down. Down into the emptiness. Sonia hadn't talked. She was just a saru, a nothing girl, but she had defied them. For me? A smile lifted my lips. I'd made the classic mistake of underestimating a saru. She still lived. I would find a way to thank her.

Turning my head, I wondered if Sjora realized how precarious her position was. "If you put me in the arena against Kellee, I will not fight, and all of this will be for nothing. You'll look like a fool."

The breeze stirred her cloak around her.

"You'll fight." She closed the distance between us in a single step and dragged her glass-tipped thimble down my cheek. The look in her eyes was pure arrogance. "Did your Master Talen tell you he had a plan? Did he ask you to trust him?"

I gritted my teeth and glared back.

"He is not the fae he once was. And make no mistake, he is mine. You will fight the vakaru or Death will find your Lord Talen."

Death. The Hunt.

Sjora knew why he was running.

He had escaped the Hunt by coming to Halow, by hiding in tek-enforced prisons, but New-Calicto was built on magic foundations strong enough to summon the Hunt. Sjora would have him killed if I didn't fight Kellee.

I tried to school my features, trying to keep my face blank, and failed.

Sjora laughed. The wind tore the sound away, taking it deep into the arena where it echoed. "All you have to do is be a good saru and die for your masters."

The breeze tugged at my coat, and with it came a whirring like a swarm of pixie wings, but the more the wind lashed my hair around my face, the more I recognized the electronic buzz. But it was impossible. That sound had no place here.

I sank my hand into my pocket and withdrew the tiny spy, then leaned into Sjora and rested my hand on her shoulder, planting the paper-winged tek under her collar. "Your confidence will be your undoing."

She sneered, her gaze following me as I moved away from the edge. She didn't see the drone rise from below the balcony. Its matte-black coating rippled, sloughing off the invisible cloak, and a single red eye blazed.

"Run, Kesh Lasota," a robotic voice said.

The drone's outer casing split apart, shield cracking open, revealing twin firing ports. Sjora barked an order and moved in a blur of red and green, vaulting over the balcony. My gaze fell to the doomed line of fae lifting their crossbows. But they were too slow. Motors whirred. Dancing red dots highlighted the fae's torsos. The drone fired, strafing the line with impact-rounds. The soldiers twitched and bucked, but the rounds were little more than a nuisance. But it wasn't over. The guards nocked their crossbows but didn't get a chance to fire. A high-powered microwave laser cut through the line of fae as easily as a scythe felled wheat. Leather peeled apart, fae skin broiled, blood flash-dried and exploded into the air like rose petals.

Their immortality did nothing to shield them from the clinical precision of a SOTA drone.

When the motors stopped whirring, I stood in front of the dead, blood petals raining around me, the bitter smell of hot tek on my tongue. I looked up. It couldn't be? "Sota?" The drone swiveled, fixing its single killing lens on me. But there was no life there, no flicker of recognition.

"Run, Kesh Lasota."

A bolt shot in from above and thwacked into the drone's casing. It swiveled up, searching for the shooter. Fire flared so brightly that heat scorched my face. Then the explosion hit, throwing me backward. Ears ringing, I stumbled back to my feet.

Run.

I stumbled through the doorway. Shouts bounced around the corridor or my head, I wasn't sure which.

Run.

A fae stepped around a corner. Talen's coat shimmered around me, seemingly of its own accord, throwing up a protective shield like a shimmering bubble.

I slammed into the fae, knocking him into a wall, and sprinted away. He shouted a warning, but I was already across a hallway and dashing down steps. I ran like Talen had taught me, ran even as Faerie's creatures wailed and the ships above shifted, releasing their clutches of single-pilot vessels.

Run.

Talen's magic swirled across my skin, pouring inhuman strength into my muscles. Our bond throbbed, his strength now mine. Leaving the compound, I darted into the nearest tree line. Thick vegetation swallowed me whole. I tasted Talen's magic in the air, seeping from the

176

coat, and breathed it down, letting it fill my lungs and race through my veins.

I ran, fueled by Talen's strength and the taste of freedom. I ran until I stumbled up a mountain of vine-covered steps and in through filthy glass doors hidden behind wet, trailing branches.

Arcon.

Roots entwined doorways. Choking blankets of undergrowth smothered walls and floors, sprouting bright toxic flowers.

I jogged deeper into the building, fighting my way through the jungle-like foliage deeper into Arcon's heart.

CHAPTER 17

Faerie's touch had embraced Arcon. The walls, the floors, everything had been taken and twisted into the organic. Arcon was alive with magic, but its bones were tek. Its human-made skeleton still existed beneath the rich smell of greenery and the rustle of plump, sticky leaves.

Muscles aching, lungs burning, and head spinning, I stumbled, taking wrong turns, turning myself around and around—or perhaps it was the building changing around me. Anything was possible now that Arcon grew on a well of magic. Thorns cut my hands and tore at my coat and hair. Roots tangled around my feet, tripping me, trying to pull me down and bury me. I pushed on and on and on until I found the room with a broken oak throne at one end and a missing window overlooking the tropical paradise that was now a new Faerie-made Calicto. Eledan's laughter lived in the memories here. Ghosts crowded every corner. I ignored the past sinking its claws in and scrabbled around the organic debris, tearing away finger-like branches to get to the prize buried inside.

And there he was.

SOTA.

My Sota.

I dropped to my knees and let the laughter bubble out of me. All around, life magic throbbed, and in my hands, I held the pieces of an old friend. I had promised I'd save him, and now I would. I might even save us both.

Arcon was a treasure trove of tek, all of it buried under the primordial jungle. I scavenged its abandoned tek-development levels, remembering exactly where to find Arcon's defensive weapons, and took all the best bits to help rebuild my friend.

Kellee's claws had torn through Sota's undercarriage, ripping out the drone's vital components, but the master CPU was intact. I cradled the innocuous tek-tile in my hand. Only when I rebuilt his body would I know if his mind was unharmed.

I worked feverishly—desperately aware that the day of the arena celebration would soon arrive and if I wasn't there, Kellee and Talen would pay. I *would* be there. And I'd give the hundreds and thousands of fae a show they'd never forget.

"The nothing girl and her tek trinkets."

Eledan casually leaned against the broken table, arms crossed. Humidity had dampened his shirt, making it cling to him in all the wrong ways. He tilted his head as he watched me work. I'd seen him there hours ago, caught him in the corner of my eye, and waited for him to attack. But he hadn't moved, probably because he wasn't real. My stretched mind, coupled with the fallout from his abuse and Faerie's poisonous blooms sprouting all over Arcon, were messing with my head. This pretend Eledan was an illusion. I ignored him.

Spread across the floor in front of me were all the bits of tek that made up Sota. Some areas were empty, waiting for the parts I still needed to find. And some held mangled pieces of wreckage I couldn't save or replace. I had two days left. Two days to rebuild a tactical wardrone was difficult enough, but Sota wasn't just any drone.

"You won't do it in time," Eledan said.

"Go away." I shooed him with a wave. He didn't budge. His lips almost smiled, like he might laugh at any second. Laughter sparkled in his eyes. I'd heard enough of his laughter since I'd yanked out his heart and didn't need to hear it here.

I pinched the bridge of my nose and squeezed my eyes closed. *When I open my eyes, he won't be there.* I swallowed, counted down from five, and opened my eyes.

"I'm not that easy to be rid of." His sloping smile wasn't even fae. It was the kind of look tired predators gave their prey when they knew they could kill it but didn't feel like right now.

Fine. Whatever. He could stand there and try to distract me. It wouldn't work. "You're not real. I'm not listening to you."

"Are you so sure?" He lifted his head and looked around him. "I like what you've done with my office. Very... Faerie."

I crouched and worked on a particularly fiddly tek

module. To solder the elements together, I'd been using the acidic resin from a tangling vine, but its smell tickled my nose and left me lightheaded. Eledan was here because I was high, and exhausted, and hungry, probably dehydrated too. That was all. *Not real.*

"She killed a queen, made a king, but they say she thinks it's all a dream."

Ha! "See, you're not real." I pointed at him and laughed. "I made up that song—*in my head*. You can't know it."

He nodded, apparently turning my denial over in his mind, and then tapped a finger against his collarbone. "No collar. And this place is flooded with magic. Everything you know your mind tells me. Those human thoughts of yours are exposed."

I scoffed. "You're not that powerful."

He grinned like he knew a secret, like he had when he'd offered me water and knew I would drink it eventually.

I rocked back on my heels and sighed. "I killed Devere because I believed he was you. If I believed you were here, for real, I'd rip your heart out of your chest all over again and eat the vile thing—tek and all." I flashed him my own acidic smile, but it fell away when I saw how his unlaced shirt hung open, revealing metallic veins crisscrossed over his heart. That had to be another sign he wasn't real. The fae would have fixed him. *If they could...*

"I can taste the bite of your hatred." He dragged his fingers down his chest, snagging on the tek-infested scar. "I almost wish I were here so I could feel it again."

I shifted to my knees and continued working on Sota. He would go away eventually. I just had to concentrate.

"Was the illusion of me as good a fuck as your memory tells me?"

My memory, rotten place that it was, helpfully provided the image of Devere-Eledan peering up from between my legs, his tongue working a new kind of magic.

I fumbled a piece of tek and swore. "No. Lasted all of three minutes. Imaginary you should be ashamed." The silence stretched on. I glanced, and he was gone. "Good. Stay away. I have work to do."

HE STAYED AWAY until exhaustion claimed me, and then the dreams came and he was there and everywhere all at once, filling my head, filling me. It wasn't real. And yet I still reached out to him, wanting to carve out his heart all over again and fuck him while I hacked at the tek keeping him alive.

I woke to the sounds of my own laughter, my face wet with tears or sweat. I couldn't change what he had done to me or stop my body from craving more dreams. None of that was in my control. Sota was something I could put right. *That* I had control over.

Sota started to take shape. I replaced damaged shielding, but the matte-black outer casing would always bear a few dents and scratches. I'd considered replacing it using drones I'd found in Arcon storage, but I liked the scars. Sota would love them. *Battle scars*.

As I worked, I wondered about the drone that had microwaved Sjora's soldiers on the balcony. Someone had sent it. Someone who knew tek. It didn't feel like Talen.

He had built up a resistance to tek, but he still didn't like it. Perhaps Talen and Kellee had worked together? It seemed unlikely, but how else had the drone known me by name?

I sealed Sota's outer shell and set him down on his dock. The dock didn't have a power source, but it had enough of a charge left to fire him up.

"Here goes nothing."

I flicked him on.

The whirring started up. The lens flared bright red. Sota swiveled upward, flew into the air, and shot over my head. He hit the wall with a resounding crack and collapsed.

Eledan laughed that horrid, deeply seductive laughter.

The drone rolled my way and came to a rest against the leg of Eledan's oak table.

Eledan doubled over, the words coming in clutches between hilarity. "That's the funniest thing I've seen... since the last vakaru walked... into my office and tried to save you."

I scooped Sota under my arm and stepped up to Eledan, glaring into his blue eyes as he straightened to his full, overbearing height.

The laughter faded, but the dregs of it still flashed in his eyes. He looked real. If I touched him, would he be solid beneath my fingers? What if he was?

I clutched the drone tighter and peered defiantly at the Mad Prince. "Say what you have to say and go away. This is important, and you're making me make mistakes."

"No, you're doing that all on your own, *nothing girl*."

"You talk like I'm nothing to you, but if that were true, you wouldn't be here."

184

"Dreams are wild things. Left to roam free, who knows what trouble they'll cause. Is this your dream or mine?" His smirk slid sideways. He leaned closer. "What if reality is the nightmare?" he whispered. "Come back to me, Wraithmaker. I'll take all your pain away. We can dream together."

A dangerous thought wormed its way through the others: what would it be like to walk the nowhere spaces with the Dreamweaver? I dismissed the idea, pushing it down into the dark. "You, your words, it's all poison."

His eyes narrowed. "What if my dreams are saving that fragile saru mind of yours?"

He was close, so close the sweetness of his magic tingled on my tongue. "I don't need saving."

He straightened, and his smile faded. His deep blue eyes turned icy. "From the moment you revealed yourself in this room and threw yourself out that window, I knew you were a creature of lies, but I couldn't have known the deception was my brother's." His gaze darted over my face, reading my reaction or searching for the truth. "I don't blame you. You are saru. I blame him. There are lines we do not cross. Through you, he murdered our mother." An odd parade of emotions crossed his face—pain, disgust, anguish—before he covered them all with a blank mask. "He would have murdered me."

"My saru heart bleeds for you."

He reached out to touch my chest. I jerked back, but I'd felt something brush my shirt. *No, no...* He was the lie here. He wasn't real. It was all a Faerie hallucination. He was in my head, another ghost like all the other memories.

"Not so sure now, are you?" He chuckled. "There's a great deal of life magic here, saru. *My* magic. If I were incapacitated a long, long way away, my mind drifting, where do you think I'd let my consciousness wander to? Back to the home I've known for so long? Back to a life I built. And when I get here, what do I find but the nothing girl rummaging around the remains of *my* Arcon."

That sounded entirely too plausible, and I wouldn't give it another moment's thought, lest it undo me. If I started to believe, I'd start to fall and never stop. "Go and haunt someone who cares."

I set Sota back down on his dock and peeked out of the corner of my eye. He was still there, watching. Always watching, his smile held a promise. One the threat in his eyes would keep.

Under his scrutiny, I stripped Sota down again. Water streamed down the inside of the clouded windows and dripped from the ceiling, gathering in pools where I worked. My fingers were wet, and the smallest pieces of tek often slipped from my grip and plinked into puddles.

"I don't blame you," Eledan said again after hours of silence, hours of watching. "It is uncouth to blame the saru for the actions of its master."

I couldn't get Sota to fire up, and the light outside had changed from the pinks of day to the darker mauves of night. I didn't have long. I wiped perspiration from my forehead with the back of my hand and looked over at where he stood, expecting him to look smug. He didn't. He blinked back at me with far too much compassion in his eyes. He almost looked *human*. I hated him for that. He shouldn't look as though he understood. Shouldn't look as though he cared. It wasn't fair.

"Well, I blame you," I snarled back.

"You butchered my heart."

"You mind-fucked me for nine months."

He purred smoothly, the sound all fae made when stimulated. "And I enjoyed every minute of it... and so did you." I opened my mouth to deny it. "Don't lie, Wraithmaker."

Damn him. I hated him. I did. *That* feeling was real, and it boiled inside, turning dangerous. "I didn't have a choice," I murmured. Bits of Sota were scattered in front of me, and time was moving too fast. There was other tek in the building that I could splice together and make something to take into the arena with me, but I needed Sota's mind. I needed his ability to cut through all the illusions and see things for what they were. There wasn't time to build something else. This had to work.

"You were ordered to kill me. You didn't. You went against your master's commands. The King of Faerie, no less. A master you loved. Still love... probably."

He talked too much, and I didn't like the way his words made me squirm. "It wasn't all about you. I did it for the people."

His sudden laugh startled me, rattling my nerves. "Is that what you tell yourself? You didn't kill me to save a bunch of people you'd hardly met? Oh, please... that doesn't sound like the Wraithmaker."

"I'm not her anymore."

"And the lies keep coming." He moved from the table for the first time since appearing and approached slowly, either to keep me from getting spooked or because he knew, in my dreams, I liked to watch him move. His arrogance, his power, his lineage, it was all there, marked with every single step. My pulse quickened, instincts readying

187

me to run or fight. "Those two males you hope to save." He crouched beside me, rested his arms on his knees, and cast a light glance over the bits of Sota. The humidity had sprung some of his silky black hair from its braid so it curled and licked at his jawline. His shirt was ruffled and creased like he'd worn it for days, and for the first time, I realized he wasn't wearing shoes, just wrinkled black pants and bare feet. Had my mind concocted all this? Was he the mad one, I wondered, or was I? "If the vakaru doesn't kill you, he'll hate you because it's all they know, and the fae you're partially bonded with..." Eledan's lips twitched. "I suspect he has another name, one he guards like I guarded my heart. Ask him. He can't lie."

I listened to my heart pounding and told myself the addictive taste of Eledan on my tongue was just the magic rising from the foundations of Arcon and not because he was here, right beside me, close enough to whisper to. His words were slippery and poisonous, like him. I knew better than to let them in. "If you're truly here, make yourself useful. How do I fix Sota?" As Larsen, he had spearheaded all of Arcon's tek-development and reprogrammed Sota to protect him. It hurt my pride to ask him for help, to admit I needed him, or at least the memory of him, but there was more at stake than my pride. If my subconscious wanted to fantasize about him, it could damn well make him useful.

He looked once more over the debris of my tek-friend, rolled up his sleeves, revealing the warfae tattoos snaking up his golden skin, and nodded. "You've misaligned the gyro and navigation modules." He pointed. "It's a simple mistake, especially without the use of a UI to guide you."

I looked again at Sota's parts. Eledan's solution made

sense. And it was an easy fix. I should have seen it. A thank you balanced on my tongue. I swallowed it like a bitter pill.

"You had better get to work, Kesh Lasota. You don't have much time."

CHAPTER 18

$\mathcal{T}$he drone buzzed to life and lifted off his dock, hovering a few feet in the air. Something inside his casing clinked, and he dipped an inch and then leveled out. I needed to work on that gyro, but at least he wasn't throwing himself against a wall. His lens whined, telescopic focus shifting in and out and swiveling to take in his surroundings.

I glanced at Eledan sitting on the floor, legs stretched out, arms propping him up. He watched the drone, intrigued but not surprised.

And then Sota swiveled to me. His lens flared. The gun ports snapped open, rocking him on his axis.

I lifted my hands and scrambled to my feet. "Sota?"

"*Kesh Lasota,*" the drone said, sounding exactly like its twin that had exploded over the balcony. "*Cease all aggressive action.*"

"I'm not a threat." Seconds ticked by. His processors could still be reacting to the last scenario, right before Kellee had torn out its insides. Eledan had programmed

191

Sota to kill me if I hurt him. If he fired, I'd be as dead as those fae on Sjora's balcony. There was no coming back from incineration by drone.

Sweat trickled down the side of my face. "Sota, disarm."

The lens retracted. "K-Kesh?" His voice was fragmented, but it was a voice, not the robotic AI auto-responses.

"Yes," I breathed out. "Disarm. *Please*."

The gun ports closed. Sota lifted into the air another few inches. "Did you get shorter?"

"What?" With a laugh, I lowered my hands. "No." He was Sota. My Sota. Finally, I had my friend back.

He whizzed around me, causing me to stumble as I turned with him.

"I must have gotten bigger," he mused, voice cracking. Around and around he hovered, making me dizzy, until he abruptly stopped and hovered perfectly still at eye level. "Are we underwater? We're underwater. Where are the fish?"

Okay, so maybe I needed to calibrate his sensors. But he was awake and alert. This was good. I had my drone back. Delight fizzed through my veins. I would survive after all. I beamed at Eledan, caught the fae's oddly humble closed smile, and flinched, remembering he wasn't supposed to be real. "Sota?"

"Yes, Kesh."

"Are we alone?"

The drone did a 360-degree turn. A dancing red line brushed over every surface, scanning Eledan, still relaxed on the floor. "No."

Eledan shrugged a shoulder and lazily got to his feet.

He dusted off his hands and combed his fingers over his hair, sweeping the loose strands back.

"Who else is here with us?" Now my voice sounded broken, the words trembling. The edges of my consciousness started to crumble. The Dreamweaver was here with me. He'd been here the whole time.

"Approximately five thousand insectoids commonly found on Faerie. Two piskies, also called pixies, sprites, nineteen wisps, and one rodent-like creature, status: unrecognized. Are we on Faerie?" he politely inquired.

"Are there any fae here?"

"No. Though you are exhibiting some new and interesting fae-like characteristics—"

I took three strides across the tek-strewn floor and thrust a hand through Eledan's chest. His image shimmered and exploded into dust. His smile was the last thing to go, swirling in the air before settling like glitter on fat green leaves.

He wasn't here.

He'd never been here.

A waking dream. Or something. Whatever it was, he was gone now and I had Sota. I had my friend back for the first time since Eledan had stolen him from me, and for the first time since then, I almost felt like Kesh Lasota again, the renegade messenger. The girl with a life to call her own. I could be her now. "I'm sorry I took so long to save you."

Sota bobbed happily in the air. "I never d-d-doubted you," he stuttered.

"All right, let's get you fixed up and find us some kick-ass tek. We've got a show to attend."

"Oh, we do?" He dropped into his usual hovering position over my shoulder. "Is it good?"

I rolled up my sleeves and plunged through the undergrowth, deeper into Arcon. "I'll blow them away."

I FOLLOWED the rise and fall of the noise of thousands of people and walked from the jungle back into New-Calicto with Sota at my shoulder, my coat shimmering, and a new whip at my hip. Not a single fae soldier stepped in my path. They watched me pass, eyes cold, but they *saw* me. When I stopped outside enormous double doors, they swung open into a long tunnel, and beyond, inside the arena, the mass of waiting fae sounded like the roar of waves.

Sjora had known I would return. She'd given me no other choice. Kellee or Talen. Fight one to save the other.

I walked out into the light and heat, watching the gusting breeze kick up dust devils and spin them across the sprawling arena floor.

"The Wraithmaker has arrived!" The wind carried Sjora's voice through the open air and tossed it around the terraces. The audience cheered so loudly the ground trembled, anticipating the show ahead.

Fear and the thrill of what was to come danced down my spine, tingling outward, sparking like electricity across the warfae markings. I opened my arms and turned on the spot. Cheers lifted my smile and soaked into my saru skin. I had been built for this.

"Can we kill them all now?" Sota whispered, buzzing by my ear.

"Patience," I replied through a grin.

"But it's what I do."

"I know the feeling." I flicked my fingers against my palm, firing up Sota's ocular link. The image floating bottom right in my vision showed an aerial view of the arena, including the red dot of my active spy-bot pinpointing Sjora's exact location. "Gotcha."

"The Wraithmaker has been accused of heinous crimes," Sjora announced from her spot on the balcony high above. *"Regicide of our beloved Queen Mab. And more recently the vicious murder of Lord Devere. Plus, a slew of fae who happened to have the misfortune to cross her path, including a flight of mine, callously cut down by the same drone you see with her now."*

A wave of hisses assaulted my ears. Oh, the fae didn't like that.

"You had another drone?" Sota asked, in alarm.

"Not mine. It exploded."

"It *what?*"

"Like I said, not mine. You won't explode."

He muttered something I didn't hear and asked, "Did you do all those things she said?"

"Some," I admitted.

His whirring noise pitched up a note. "You are so bad-ass."

I chuckled and walked farther into the center of the arena.

"It is by the decree of our king that she fight in a trial by combat for your entertainment. She will fight for us today, and if Faerie favors her, the Wraithmaker shall earn her freedom."

More hisses.

"I don't like the green and red fairy," Sota grumbled.

Fairy was a derogatory term. I'd missed him more than his electronic components could ever understand.

"Now, let us begin!"

The ground trembled, pebbles dancing.

Sota shot fifteen feet into the air above me.

I hunkered down and freed my whip, turning quickly so nothing could leap at me from behind. I'd expected to go straight into a fight with Kellee—but this was something else. Clouds of dust grew, rolling upward from the arena floor, and coalesced into eight or nine huge funnels. Darkness crept across the arena, silencing the audience.

The funnels spun tighter, sucking up all the air, whipping my coat and hair around me, and then abruptly, the chaos ended. The wind dropped, and the funnels dissipated.

Silence as thick as the darkness fell over Sota and me. My drone quietly descended. "There are three distinct signs of life approaching fast from the east, north-east and west."

I turned, squinting into the haze. "Where?"

"They do not appear on your visual spectrum."

Well, great. "Stealth."

Sota's casing cracked and shimmered. The drone disappeared, and overlaid in my vision, I saw the three rippling sources dashing fast toward us like heat-seeking tek.

"Banshee." I tugged my coat closed, hiding my whip inside, and mentally pulled on Talen's magic, hoping he answered. Warmth plunged over me, and like Sota, my outline rippled and folded in on itself, turning me invisible. But the banshee kept coming.

The thrill of the chase buzzed through my veins. I fell into a jog, heading straight toward the westward mass of energy. They would stay invisible until the last moment. That was how they trapped their victims. I'd fought one in an arena before, subduing it only after it had swallowed the souls of three of my fellow saru.

I ran, clutched my whip, and closed the distance in seconds.

I hope you're watching, Kellee.

At the last second, I freed the whip, the thrashing metal links exploding through my illusion, and sprang. The banshee's skeletal hand reached, its yawning black mouth opened. I slashed the whip through the creature's shadowy robes, slicing it clean in half, tek-severing the banshee's hold on this Faerie-enriched world.

"Behind!" Sota warned, breaking stealth to bark the alarm.

I landed in a roll, sprang back to my feet, skidded in the dirt, and faced the two remaining horrors. Sota's laser scorched through one, tearing out a chunk of its middle and turning the rest to ash. The final one tried to slam into me. I yanked on one side of Talen's coat, pulling it around me and brandishing it like a shield. Fae magic blazed in a wall of orange light, seemingly from nowhere. The banshee screamed and recoiled. It fell into Sota's line of sight and was nothing but dust a moment later. Wherever Talen was, I thanked him.

The dust settled, and so did the silence.

"Poor things," I brushed the dust off my coat. "They were hoping to see blood."

I lifted my hands, tossed the tail of the whip into the air, and cracked it dramatically. "IS THAT ALL YOU'VE GOT?!" I yelled, sending my voice out as far as the arena's outer edges, riling up the crowd.

"We're just warming up."

It would take a lot more than a handful of Faerie's monsters to bring me down.

I lifted my chin and peered up at the balcony. Sjora was there, a shimmering picture of greens and golds. Her prickling aura of magic gave her an iridescent glow. She thought she was safe all the way up there. They all thought they were safe...

"Round two! Begin."

Again, the ground shook, but this time giant cracks darted through the earth, and dirty water bubbled through. In seconds, its surface sloshed around my knees.

"Sota?"

"Yes, Kesh."

"Did I ever tell you I can't swim?"

He hesitated. "Neither can I."

And it wasn't our only problem. A high-pitched keening cut through the sound of roaring water, and all around, black beasts emerged from below the surface. They bore a passing resemblance to Faerie horses, but these were no tempered stock animals. Wildness blazed in the whites of their eyes. They tossed their heads, sharp hooves churning the waters. A single jagged spear-like horn protruded from their foreheads. Kelpies. Water horses that lured the unsuspecting in and dragged them into their watery depths.

I almost laughed and wondered if that was the madness in me. Faerie wouldn't let me live through this.

Water sloshed around my waist, lifting my coat and rendering any low swings of the whip useless.

"Things just got interesting."

The beasts thundered forward, water rising with them

until they rode a cresting wave the size of a container stack. I pulled on the knot of magic inside, the one Talen had tied to me, and summoned everything he could spare. But as the wave towered over me, Kelpie hooves relentlessly beating the crest, I doubted it would be enough.

I stood facing a wall of water, and all I could feel was anger. Talen had said I wouldn't die, and he'd been wrong.

Water crashed in. I rolled and tumbled, tossed around like a doll at the mercy of the currents. A hoof cracked against the side of my head and another hit me in the back, popping something out of place. I gasped, pulled water into my lungs, and felt the hot, thudding beat of desperation pounding inside my head.

Something nudged my hand. I sank my grip into a fan of hair, and held on. The surface shattered a second later. I spluttered and threw my leg over the back of the Kelpie. The beast swung its head and gnashed its teeth, trying to bite my face off. Talen's magic flared in a heady snap that jolted the kelpie into a gallop and acted like a slap across my face. I gasped, filling my lungs with precious air. Water churned and swelled, but the faster the beast ran, the more my heart raced with it, until I felt the beat of its blood between my thighs, its rapid breathing billowing its lungs, and the wildness of Faerie driving it forever onward. *To run and run and run and never stop. Never let them catch you.* Obscure, mad-like joy ripped a laugh from me. *Run.* I heard Talen laughing all those times we had sprinted through the prison, telling me to keep up with him. I never had, but I could now. Magic swirled like the waters, building higher, feasting on new wildness I hadn't known I had in me. The thrill felt the same as when Talen looked in my eyes and warned me of all the terrible things he could be.

I let go of the beast's mane and gripped it with my thighs so I could straighten and truly feel the touch of Faerie flow down my spine. Love, ecstasy, madness. It strummed my human body alive, lifting me up and making me something more. The back of my hands shimmered, lit from the inside, throwing my tattoos into stark contrast, making them almost... living.

My kelpie slowed and tossed its head. Its hooves danced on drying ground, and we whirled, the beast and I breathless but alive—so very alive. The herd surrounded us, toeing the muddy earth with their heads bowed, sharp horns sparking with magic.

I almost forgot the arena, forgot the crowd, forgot Sjora, because somehow, I was connected to these beasts, connected like I was to Talen, and it felt glorious.

I dug my heels in, shifting the beast to the side, and peered up at Sjora on her balcony. I didn't need words. I could feel her anger bubbling the rest of the water away. She had thrown Faerie at me, and I'd ridden it into submission.

"It's not over. Faerie's latest arena champion—your successor— has waited a long time for this, as have we." The crowd roared. *"Prepare to meet your match, Wraithmaker."*

Another champion? The herd of kelpies stirred, nostrils flaring. My beast reared. I kicked off and landed in a crouch. The animals scattered to the far fringes of the arena, parting around a human male as he casually approached.

Sota buzzed in. "I was absolutely about to save you."

A rough scarf wound around the champion's neck and

covered the lower half of his face. He wore scout leathers that were well equipped for stalking through shadows. A dagger sheath adorned each hip. Curved steel daggers glinted in his hands.

So, he was their champion now, the one they all cheered for in the arenas back on Faerie. A champion who would always be second to the Wraithmaker unless he took my crown here and now.

Cheers from the countless fae reminded me that this was all a show to them. Saru lives were worth no more and no less than their entertainment. They were about to watch one of us die, and they *adored* it.

I sank my hand into my pocket but found the flash-tek soaked through. Even my whip felt clunky in my hand. *Another saru.*

"Who's this guy?" Sota asked, finding his spot behind my shoulder.

"Doesn't matter. He's a dead man." *I have to get to Kellee, and this gladiator is in my way.* I strode forward. "Don't attack him. Let's give the fae what they want." I needed them to believe in the Wraithmaker one last time. I needed their eyes on me.

"And if he's about to kill you?"

My mouth ticked at the corner, and Talen's magic skittered from my hand down the whip. "He's not that good."

CHAPTER 19

The champion stopped a good fifty feet away. The tattered and dusty leathers he wore had survived many fights. Like him. He wasn't as tall as Kellee, but he had a similarly honed physique that told me he was ready for anything. If he'd risen in the gladiator ranks right after I'd left, that gave him five years in the arenas. A long time for a saru. He would be skilled. But it wouldn't be enough.

Kellee had said I could stop killing. If only it were that simple. One day, maybe. But not today. Today, I needed to be everything the fae expected of the Wraithmaker.

"Put down the blades and kneel." I raised my voice, letting the wind grab it and toss it around the arena. The jubilant noise from the crowd swelled. "It's the only way you'll survive this."

He didn't move, didn't reply. His eyes might have crinkled, but I was too far away to tell for sure.

I read his easy stance, one foot slightly behind the other. He'd spring off his back foot and swing with the right dagger. He wasn't heavy like some saru I'd fought and killed, which meant he was fast and probably had the stamina to outlast his opponents. How many saru did he kill as a child so he could step out of the crate into a new life serving the fae?

I flicked the whip, letting it lick the arena floor, testing for any fear reaction. He gave none. Not even a twitch. We both understood how this world worked. One of us would die, and it sure-as-cyn wouldn't be me.

"Back up," I told Sota. "I've got this."

The drone whirred backward, reluctance making his movements clunky.

I had a pistol inside my coat. I hadn't used it yet because everything they'd thrown at me had been magical, and a pistol shot wouldn't have done much beyond pissing off Faerie's creations. I could draw it now and shoot this gladiator between the eyes. But where was the showmanship in that?

I flicked the whip again. "You've been waiting for this?"

He jerked his chin but remained silent. Had he lost his tongue over an indiscretion against his masters?

"Then I'd better not disappoint you." I stepped forward, ending the stand-off.

His right hand flicked, launching the dagger at my head. It was a strange opening and a move I easily jerked away from. I moved closer, striding faster. Magic trickled through the whip, lending it more than physical strength.

"Look out!" Sota barked.

I heard the hiss from behind and ducked. The dagger swept past, and the champion snatched it out of the air.

"Nice." I straightened. His dagger had returned to him. Tek? Or magic? I appreciated a few tricks. We were both entertainers, after all. "Now let me show you mine." I ran my hand down the trim of my coat, pulling a string of metal buttons free, and tossed them into the air. Their watertight casings burst open, instantly turning into deadly razor-edged stars. They lunged. The champion brought his arms up, shielding his face, and flinched away, but the flying blades sank into his forearms and lower torso, peppering his leathers and sticking fast. Now every time he moved, they'd dig deeper.

I sprinted forward.

He must have heard the whip slice through the air because he rolled away a second before its tails could snag his arm. He was up, the left blade catching the light as it plunged. I twisted, heard fabric tear, and cracked my elbow into his jaw. We sprang apart, him nursing his jaw and dripping blood from a dozen cuts, and me frowning at the huge tear in Talen's fancy coat.

The champion dashed forward, using my momentary blip in concentration to tackle me low, but he didn't throw his arms around me as I'd expected and braced for. Instead, he shot out a flat palm, fingers locked, hitting me with the ball of his hand square in the solar plexus. Pressure crumpled my lower ribs, knocking the air from my lungs. My back hit the arena floor, then the back of my head cracked against the stone, and I skidded a good few feet in the grit before coming to an unceremonious halt, blinking at the sky. I looked down my nose as my lungs figured out how to breathe again. He stood in the same spot, hands at his sides, waiting. Had he followed through with those daggers, he could have cut my throat. Damn, he was good.

"Kesh?" Sota inquired, buzzing above our heads.

205

"Still got this," I wheezed and climbed to my feet. Cheers thundered through the air. I couldn't tell if they were for me or him, but given my crimes, I suspected he had all of New-Calicto on his side.

He shook out his right hand, feeling the effects of the open-handed punch. He had the moves, but did he have the fire?

Instead of running from him, I ran at him, feinted left as he swung a solid right hook, and snatched his arm, jerking it upright. We grappled. He blocked every punch, every knee thrust, and every elbow I threw at him—until one got through. I got lucky and hit him in the gut. He grunted in pain, rolling over the impact. I grabbed his wrist, twisted harder, and he buckled to keep his arm from breaking, falling backward in the dirt.

I pressed my boot to his neck and dislodged the scarf from his chin, revealing the corner of a partially smiling mouth. Dust lightened his short, ruffled hazel-colored hair. Dark, sweeping eyebrows accentuating graceful tear-shaped eyes. Old knowledge resided in those young eyes, and the arena, the fight, Sjora, the fae—it all came crashing down. I knew him.

Shock hit me like a fist. I lifted my boot off his neck and stumbled backward.

"No." The denial fell from my lips. More might have babbled free, but I wasn't listening.

It's not possible.

He brought his legs up and flipped onto his feet.

I felt my mouth twist into an ironic smile. This was a trick. An illusion. It had to be.

"Kesh Lasota..." he said. And I recognized the voice, though it had deepened and become abrasive. He casually tossed a dagger into the air and caught it. "That's what I should call you now?"

This isn't real.

I staggered, almost falling over my feet.

"Kesh?" Sota asked again.

The champion yanked down his scarf, tore it from around his neck, and tossed it into the air. It fluttered downward. I would have recognized him anywhere, could have picked him out of a crowd of thousands, but it was the smiling scar across his neck that undid me.

I dropped my whip, and somewhere distantly, I registered that I should pick it up again, but I couldn't. This man... this saru champion... I had once reached through cage bars and held his hand to stop us both from trembling. I'd listened to his fantastical stories in which the saru would find a leader to unite them. I'd laughed and told him his dreams were foolish—worse, they were dangerous—and then, in the end, I'd cut his throat.

"Aeon?" The name left my lips, spoken to test if this was real.

No, no... Not real, not any of this. I'm losing my mind.

No more. I can't do this anymore. I eyed the imposter while shock wrapped me in detached bliss and yanked out all feeling. "This ends here."

Turning my back to the champion, I lifted my hands and pinned Sjora under my glare. "You have been entertained. It's over." Aeon moved behind me, boots deliberately scuffing the dirt so I knew where he stood. If he moved to stab me in the back, Sota would fry his insides before he could sink the blade home.

He kept his distance and stopped to my right, far enough away to not pose an immediate threat. He lifted

207

his head, looking up at those looking down on us. Aeon and I had bowed to them before while covered in the blood of our kin, and here we stood, together again, but not bowing. My thoughts stuttered at the symmetry. *It can't be him...*

"They came to see blood spilled," he murmered so they wouldn't hear.

"They'll get their chance," I told him, grateful for the cold edge to my voice. I waited for Sjora to speak and end the game. I still had one move left, my closing gambit.

"But it's only just begun, Wraithmaker." She laughed, and a rush of excitement crackled through the air. Beside her on the balcony, a regal figure appeared, cloaked in royal blues and shimmering with a golden aura, the same aura that had touched me. Talen.

The kelpies gathered at one side of the arena, letting out their screaming cries and frightful whines.

"THE LAST VAKARU," Sjora boomed. Thunderous cheers and applause assaulted my ears, so loud it almost drowned out my thoughts.

Kellee approached through the heat haze, his outline a ghostly ripple. A telltale flutter of fear kicked all my senses up a notch.

"Sota," I said. The drone zipped in low. "Now."

Sota's subsonic blast throbbed at the back of my skull and beat through the air. For a moment, nothing happened. The wind still swirled through the area, the fae still watched, the kelpies stirred up clouds of dust, and Kellee kept on coming.

I threw a warning look at the champion—I wouldn't call him Aeon because Aeon was dead. "I don't care who you look like, touch that vakaru and you're dead."

The champion raised an eyebrow in an expression so familiar it cut me to the bone.

"How long?" I asked Sota.

"One minute fifteen seconds."

This had to work. If it didn't, I had nothing left. I clutched at the trim of Talen's coat, hoping he understood, hoping we were on the same side.

The champion took a few steps forward. A frown tightened his eyes and the corners of his mouth. He studied Kellee's approach and then lifted his face to the sky. His lips twitched. "After all this time, I was right," he said.

Not Aeon. "You're only alive because of the face you wear. Now stay out of my way and you might survive a few minutes more." I drew my pistol and approached Kellee's moving silhouette. My whip lay behind me. Hopefully, I wouldn't need it. "If you're smart," I called, "you'll run while you can." The words were meant for the champion, but the fae took it to mean Kellee and hooted their approval.

They'd given Kellee a three-quarter-length coat but no shirt and no shoes, just dark pants. His hair whipped loosely around his face, and his eyes burned with the true wildness I'd only seen once before. He was Faerie untamed, molded into the male form.

Kellee's skin barely contained the threat radiating from him. I told myself he might not know me, that I just needed to buy time to keep him and the crowd preoccupied, but with every step that brought us closer together, the growing sense of fear tightened around my heart, leaving a bitter bite of terror on my tongue. The fear stemmed from a primal part of me that recognized the monster approaching. And I knew the truth of what I faced. The fae hadn't wiped out the vakaru for turning on their masters. They had killed an entire race because of what I witnessed in the beast's eyes now: the depth of the darkness, the raw, dangerous threat rippling around him like a fae's lighter magic. Only this last vakaru wasn't made of the light. It wasn't pretty, it didn't seduce, and it was a nightmare made flesh. Seeded inside him, Faerie's darkest creation waited. The fae had killed every vakaru because, inside, they were unseelie.

I was afraid like those fae who had faced the vakaru before me. Afraid of and for Kellee. Afraid that I was doing the wrong thing. Afraid this was another mistake. Afraid I was never meant to be anything but a killer.

I want to save people, Kellee. I'll start with you.

Dust swirled off the arena floor, sweeping Kellee out of sight.

"Sota, how long?"

"Fifty-one seconds."

A lot could happen in fifty-one seconds. I lifted the pistol, cupping my grip in my left hand, and waited for the dust to clear. The kelpies' cries circled the arena, sounding like the screams of the saru I'd killed.

C'mon, Kellee. Let's dance.

My heart pounded.

"I know him," Sota said from somewhere behind.

I still couldn't see more than a shadow moving inside the dirt cloud. "Hold," I told the drone.

Sota's whirring turned heavy, and his casing hissed open, revealing the guns.

"Sota. Do not fire."

More dust rolled in, and then the wind finally dropped

and the dust settled. I blinked at the spot where Kellee had been, eyes scratchy. He'd vanished.

"I know h-him," Sota repeated, falling into the deadly monotone of an attack drone.

Claws cut through the air. I twisted away, but not fast enough. Crackling pain sank into my right arm, igniting the nerve endings. The metallic bite of spilled blood wet the air.

Sota fired.

CHAPTER 20

*I*t hadn't occurred to me that my drone might harbor a grudge, but as Sota opened fire on Kellee, I realized my oversight was about to cost Kellee his life. Rapid bolts of energy tore through Kellee's body. Holes punched through flesh, and blood and muscle ignited. I turned the pistol on Sota and fired. Sota whirled on me, his single lens aglow with the shock of betrayal, and then one of the champion's crude daggers *thwacked* into the drone's weakened outer casing, plunging home.

Kellee collapsed to his knees, blood pooling around him.

"Stop. Dammit, Sota, STOP!" I threw myself between the drone and Kellee. *"How long?!"* I yelled.

Sota bobbed in the air, ports still open and smoking, but he wasn't firing. "Twenty seconds."

A rumbling sounded. The air trembled.

The champion searched the sky, his remaining dagger clutched in his right hand.

I dropped to Kellee's side, kneeling in muddy puddles

drenched in too much blood. He crumpled onto his side and blinked at me as though he barely understood where he was. The monster inside him had fled, leaving behind the marshal I knew so well. "I've got you," I told him. "It's over now. No more killing. Okay? No more fighting. Not for you."

His green eyes widened. "Did you just *shoot* me, Kesh?"

"No." I peeled back his coat and winced at the minced meat Sota had made of Kellee's side. "The drone... I..."

A cloud passed over the arena, the temperature plummeted, and the trembling grew into a thunderous roar.

"Is it bad?" he asked, watching my face.

"Just a scratch." Thick, dark blood pulsed from the countless wounds.

Wincing, teeth gritted, he rolled onto his back, his eyes glassy. "The sky is falling."

I looked up. The sky *was* falling. A cloud of black drones swept downward in an endless stream of tek I'd resurrected from the bowels of Arcon. Thousands of drones formed an enormous wave and poured into the arena. Their lenses glinted, cold, hard, efficient. They were... beautiful.

The reflection of the drones passed across Kellee's too-bright eyes. "I was wrong," I told him. His lashes fluttered. "Halow needs the Wraithmaker."

He let his head fall to the side, and the sadness on his face almost broke my resolve. He didn't want this, not like this...

I understood. Despite the darkness at his core, or perhaps because of it, Marshal Kellee was good. He believed in Kesh Lasota. But sometimes goodness wasn't enough. Right now, Kesh Lasota wasn't enough. Sometimes the monsters needed to win.

"Open fire."

Two words. Two simple words that Sota transmitted to every drone inside the arena. They obeyed. A tek-storm of light and noise erupted around us. I had only heard the fae scream like that once before, when the Hunt had harvested the night back on Faerie. I'd huddled in my cell then. I wasn't cowering now. Fire and blood—the smell of hot metal and weeping flesh—saturated the air. Thousands of immortal lives blinked out like stars consumed by darkness, and I was that darkness.

"Kesh, stop!" Talen's voice pierced the uproar.

I turned and saw him reach for me.

The champion pressed his last blade to Talen's throat, holding him back. Talen froze, his hand outstretched, eyes wide with disbelief.

"One wrong move and that smooth throat of yours gets a bright new smile," the champion warned. *So much like Aeon...*

Talen's gaze turned from pleading to menacing. He lowered his hand and lifted his chin. "Stop this slaughter. You've won."

"No, I haven't. *We* haven't."

The drones continued to fire, their staccato blasts peppering the air, but the screams were fading, with fewer living sources to hunt down. Sota hovered behind Talen, observing.

Talen's gaze dropped to Kellee sprawled on the arena floor behind me. His throat bobbed against the champion's blade. "Do this and I can't keep you safe," Talen said.

"It's done." Silently, I begged him to stand with me,

not against me, but his eyes remained hard, his expression fierce. I was butchering his people. But it was nothing less than his kind had done to Halow's cities. We were on two different sides of the war, he and I, and I'd drawn my battle lines. But had he?

Overlaid in my vision, the red tracking dot blinked into motion. Sjora was alive and moving. This wasn't over.

Talen stepped back. The champion lowered his blade. A teardrop of blood dribbled down Talen's neck. He wiped at it and cut the champion a scathing sneer. The champion winked, and my wrecked heart wanted so badly to believe he was Aeon, but now was not the time.

"Help me get Kellee—" I began.

Talen turned away.

I'd lost him.

I'd crossed the line Eledan had spoken of. I'd gone too far. But I'd had to do it. This was war. Halow had some fight left in it, and I planned to find it and stoke the last dregs of humanity back into the fight. Me and Kellee, and Talen…?

Talen looked up at the sky through the swarming drones. "I told you to trust me."

The ground shuddered again like an ancient beast was rising from beneath the ground. The light faded, plunging the arena into true darkness, and above, a colossal ship groaned into sight. Sjora's warcruiser.

The champion's hand closed around my upper arm. "We have to go. Now!"

I almost yanked out of his grip, but his eyes held all the honesty and pride I'd admired in Aeon. After all this time, after everything I'd done, could he really be Aeon?

He cupped my face in his hand and pressed his forehead to mine. "I'm real. I'm with you."

I remembered the boy who had taught me to survive, to dream of better things, to see outside my cage. And I saw that boy in this man's eyes. "This is no trick, *Mylana*."

I gasped, and the world froze around us.

Mylana.

It was our secret.

My saru name.

Only Aeon knew.

The truth was right there, his hands on my face, his eyes pulling me in. "I'll explain it all, just leave with me now—"

A lazy string of slow claps announced Sjora's presence. She emerged from the darkness, her skin glowing green with magic. "You certainly know how to deliver the theatrics."

I lifted the pistol, but vines sprung from the ground and ripped the weapon from my hand, tossing it out of sight. More vines punched from the ground and laced around Kellee. He cut through some, but more tangled around his limbs, tying him and his claws down.

"Run!" I shoved Aeon away. *"RUN!"*

Defiance shone in his eyes, just like it had when he'd stood up to Dagnu time and time again. "Not from them."

Sjora flicked her wrist and the whiplike vines lashed in, cutting down Aeon's back. He jerked but let loose the dagger with a lightning-fast crack. The blade slammed into Sjora's shoulder. She merely laughed, plucked it free, and tossed it away. "Do you even understand what you have done?" She looked at me. Too calm. Too controlled.

Vines wrapped around Aeon's ankles and snagged his

wrists, yanking him to his knees. Before he could open his mouth, vines wrapped around his head, gagging him.

I faced Sjora. Vines tightened around my wrists, knotted up my forearms, and pulled, trying to force me to my knees. I stood firm, drawing on the fire inside to keep me strong. Thorns dug in, clawing across my shoulders, sinking into my coat, and puncturing my shoulders.

Sjora stopped so close that her heady magic lapped against my skin. "When Oberon learns of his Wraithmaker's betrayal"—she dragged her glass thimble down my cheek—"he will bring the might of Faerie down upon the humans. Halow will not be enough to satiate his rage. Sol will not be enough. As much as I despise our king, his vengeance is glorious to witness."

Talen's magic beat through my bones, and just like with the kelpie, I took it all in and let it open something hidden inside.

"You may have created us," I hissed, "but you don't own us. Not anymore. We are free because we choose to be free. And we will fight because we choose to fight. I am saru and you have no power over me."

If I died here, it would be for something. It would be for hope, for freedom, for all the things the saru had been denied. It would be for the last vakaru and his long-forgotten people, for the humans and their relentless strength and courage, for all of Faerie's mistakes.

She took my chin in her hand, dug her fingers into my cheek, and yanked me close. "You are *nothing*."

"You are wrong," Talen said. "She is everything."

His power poured in, igniting an aura of light from inside my soul. Sjora threw herself away, her attention no longer on me, but on Talen.

Light spilled from the ship above in a column of magic, illuminating Talen inside the spotlight. His power blazed all around him. His hair snaked outward, and his eyes shone golden. He wasn't seeing me, not anymore, though I felt the depth of his sadness tug at my heart. A sadness for something lost before it had been found. This felt like a sacrifice, like he was giving up, but it looked like victory.

Sjora laughed a giddy, childlike laugh, and then the light blinked out, plunging the arena into darkness once more. Thumps hit the ground all around. *Falling drones.* The ship likely had short-range EMP that knocked my drones out of the sky.

The vessel thundered above, blasting the ground with back draft. Its enormous bulk steadily rose into New-Calicto's sky.

Talen and Sjora were gone, and so too were the strangling vines.

Kellee lay panting, trying to stand, and Aeon looked at me as though seeing me for the first time.

"We have to... go after him." Kellee stumbled to his feet, then staggered backward.

I grabbed his arm and threw it over my shoulder, heaving the marshal against me. "He's made his choice."

"Yes, he did." Kellee clutched at the mess that was his side and glanced at Aeon. "He chose to save us all."

"He made it clear, Kellee." I shifted his weight, trying to get a good hold. We had to leave. More fae would come. "He's not on our side. I should have seen it. You were right. You're always right—"

Kellee laughed, the sound tight with irony. "Kesh, I know you can't see it, but even your stranger friend here sees the truth. Sjora was about to kill us all. He gave himself to her."

I stopped, absently eyeing the fallen drones and twisted fae bodies.

"She was about to kill us," Aeon agreed.

I blinked at them. What I'd seen was Talen leaving with Sjora. "I don't understand."

"You saved me once, held a blade to your throat and told the Mad Prince you'd kill yourself if he didn't fix me up." Kellee shoved out of my grip and swayed. "What Talen did is the same. Don't you see? She has him. All of him."

"She always had him."

"No... No, Kesh." He smiled sadly. "He was yours. That's why he held out, but now..."

"What?!" I snapped. "Dammit, Kellee, I don't understand what you're telling me."

"If we don't get to him, he'll be lost forever." Kellee shook his head. "He's her pilot. Once he's bonded with the ship, he'll be gone forever."

CHAPTER 21

*I*t was a long walk to the docks, trudging through tightly knotted undergrowth. Thick leaves dripped heavy water droplets over us as we passed, drenching us to the bone. Kellee kept a decent pace, but the strain showed on his face. His wounds were healing but slowly. Aeon scouted ahead, moving like a ghost through the undergrowth with the EMP-unconscious Sota slung in a sack over his shoulder. We'd—I'd killed the fae in the arena, but there could still be some out there looking for us. In the chaos and revelations, I'd left my whip behind, another one gone.

Gone forever. Kellee's words haunted my every step. I still didn't understand what had happened, not really, but Kellee did. I wanted to ask him all the questions, but he was in no condition for me to grill him on Talen's sacrifice or if he knew the thing inside him was unseelie. If he did, would he care? There was nothing anyone could do to save him from himself.

Kellee grunted and fell against a young tree trunk. His

drenched hair clung to his face, dripping water across his chin and down his neck. "I have to stop," he admitted, grinding out the words as though they hurt. "To rest…"

I whistled, thin and low, wondering if Aeon remembered our secret signals. He peeled back a curtain of ivy to my right as though he'd been there all along. His stalking ability was second to none, including mine.

"Get to the docks and see if there's anything we can use to get off Calicto. I'll find somewhere nearby to rest up while Kellee heals."

He nodded once, dropped Sota, and left. I swung Sota's sack over my shoulder and helped Kellee to his feet. We struggled on until the vegetation opened into what had once been a street stacked on either side with containers. It now resembled a tropical valley. But the containers were still there, their rusted corners poking through in places.

I kicked open a container door, scattering a cloud of bright pixies out the open window. Vines and roots had wormed their way inside, but recognizable bits of moth-eaten furniture remained.

"Here." I helped Kellee to the couch and eased him onto the cushions.

He dropped his head back. The wounds on his chest opened and wept fresh blood. He saw me looking. "I'll be all right. Nothing vital is broken." He tried to smile his don't-give-a-damn lawman smile, but it didn't stick.

"Sure you will, tough guy." I tore open hidden storage units and found blankets, a med-kit, plus a few critters that blinked at me before taking flight on double translucent wings.

"Why didn't he tell me he was a pilot?" I'd been turning over the revelation while we'd been walking. Talen had had plenty of opportunity to tell me why the fae were fawning over him, and he hadn't said a single word.

Kellee snorted. "They guard their words like we guard family. Would it have changed anything?"

I tore open a med-wipe and cleaned my hands with angry swipes, aware of Kellee's gaze warming my back. It might have changed something, but how was I supposed to keep them safe if they kept secrets from me? Or perhaps I was a fool to think I mattered enough for either of them to bother telling me anything.

"Don't like being lied to, huh?" Kellee asked.

I stopped wiping my hands and gripped the counter-top. I deserved that and worse. "He didn't lie. He just... didn't say anything."

"Spoken like a professional liar." Kellee laughed, then spluttered and hissed. I dumped the med-kit on the couch beside him and knelt next to his leg, nudging it aside so I could get closer. He looked down, his gaze holding the weight of everything that had passed between us. His hand resting on the couch arm twitched.

I looked up, not about to dive into cleaning him up if he was going to go all vakaru on me and try to tear my throat out. The unseelie in him was buried deep, but knowing it was there made me think twice around him. "Will you let me take a look?"

"There's no need."

"Right. You're a big, brave vakaru who doesn't need help from a little saru, but for the sake of getting you moving again, let me take a look?"

His claws slowly stretched from his nails. He noticed and flinched, struggling to stop his instincts from taking over. Licking his lips, he let his head fall back and closed his eyes. The claws receded. "Look, if you have to."

I peeled his coat open and paused. Sota's blasts had torn through Kellee's hip, cauterizing the skin, which was probably why he was having a hard time healing. I'd seen worse—on the dead.

Grabbing a few wipes from the pack, I cleaned away the dirt, gently working my way inward. Kellee's breathing remained steady, his eyes closed. He might almost be asleep.

"What's with you and the new guy?" he asked.

"Nothing."

He flinched when the swab snagged on something raw and painful. "Uh-huh. If this wound doesn't kill me, the tension between the two of you will. Talk to him." I frowned at Kellee. He cracked one eye open and smiled when he saw my expression. "Always right, remember."

"I can't *talk to him*," I said, mimicking Kellee's voice. His eyebrow arched, giving me *the look*. "It's complicated."

That earned me a smile. "Nothing is simple around you."

Where did I start explaining who Aeon was, if he even was Aeon. "If he is who he appears to be, we knew each other... from before."

"*Knew?*"

I prodded around a nasty gaping slice near Kellee's hip. "I thought I killed him. Like I said—complicated."

"Are there any males you've had a relationship with and haven't killed afterward?" I jabbed a nail into the cut, and Kellee arched off the couch. "Ah, *fuck*."

"Oops, I'm so sorry," I drawled. "My finger slipped." When I lifted my gaze, he was grinning. Bastard.

"Too soon?" he asked.

I smiled anyway. Kellee had a way of brightening even the darkest corner, which was crazy considering what he had inside him.

"You're like a spider that eats its mate right after s—"

I poked at another raw bit, and Kellee shut up. "That smart mouth of yours will get you into trouble." I rocked back on my heels and sighed heavily. His smart mouth had a quirk to it that had me wondering what it would be like to kiss its corner.

"It often does."

I knew what he was doing: distracting me from all the things I didn't want to think about. "You're talking about the Blaksrach spider. They eat their mate during copulation. They're about the size of a shuttle on Faerie."

He was already pale, but he might have gone a shade paler. "I'll make a point of not meeting one."

"I thought you said I was one, and you've already met me, sooo..."

"Well then, I guess I was lucky to escape your clutches."

"I guess so..." That damn ache started in my chest again. The one that came when I thought of what would be like to be alone again, thought of Talen turning his back on me and Kellee locking the door and throwing away the key. "I can't do much more without proper equipment, but the wounds are clean." I reached across him to drop the used swabs. "The conditions here aren't ideal—" He grabbed my wrist. I pulled, and he loosened his grip, but his warm fingers a firm hold.

"There is something you can do." His voice had hardened, turning gravelly with menace. I'd seen the same

225

change in him many times. His smooth lawman act sometimes cracked open, and the hard, monstrous thing inside
peeked out. Now that I knew the truth of it, I felt a
genuine flicker of fear.

When he next spoke, the points of his canine teeth
seemed sharper. "Oberon designed us for war."

"I know," I said carefully.

Kellee's fingers stilled around my wrist. I could pull
away, but the rawness in his voice held a tempting ragged
edge that spoke of a vulnerability, a need.

"They poisoned our blood so, on the battlefield, our
fallen continued to kill, and they made us crave the kill."

I shifted, resting my free arm against his thigh so I
could face him and punch him between the legs, as a
precaution.

"They made us... *hunger* for death." He leaned forward,
lips pulled back in a grimace as his wounds protested. His
grimace revealed sharp, curving vakaru teeth designed to
dig in and clamp onto their prey. "I heal faster when...
satisfied." He lifted my wrist and bowed his head. His
green eyes locked on mine, seeking permission. I
wondered if he'd take what he needed anyway. He
breathed too fast, and the flecks of hazel in his eyes
dilated, turning the green dark. I knew he was dangerous,
but I hadn't known the extent of his control and the battle
he fought every day.

"Will it hurt?" I asked. It didn't matter if it did. I'd do
this for him. I owed him my life. If it weren't for him, I'd
still be dreaming my mortal years away.

He swallowed. His lips parted as he raised my wrist to
his mouth. "Yes." He opened his mouth, drew back his
lips, and plunged the fangs in deep. The flash of white-hot

pain seared through me, too acute for it to be a mere physical attack. I almost tore my arm free, but Kellee's bite clamped harder, teeth sinking impossibly deeper. I clutched at his shoulder, half trying to push him off and half trying to hold on. My fingers dug in, nails biting into his back. A chaotic panic I hadn't felt in years tried to sink its claws in and tear me away.

I found his gaze, tried to tell him it hurt too much, that it was too deep and pulling something vital out of me, but his scowl burned, his eyes fierce, and the beast glared back, daring me to run so it could hunt me down and tear me open. The wildness of Faerie challenged me—*run*, it said.

"Kellee..." I pleaded.

The room spun and dipped, taking the weight of me with it, leaving a lightness so bright I might drift far away.

"Kellee, stop..." I wasn't sure if I'd spoken or even if he'd heard. Madness blazed in his eyes. His bite crunched down, pulling a whimper from my lips. He wouldn't let me go.

I switched my free hand to the back of his neck and squeezed, pulling myself up, almost into his lap. My forehead bumped his, and his eyes widened so that their ancient, hungry depths were all I could see, and the unseelie thing inside him saw me. "LET. ME. GO."

He jerked back, yanking his teeth free, but he still had a hold of my wrist. His tongue flicked out, sweeping across the ragged, bloody mess that was my wrist.

"Whatever you do... next..." he panted. "Do. Not. Run." A primal part of him wanted me to do exactly that. There was no doubt in my mind he would kill me if I ran.

I pulled my arm free and staggered back, fighting the

prey-like urge to tremble. Acting weak would only arouse him further.

Kellee sat poised on the edge of the couch, breathing hard like we'd spent hours sparring. His claws glinted, savage and sharp. If I ran, I wouldn't get far.

Run, run, run... my instincts clamored. But they were wrong. You never ran from something ancient and hungry. I held his stare, my standing position helping to pin him down.

His eyes rolled, and he threw his head back, ran his tongue across his teeth, and caught his breath, holding himself still and under control. His chest wounds pulled and twitched, closing as though stitched by an invisible thread. I had never thought of Kellee and his people as magical. But what I witnessed was pure Faerie engineered into the template of a man. It was savage, and brutal, and raw, and beautiful, and dangerous. All things Kellee.

His eyes fluttered open, and without looking, he ran his hand across his lower abs, sweeping off the last of the spilled blood. Shuddering, he rose to his feet, his motion smooth and unhurried. And then he was moving toward me, his head tipped downward. He took my damaged wrist gently in his hands and turned it over. His thumb brushed through the blood, revealing unblemished skin beneath. He'd somehow healed me, and that made it worse, as though he could just wish what had happened away. I still trembled, coming down from the arena rush and the shock of my actions, of Aeon, and now him—this monster I'd do anything for.

He blinked heavy eyelids. "Are we good?" His teeth were small again, and his mouth slanted coyly. He had that lazy, gratified look in his eyes that said he'd enjoyed his meal more than I had.

"I don't know what we are." I pulled my wrist free and scooped up Sota's bag on my way to the door. "C'mon, we have a shuttle to catch."

CHAPTER 22

*a*eon had found a shuttle and untangled it from the blanket of roots. Kellee fired up its engines, and we were flying free of New-Calicto's gravity not long after. Our new shuttle was luxurious—the kind Eledan's alter ego, Istvan Larsen, would have owned. A quick search through the various cabins revealed clothes, medicinal supplies, and enough food and drink to last a few days.

"We're riding Calicto's atmosphere. I'm not picking up any local signs of life," Kellee announced, emerging from the pilot section at the front into the communal area that resembled a living room. There was probably some ship term for it, but I had no idea what. Benches hugged the outside walls. Aeon lay on one, his hand thrown over his eyes and a leg drawn up. His slow, regular breathing suggested he was sleeping.

"Any idea how to find the fae warcruiser before it gets to Faerie?"

Kellee approached me from behind and watched me

lift Sota from the sack and dump him on a counter. "It's not going back to Faerie."

Keeping his distance, the marshal eyed Sota like the drone might spring to life. "Will that thing try to kill me again?"

"This *thing* is Sota, and he's my friend."

"Why am I not surprised something of yours took chunks out of me?" Sota wobbled, and Kellee reached out a hand to steady him. "Wait, is this *the mythical friend* you were trying to save from Eledan?"

"Yes." I scowled at Kellee. "And I was planning on saving him, but I also needed Eledan to find the truth I'd hidden inside Sota so he'd reveal his true identity."

"You used your friend to assassinate Eledan," Kellee reworded succinctly.

Aeon stirred and muttered, "Old habits die hard."

Kellee canted his head, hearing all the unsaid things in Aeon's accusation.

I spread my hands carefully on the countertop and breathed in. Nerves already stretched to their breaking point threatened to snap. I felt like a paper thing tied together with a string of lies, and at any moment, I might unravel. I was tired and angry, and cold and empty, and the weight of all my crimes was right there in the room with us. It always would be until I made it right.

I turned to face them. "Fuck you both and the heroic kelpies you rode in on. Do you think any of this has been easy for me? I'm not proud of the things I did, but I'm trying to do something about it. Either help me or get out of my way."

Kellee decided now was a great time to scrutinize Sota's outer casing, and Aeon hadn't moved beneath his hand. Both stayed silent. The ship's engines burbled, and circulation fans hummed.

I puffed out a sigh. Kellee was right. The tension was suffocating. Aeon was impossibly here, I'd slaughtered countless fae, I'd been speaking with a fantasy version of Eledan, and I'd lost Talen. I brushed Talen's coat between my fingers and looked down at the huge tear. I was coming undone.

"Your plan?" Kellee asked, drawing my eye back to him. He had moved closer, but I didn't recall seeing him do so.

Every muscle and bone in my body ached. I needed rest and food and somewhere Kellee wouldn't see me break down and cry.

"I planted a spy-bot on Sjora," I said. "I'll to reboot Sota and see if we can boost the signal. Hopefully, it'll lead us straight to the ship."

Kellee nodded then startled me by sweeping my hair away from my face, and tucking it neatly behind my ear. He leaned in and whispered, "Talk to him." The little touch and whispers sparked a riot of shivers that had nothing to do with the cold. I was running on fumes racing from A to B, because if I didn't, I'd stop and see the look on Talen's face when he'd asked me to stop killing and I'd refused. I'd see Aeon's scar, and Kellee's teeth in my wrist, and the terror in Devere's eyes when I'd tightened the whip.

Kellee's fingers skimmed my jaw, and then he left, returning to the flight controls. The door closed behind him with a soft puff of air.

Aeon still lay there. The laces had unraveled from his scout leathers so that the jacket hung open by a string. Dust and mud caked his boots and scratches marked his pants, where the thorns had captured him. After ten years, the evidence of my attack had faded, but there was no hiding the smooth smile of scar tissue around his neck.

There wasn't time for this. I had to fix Sota, find the signal, and track down Talen. But I also needed to know who he really was. I needed the truth, right here and now.

"Do you remember what Dagnu used to call you?"

Aeon didn't move. Seconds passed, and then he slowly rolled onto his side and propped his head on his hand. His eyes opened, his gaze heavy with tiredness. *"Saru nechet."* Tiny lines cut into his forehead. *Saru nechet*, had no direct translation, but it implied the person wasn't there, as though they were gone. Saru nechet was Dagnu's way of saying, Aeon was nothing. "He's still alive, still keeps the gladiators in line. I stopped fighting him after..." His words caught in his throat. He flicked his fingers at his neck and smiled ironically. "I asked myself what you would do, and I used his infatuation against him, true Wraith-maker style." His smile grew and twisted with a hint of malice. "You taught me how to deceive, among other things..."

I leaned back against the counter and tried to swallow around the painful lump in my throat. I was breaking inside. I could feel all my pieces cracking open, and I wasn't sure I could put them back together again. I couldn't afford to fall apart, but when I looked down at my hands, they trembled. "I want to believe you're him." I couldn't even lift my voice above a whisper. "I want to believe it so badly that I'm afraid I'll make you him even if you aren't."

Aeon got to his feet. "Whispers of the Wraithmaker reached me in the cells. How she helped the hero Eledan return from ancient history. I thought if I could find you, I'd do to you what you did to me."

I didn't want to look at him, but I forced my head up. "In the arena?"

He stopped a few strides away. He was unarmed but still dangerous. Anything not tied down was a potential weapon. If he acted on the hatred in his eyes, would it be justice?

"Sjora shipped me in especially. The Calicto arena was going to be my moment." He looked away and studied the room. "But I saw you—" His voice cracked. "And I remem —" He swallowed. "I remembered the girl who had listened to my stories and laughed at my dreams." His blunt teeth sank into his bottom lip, and his mouth twisted. He tried to school his expression, tried to keep his emotions from his face, but he was coming apart, just like me. "I saw you and I knew I could never hurt you." Tears glistened in his eyes. "Even after what you did."

The pain on his face cut me open.

"I missed you, *Mylana*." A tear fell. "For ten years, I tried to hate you, but I can't. You're saru." He angrily swiped the wetness from his face. "You survived."

I took a step, then another, and threw my arms around him. He stiffened, but I didn't care. I clutched him so damn tightly that his heart beat against my cheek. "I'm sorry—I'm so sorry," the words tumbled free.

His arms closed around me, their strength hemming me in. His fists trembled where he grabbed my coat against my back and crushed me against him. *So sorry...* I said it over and over. I'd never said it aloud because I hadn't really been sorry, not until now. The guilt piled on. I'd broken his heart and cut his throat. There was no forgiving that, yet he held me in his arms and sobbed. He had tried to hate me and couldn't. Aeon, the defiant one. Aeon, the dreamer. The boy who had dared to stand against them.

We crumpled together, falling to our knees. Sobs shuddered through him, breaking me open even more. I cried out the hurt and the pain and the guilt until I pulled away enough so I could run my fingers over his face, his mouth, his lips, and brush the tears from his cheeks. He had tried to save me once, and I'd killed him for it. I didn't deserve to have him back. I didn't deserve that look in his eyes that spoke of understanding and compassion. He was back: my Aeon, my friend, my love.

I WOKE ON THE BENCH, stiff and aching all over. Male voices rumbled close by. I kept my eyes closed and let the comforting noises roll over me. It took me a few moments to first identify what I was feeling and then believe it. Safety. But more than that, I felt warm and unhurried. I felt as though I were home. But it wasn't the place; it was the people.

Kellee and Aeon stood across the room with their backs to me as they discussed Sota. Aeon was shorter, but most people were next to Kellee, unless they were fae. He was also slimmer, likely grown from two impressive saru breeding stocks. The fae liked to keep their saru svelte so they didn't appear too human. If he wanted, Kellee could probably floor Aeon with a single punch, and Aeon wouldn't see it coming. Luckily, they were getting along just fine.

"How can you fix tek?" Kellee asked.

"My—Kesh taught me." He caught his slip so it sounded as though he were claiming me instead of revealing my slave name. I wasn't ready for Kellee to know it, and it wasn't Aeon's place to reveal that sacred piece of me.

"But you grew up as a saru on Faerie, right? Not much tek to play with."

"It wasn't easy. We scrounged for a time between arena battles, and when Dagnu wasn't looking, or when one of us distracted him, we'd sneak out and find the components. Kesh was quicker than me. She always brought something back. Jewelry, books, feathers, trinkets... and tek."

Books... of course. We would steal fae books and spend hours each night deciphering their pretty writings. Aeon had left the books outside my cell with the tek tucked safely inside. Not Talen. Even before the arena and against his own desires, Aeon had helped.

Kellee glanced behind him. I quickly shut my eyes, and after a few seconds, I peeked out. While Aeon worked on Sota, Kellee watched over his shoulder like a studious parent. Aeon had been around fourteen years old when I'd stopped him from assassinating Oberon. Where had he been before emerging as the latest arena champion?

He's here. He's really here.

Then I remembered where here was and what I'd done to most of the fae population on Calicto. And Talen's sacrifice. The warmth of safety fell away.

"You shouldn't have let me sleep," I grumbled, forcing my tired body to its feet.

"Your drone should reboot," Aeon said. "Try it."

I slotted myself between them at the counter and

placed a hand on Sota's shell, but I didn't switch him on. Not yet. Aeon waited, a touch of pride in his eyes. The drone... He had sent the drone to Sjora's balcony. It could only be him. *Run, Kesh Lasota.*

I was lucky, wasn't I? I had Kellee beside me and Aeon back. But it wasn't over. Talen was mine too, and I wasn't giving up on him, even if he had given up on me.

I flicked Sota's switch on. The drone whirred back to life. His lens scanned all three of us, reading our heat signatures and pulse rates, and then zeroed in on Kellee.

The marshal growled a low warning. "Don't even think it, sparky."

"You attacked first," Sota said flatly.

"And you fried my insides. We're even." Kellee shrugged. "That AI memory of yours has forgotten you were under Eledan's control when I took you out all those months ago. If I hadn't, you'd have killed your friend, Kesh. You're welcome."

The drone buzzed a few inches into the air. "Kesh?"

"Yes, Sota."

"I don't like that one."

"We all noticed." I patted Sota. "He'll grow on you."

"Like rust."

Kellee chuckled.

"Who's the new guy?" Sota turned his unwavering single-eyed glare on Aeon. His lens jutted outward, taking in Aeon in minute detail.

"Sota, it's rude to stare."

"Aeon." Aeon's keen gaze examined Sota's patched-up outer shell and various tek improvements. "I helped patch you up."

"You can stay." Sota shivered. "EMP aftershocks. Tick-

238

les." His lens swelled to an impressive size again. "*The* Aeon?"

I rolled my eyes. I'd told Sota about most of my past. I'd had to, to entice Eledan. "Sota, don't—"

"Kesh told me all about you," he gushed, which, for an attack drone, was quite something.

"She did, huh?" Aeon smiled humbly.

"It's not what you think, kid." Kellee slapped Aeon on the back. "She used the memory of you as bait for the Mad Prince."

"Kellee." He just had to say it, didn't he?

He shrugged. "It's called honesty, Kesh. You should try it sometime." The marshal sauntered back through the hatchway into the pilot area.

"What does he mean?" Sota asked me.

Sota didn't know Oberon employed me. All he knew was that I'd risen through the Faerie Queen's ranks and killed her, then fled to Calicto where I hid as Kesh Lasota. I'd fed him my lies, just like everyone else. He was a drone. It shouldn't matter. But it did. "I'll explain everything, Sota, but first, can you locate the spy-bot I fixed to Sjora?"

Sota's motors whirred. His lens retracted, and inside him, his processes ticked. "Not accurately."

"Then we need to boost the signal." I found Aeon watching me. His hint of a gentle smile melted the ice around my heart. "Help me fix this?"

He nodded. "You don't have to ask."

Beside Kellee in the pilot's chair, I entered Sjora's location into the shuttle's coordinates. I pointed at the speck on a very large map. "How long will it take us to get there?"

"Not long." Kellee adjusted course, and the smattering of stars visible through the screen slid sideways. My stomach lurched, forcing me into the chair. "A few hours. They're not traveling fast, and you're right, they're not going back to Faerie. From their trajectory, it looks like they're drifting."

I rubbed my temple and recalled Talen's grim, resigned look back at the arena. "You think he's resisting?"

"I think he'll do everything he can to make it difficult for her. Bonding with that ship—that's the last thing he wants."

"How bad is this?" I asked.

"Once he becomes a pilot, he'll be gone. It's another type of bond, but not just metaphysical like the one he has with you. A pilot's bond with a ship is physical. He *becomes* the ship."

I closed my eyes and sighed, listening to Kellee's voice as he continued.

"True pilots are rare, and even rarer since the wars wiped most of them out. Talen is one in a billion. Last I heard, there haven't been any new pilots born since the wars. If Sjora successfully bonds him with the ship, she'll have herself a powerful tool."

She had already tried and almost killed him. "Did you know he was... special?"

"Not until that beam-me-up stunt he pulled in the arena. But it makes sense. I found him scavenging ships, probably looking for one he could nurse back to life. He has an affinity for all fae animals, like the kelpie."

The kelpie... the rush of life, the thrilling race through the water... all Talen's.

"You felt the bond with them, right?" Kellee asked.

I nodded. It had all been Talen. He was remarkable, and I'd let him go. "I'm getting him back."

"*We* are. I caught that son of a bitch centuries ago. I'm not letting some fancy-ass general steal my prisoner."

"Your *friend*."

"That too. Speaking of friends..." Kellee thumbed toward the back of the cabin. "Is Aeon good with us going after Talen?"

"Saru love the fae," I replied, the knee-jerk words slipping out before I could stop them.

Kellee spluttered. "Like you loved them back at the arena?"

Ten years was a long time. The Aeon I knew had dreamed of a world without the fae in it, but he'd also spent the last ten years acting like a good saru, just like I had. The truth was, he was Aeon, my friend. I loved him, but I didn't trust him at all. "I'll talk to him. Tell him how it is with Talen. I think he'll be all right."

Kellee pursed his lips. "That'll have to be enough. When we get there, how do we get them to open up and let us in?"

I leaned back in the chair and watched Sjora's location blink on the guidance screen. "Leave that to me."

THE WARCRUISER'S enormous bulk drifted in the blackness, looking limp and inactive considering how fast Sjora had hightailed it off New-Calicto.

Even Aeon frowned at the sight. He sat in the chair behind me and scooted it forward, putting him close to my right shoulder. "You think it knows we're here?"

"I'm sure it does," I said, checking Kellee's reaction. The controls spilled green light over his intense face. He had a tight hold on the shuttle, drifting it inward at a slim angle to make us less of a target. Not that it would help. If that ship locked on and decided to blow us away, we'd be dust in seconds.

"You sure you want to do this?" Aeon asked. There was doubt in his words, and I couldn't blame him. He didn't know Talen. All he'd seen of the fae were the theatrics at the arena.

We were doing it. "Not what you signed up for?" He'd signed up for revenge on me and hadn't gotten that either, but he was here with us. That counted for something.

"Not in the least, but I'll take any chance to bring down a fae general like Sjora."

Kellee's eyebrow twitched—a sign he approved and didn't want to outright high-five Aeon. They would get along just fine.

"Open communications," I said.

"Comms open."

A green light blinked in the bottom left corner of the huge viewing screen. I watched it for a few seconds, wondering if I was doing the right thing. Once the words were out, there would be no taking them back.

"Sjora, this is the Wraithmaker. How's your new pilot working out?"

Silence filled the seconds.

"They heard?"

Kellee nodded. "Every word."

Sota's calming whir sounded behind us. "There's activity."

The ship's nose turned toward us. Lining up to fire? I dug my nails into the chair.

The comms light flashed. "Wraithmaker." Sjora's liquid purr filled the cabin. "How unexpected it is to find you all the way out here in a weaponless shuttle. Did you lose your mind on Calicto, dear thing?"

"We need to talk. Face to face."

"No, that is not what *needs* to happen—" Her voice cut off, and a scuffle sounded through the comms, then her laughter rode in like a wild thing. "Maybe you can help me with something. It seems Lord Talen foolishly bonded himself with another living creature. And considering his gift to you, I will guess you know all about that."

I tucked all the fear and guilt away so that when I spoke, the words came out as cold as the Wraithmaker's reputation. "I'm not here for the fae. Keep him. Do what you like with him. My message was clear when I left thousands of your kind dead at the arena. I want to make a deal."

"Why should I deal with you?" she snapped. "What do you have to bargain with?"

"We meet and we talk."

"Meet? Here on my ship?"

"Yes?"

"Very well." Malice and confidence dropped from her voice. She held all the cards and had nothing to lose. But the fae were forever curious, and she couldn't resist hearing my offer. "I'll be waiting."

Kellee cut the comms and fired up the engines,

pitching the shuttle forward. "What do you have to trade?" he asked, his stare glued ahead.

"The only thing I've ever had. Lies. All she has to do is believe them long enough for us to get to Talen."

Yes, it was insane to deliver us into Sjora's hands. But I had Sota, Kellee, and Aeon, and the way Sjora had spoken, I may even have Talen if he could hold out. Sjora was formidable, but so was I.

"Kid, will you give us some space?" Kellee asked Aeon, avoiding my questioning glance.

"I'm not a kid." Aeon straightened. "I'm the same age as you."

Kellee opened his mouth to argue and paused when he saw my scowl. "Please?"

Aeon made himself scarce, closing the hatch behind him.

"What?" I asked, unable to stand his judgmental look a second longer.

He rubbed a hand down his face, drew in a deep breath, and angled his chair to face me. "I'm trying, all right? But this." He nodded at the ship filling the screen. "You're asking me to walk in there and back you up after what you did to Talen and me."

It was a big ask. Not long ago, I'd revealed I was Oberon's assassin. That kind of deception didn't just go away because of everything that had passed between us since then. But how was I supposed to prove I was trying to change in a way that Kellee would understand?

I opened my mouth, but Kellee spoke first. "Don't ask me to trust you." He shook his head and swept his hair back. "I can't do that." He jabbed a button on the controls.

The shuttle shivered to a halt. "Tell me exactly what your plan is or we're not going anywhere."

His eyes held his typical lawman steel, even though the laws he'd sworn to uphold were gone. He didn't blink, didn't waver. In his mind, I was still the perpetrator.

"I told you. We're going over there, and I'm going to lie to get him back."

"No. I want details. All of them. I'm not blindly marching in there beside you when for all I know you're about to sell me and the kid out in exchange for safe passage back to Faerie."

"I wouldn't—"

His laugh was sharp enough to cut me off. "Don't. I've seen you work. You're as cold as any of the fae you claim to be fighting."

I'd earned his doubt, but it still hurt to hear it in his words and see it in his eyes. Marshal Kellee would never trust me.

I bowed my head and picked at the arm of the flight chair. "She wants Oberon gone. I'm going to offer to help with that."

"Look at me."

I worked my jaw, hating how he pinned me down with words alone. I flicked my gaze to him.

"Say it again."

"I'm not lying to you."

"Then you'll have no problem saying it again to my face."

"You saw what I did back there. Haven't I done enough?" My voice shook.

He leaned forward. "You lied to the Faerie Queen for years, and then you killed her after she gave you what you truly wanted. You filled your drone with stories and made it think you were a friend. You cut that kid's throat. You killed a fae lord right after fucking him—"

I slapped him hard enough that my palm stung and his face—now turned away—flushed scarlet. "You don't get to judge me. You have no idea what it is to live as saru, to love our masters and hate them so much it burns you up inside every day of your life. I'm not lying. I'm trying to save Talen. I don't care if you don't trust me. I don't care if you think I'm a monster. Right now, all that matters is Talen. We're doing this, and you don't have to like me to get it done. Back me up or don't, but the least you can do is fly me to that ship. After that, do whatever you want. I don't need you or your judgment, *Marshal*."

He rubbed his face then dragged his harsh gaze over me. "I'll walk in there with you, for Talen. If you screw me over—"

I laughed acidly and shoved from the chair. "You were right. You don't know me at all." I opened the hatch and left him to pilot the shuttle alone.

"And whose fault is that?!" he shouted after me.

Aeon looked up as I strode past him. I waved him off when he looked as though he might involve himself.

The engines roared with too much force, and we were moving again.

Shoving Kellee's doubt to the back of my mind, I dug out the shuttle's supply drawers, emptying their contents on the floor. I would never be the paragon of virtue Kellee wanted me to be. He wanted his fantasy version of Kesh Lasota, the same way I'd wanted my fantasy version of Marshal Kellee. I wouldn't apologize for being real. I was getting Talen back. Nothing else mattered. Not my pride, not his judgments. I'd lost Kellee when I'd cut out Eledan's heart. But I knew that now. I knew what we were to each other.

The shuttle shook.

"We're in its grip," Kellee called. Minutes later, our little ship groaned and stilled.

We had docked.

Digging around the supplies produced a pistol that I tucked into my coat's inner pocket, a stubby unfussy dagger that I handed to Aeon, and a shirt I wordlessly threw at Kellee. He tugged his tatty coat over the top and raked his fingers through his hair, gathering it up into a don't-fuck-with-me ponytail, making his scowling, unshaven face look lean. Any sign that he'd been blasted by Sota had vanished, but his refined persona had faded during the last few weeks. His life, like so many others, had dramatically changed since he'd met me. It wasn't a coincidence.

Aeon wore his scout leathers. He'd lost his scarf, so the feint red smile of a scar crossing his neck was on full display. My gaze skipped around it, avoiding it completely. Aeon wore his scar on the outside, but the ones I'd given Kellee were internal. Both had their own reasons for not trusting me.

Maybe they'd team up and turn *me* over to the fae? Now there was a thought... Hand in the wanted Wraith-maker in exchange for their freedom?

Too late now.

The shuttle clunked, and the air seals hissed, equalizing the pressure.

I checked Kellee and found his face professionally unreadable. He wouldn't turn me over to the fae. He had honor and integrity, and so did Aeon. Traits I lacked. "Ready?" I asked them.

Kellee nodded.

Aeon locked gazes with me. He gripped his dagger tighter, and I wondered what thoughts occupied his mind to make his eyes so cold.

Sota sailed into position over my right shoulder. "I was made ready," my drone rumbled theatrically.

We stepped through the shuttle's airlock and into the belly of the beast.

CHAPTER 23

*N*o retinue of guards greeted us. I'd expected a fae welcome: a spear in the back and a crossbow aimed at the heart, accompanied by a symphony of mind-numbing magic. To get nothing was unnerving.

Our footfalls echoed in the vastness of the empty dock. Background lighting flickered behind the corridor walls, blinking on and off around as we ventured deeper into the ship. Doors opened ahead of us, while others stayed closed, steering us this way and that. Sjora was herding us.

Kellee's flickering cheek told me he was aware.

"Sota, engage stealth and scout ahead."

"My internal batteries will drain twenty percent faster in stealth. Should we not conserve energy for defense?"

He had a point. "All right." We were going in blind.

With Kellee's heat simmering to my left and Aeon's ice to my right, I strode on, keeping my chin high as more doors closed and opened. If Sjora wanted, she could vent this section of the ship and plunge us all into space. But if

249

she wanted us dead, we would be. Or so I told myself. This was a game. Her game. We played by her rules.

The corridors widened, and behind the walls, light pulsed, driving us forward. I should have expected something shocking, but I could never have imagined the sight as we entered a huge dome-like chamber. Hundreds of pulsing tendrils hung from the ceiling, and in their vampiric embrace hung a fae I only recognized from the tattered remains of his royal blue coat and his shock of silver hair.

I tried not to look, but I couldn't look away. I wanted to scream, but I had to stay silent, both parts of me warring. He was supposed to mean nothing to me. Just another fae caught in a web of his making. If I was as cold as Kellee believed, Talen *would* mean nothing. I almost wished I were heartless, because seeing him so thoroughly caught and watching the ship's hold cut into his skin and leech the life right out of him turned my vision red and summoned a rage I hadn't known I was capable of.

This *union* had happened before. When Devere had brought Talen back to me, his body had been lacerated. He had fought then too, and the fool hadn't told me anything. Because he knew I'd go after Sjora alone, and probably get myself killed.

I wasn't alone now.

"*Easy*," Kellee muttered, trying to placate me.

"Beautiful, isn't he?" Sjora emerged from the tunnel to our right. She looked like a monster humans had feared long ago. Her longbow glinted over her shoulder. The blood-red leathers wrapped her so tightly I wondered if a pistol shot would even punch through. Her dark green hair traced her scalp in braided lines, and each braid finished in a dagger-like point, tipped with the same glass as her thimble. She looked devastating, like a weapon forged inside Faerie's wildlands. The infamous Harvester.

I tried to swallow and almost choked. Afraid my voice wouldn't hold up, I shrugged like I couldn't care less. *Just another fae.* "All alone, Sjora?"

She ignored my question and stopped in front of Talen. She had to tilt her head back to admire her puppet hanging from his strings.

Furious tears sparked at the corners of my eyes. I willed them away.

"Pilots are so rare a gift." Awe lent her voice a musical quality. "Faerie produces a breeding pair every millennium. Many were killed in the last war, and then some... some resisted their calling. Like this one." She paused, and the silence grew thick. "He killed this ship's existing pilot. He gave me no choice."

The ship's tendrils lowered Talen to within Sjora's reach and close enough for me to see how streams of blood ran from his limp fingers. His torn clothes were soaked in crimson, just like Sjora's.

We were bonded. I should have felt his pain, but I didn't. He had to be shielding me. Or perhaps the bond was gone. My heart thumped against my ribs, blood racing too fast through my veins. The Harvester lifted her hand and gently caressed his face. His eyes were open, their violet color too bright against the pinpricks of his dark pupils. His mind wasn't here with us.

"If they are so rare," I scoffed, making sure the rage sounded like scorn, "why are you killing this one?"

She snapped her head around and snarled at my tone. "I'm not killing him! The fool does that himself. He persists in resisting the bond. He's... insufferable." She crossed the floor to me in a few sweeping strides. "This is *your* doing!" She snatched at my coat and yanked me forward. "He shares himself with a filthy, unworthy saru!"

I ripped free of her grip and drew the pistol, aiming it an inch from her porcelain nose. *Pull the trigger. Blow her away. What's another fae soul to the dead littering my path?* My aim stayed strong, the desire to pull the trigger thrumming through me.

If she died, I'd have no way of knowing how to free Talen, assuming he could be freed.

Kellee's growl threatened, swirling around the rising tension. "We're here to make a deal," he said.

Sjora blinked and gently pushed the pistol aside. "A deal. Yes. Let me hear this deal of yours, Wraithmaker. Do you wish to trade your males, perhaps? For you have nothing else." She licked her lips and eyed Kellee like he was her next meal. "I can't deny I haven't wondered what it would be like to bed a creature like him. *Namu* are so predictable. A vakaru would be... a challenge. I'm rather fond of challenges."

Kellee didn't say a word, though the highly charged tingling down my side was a good indication that he was holding himself in check.

Her gaze slid to Aeon. "And the champion. Most of the court has already ridden that one. Used him up and worn him out in every way imaginable. It's a wonder he's alive at all."

I steeled myself at that knowledge and fought not to glance back at him. Ten years as their toy? *Ten years... Oh Aeon.*

"I see the hate in you, saru," Sjora purred at Aeon. "It

surrounds you like a cloud of furious magic." She stepped closer to Aeon. His shoulders locked, and his jaw trembled as he forced himself to look up into her eyes. "I'd make your time with me your last."

Aeon lunged, but Kellee threw out an arm and hooked it around his shoulders. He growled something I missed. Whatever the words, Aeon backed down.

Sjora chuckled. "You were always the defiant one. I hear Dagnu took great pleasure in breaking your spirit. I hear"—she stepped back—"he still does."

I lowered the pistol and dragged a sharp smile onto my lips. Sjora had nothing left. Everything she was, everything she had, was here. I'd killed her followers in the arena. This was all an act, like a poisonous snake's flash of color and noisy hiss.

"Release Talen," I ordered.

She laughed and backed farther away. "Not even those male specimens are enough for me to relinquish the pilot." Sota whirred louder. She snarled at the drone. "Kill me with your tek and you'll never free him."

"Sota," I warned. He drifted lower, hanging back, for now.

Sjora grinned. "There is nothing you can give me, you foolish saru. There is nothing of yours I want. Besides, I take what I desire. I am the Harvester, after all. You walked onto my ship, and you won't ever be leaving—"

"There's one thing you want that you can't take."

"Oh please." Her laughter stroked the silence. "Do enlighten me."

"Oberon."

Something sharp and dangerous flashed in her eyes. She stilled and studied me with renewed interest. I knew her thoughts. I had killed the queen. Could I kill the king?

"We both know he ordered me to kill his mother. His brother too. The Mad Prince only survived because I failed. Like you said, I am a loose end. But what if I'm the proof you need to unseat him? I am the only living soul who knows the truth. Release Talen, let my friends leave, and I'll help you avenge Mab."

Her smile cracked, but the doubt in her eyes wavered too. "The words of an infamous liar are worthless."

"You won't have my words." I tapped my temple. "Use the Dreamweaver to get inside my head and find the truth up here. I offer you that, and know that I do not offer it lightly. Returning to the Dreamweaver is the last thing I want. But I'll help you if you let Talen go."

She backed away, peering at me through slitted eyes while her mouth curved into a grin. "You are an intriguing thing, aren't you? I understand now how Mab fell for your slippery lies. How do I trust someone like you?" She tapped the glass thimble against her chin. "I need time. Come..." She turned. "Dine with me."

I glanced at Kellee. He shook his head and mouthed, *"No."*

"All of you. Come."

Aeon frowned and shook his head, mirroring Kellee's dissent.

But they failed to realize, if we all wanted to survive this together, we didn't have a choice.

THE DINNER SPREAD COVERING the long meeting table

bubbled over with brightly colored fruits and rich, mouth-watering meats. The delicious scents and colors wormed their way into my senses and whispered encouragements. Sjora's dinner was designed to seduce. I recognized a dozen sweet-tasting dishes that would take a saru soul and turn it inside out, making them raving mad within a few bites. I'd seen the royals dine around a table arranged like this one, all of them aware they were playing the pain or pleasure game. I'd also seen saru fall victim to Faerie's fruits and die while the fae laughed and ate.

Mouth watering, I took a seat beside Sjora. Kellee and Aeon positioned themselves opposite us, and Sota hung back, watching from afar, giving him a wide angle of attack should it be required.

"Your tek is offending me," Sjora remarked as she poured herself into her chair.

She hadn't asked me to dismiss him—to do so would have made her look weak—so I ignored her and scanned the mounds of plump fruit. Aeon was doing the same, scanning for something that wouldn't kill him fast or slow. Kellee leaned sideways in his chair and picked up a fruit similar to an apple, only this one was as large as his hand and gave off a velvety dust that quickly coated his hand. Blood fruit. Had Aeon touched it, he'd already be writhing in pain.

Kellee lifted it, admired it for a few moments, and brought it to his lips.

I tensed, wanting to jump across the table and smack it from his hand. But he must have known what he was doing. Kellee was older than he looked—how old, I wasn't sure. He'd seen more than I could imagine. He knew exactly what he was doing.

He sank his white teeth in with a loud crunch, and tore out a bite. A golden halo blazed around the dark pupils of his eyes, and a flash of his fangs revealed the fruit did affect him. But he chewed and swallowed with no ill effects. "It's good." He took another generous bite. Whatever the fruit did to him, he shrugged it off.

Sjora's soft laugh was almost coy. He'd impressed her. Kellee's devastating smile lit up his face, and that glow in his eyes hinted at something hungry beyond. He had the fae general practically squirming in her seat. He was in the game. The fae were known for their art of seduction, but here, now, we were about to turn that art on Sjora.

"Talen believed he could bring my ship down upon the arena and rescue you." Sjora chuckled. "He thought I didn't know the two of you are partially *bonded*, as though I wouldn't notice the way he looks at you when you're unaware of his presence."

I masked any emotion from my face.

"It is a great gift to bond with a fae." She narrowed her eyes on me, cutting deep with her glare alone. "Powerful fae have twice gifted you with great magic, and yet I see you, and I do not understand why any of us should spend a second caring about you. Tell me, Wraithmaker..." Sjora reached for some fruit and dappled her plate with colorful segments. "Tell me something you have never told a single soul before."

"Why?" I followed her example and loaded my plate with the fruit I knew was mostly safe. Aeon did the same, his movements wooden. He made no attempt to hide his disdan and practically trembled with rage. The chances were high he had been present at similar meals, and I doubted it had ended well for the saru gladiator. I wanted to reach out to him, just a single touch would do to let him know he wasn't alone, but he was too far away and had to weather this alone.

"I want to hear the truth on your tongue so I know its sound."

I picked up a wooden fork and stabbed a sweet, juicy segment of fruit. "You believe you can read my lies when the queen herself failed to?"

Mention of the queen unnerved the general. She covered the twitch by crunching down on something hard and sharp, probably wishing it was my neck.

"If I am to deal with the Wraithmaker, I need to be certain."

"I wouldn't eat that," Kellee murmured to Aeon.

I spotted the culprit sitting on Aeon's plate—a starlike piece of pink fruit. One bite and Aeon would forget his entire life. All of it. He'd be a whole new canvas, one that would believe anything a fae told him.

Aeon looked down, knew exactly what piece of fruit Kellee was referring to, and looked straight into my eyes. He wanted to forget.

Don't.

He wet his lips.

Please don't.

He would forget the crates we'd been forced to fight our way out of, forget the years of abuse, forget the nights drenched in tears, forget the arenas, forget my blade cutting him open. Forget me. The longing on his face reminded me of the look on the faces of saru who had chosen to take their own lives rather than live another day as a slave.

I couldn't do this. I couldn't manage him and deal with

Sjora at the same time. I prized my attention away from Aeon and smiled at Sjora. The fae general blinked her dark, shallow eyes, waiting. "I killed my first love," I told her. It was the truth. The whole terrible truth I'd carried with me for ten years. And I'd never told a soul, never even whispered it to Sota.

Delight brightened Sjora's face. "That is the truth and exactly why you're so dangerous."

Aeon shot to his feet. "I'm not doing this." He staggered from the room. I wanted to go after him, but I stayed seated.

Kellee took a noisy bite of something poisonous. His sideways cocky smile broadened, and he leaned his elbows on the table. "What d'yah know, the Wraithmaker can speak the truth."

I smiled back at him like the words didn't hurt and turned my gaze on Sjora. The fae general's pretty eyes flashed with curiosity. "I love Oberon," I told her, seeing Kellee's smile die in the corner of my eye. "But a saru can love and hate in equal measure. The fae fall in love so completely that it doesn't cross your mind that we saru have room for both emotions. That's how I can help you bring down Oberon and why he won't ever see me coming."

Sjora's bow-shaped lips parted in pleasure. "What you speak of is treason," she whispered.

"Yes. It is. It's also true."

She studied me as we slowly cleared our plates. "You speak the truth. Now tell me, what is Talen to you?"

"A friend."

Kellee broke open something that filled the air with sweet, intoxicating pollen. It didn't appear to affect him, but the airborne spores landed on my lips like tiny kisses, spilled down my throat, and raced into my veins. Kellee saw his mistake and scowled at me or himself. I shook my head and pressed the balls of my hands to my eyes. It would be fine; it just left me vulnerable to suggestion. Kellee needed to stop screwing around with the damn food and get his head in the game.

"The Wraithmaker has friends?" Sjora asked.

"Not many," Kellee quirked, delighting Sjora.

"Apparently." I beamed back at him.

"She kills the good ones."

"Just the assholes and pretty boys."

What, by-cyn, was he playing at? Was this all because I'd slapped him or because he didn't trust me? Or was there something insidious at work here? I checked the remains of his meal. Most of it would have killed a saru, resurrected him, and then driven him mad so he killed himself, and all the while the fae would eat and enjoy their meals. Kellee had devoured it like it was harmless candy.

Sjora's attention had fixed on Kellee in an entirely fae way, like a cat with a mouse pinned beneath its paws, but as mice went, Kellee would bite back. He tossed something like a grape in his mouth and bit down so it popped while flashing a bit of fang. The fae general watched him like she wanted to leap across the table and fuck him dry.

She lifted her hand and clicked her fingers. "Wine."

Maybe Kellee had some namu in him—the slaves the fae had bred for sexual entertainment. Or maybe this was all just Kellee distracting Sjora. It *was* working. He had caught her eye in a wholly female and predatory way.

A saru girl whispered in, drifting on slippered feet.

Sonia.

Her dark hair had been hacked short at messy angles, and grazes stood out red on her chin. My vision blurred at the thought of her losing her tongue to keep Devere's murderer a secret, to protect me.

My stomach rolled, the sweet Faerie food turning sour.

Sonia ignored me with all the professional training I'd expect of a saru. I couldn't look away from this girl who had nothing, who had denied the fae their answers for me.

"I am tempted by what you offer, Wraithmaker," Sjora was saying.

Wine sloshed into our cups.

"But I want a sweetener. I will release Talen. I'll find another ship. There are several currently cleansing Halow. You'll stay with me, under my protection, and we'll return to Faerie without the king's knowledge. But I want your vakaru in Talen's place."

I didn't hesitate. "No deal."

"Deal," Kellee said.

I shot him a look. He lifted his cup and drank long and deep, knowing Sjora and I both watched. "Kellee," I snapped.

He licked his lips and set his cup down, eyes flashing gold. "I want this."

What? How could he... No, this wasn't part of the plan. We would get Talen back together. We had our problems, our disagreements, our distrust, but Kellee was my friend too, and there was no way I was leaving him with Sjora.

Kellee lifted his cup to Sonia. The saru refilled it, her eyes far away. "What did you think we were, Kesh? Did you think we were something special? Did you think we had a *spark*?"

I felt the corners of my mouth turn down and couldn't stop it, couldn't hide how his words hurt.

"You thought we were friends?"

This wasn't him. Something from the table had twisted his emotions and made him bitter. There was a handful of poisons that could do that to a saru. Who knew what the impact was on a vakaru.

Sjora's gray eyes had turned stormy.

"You don't know what you're saying. You don't need to do this. Sjora will take my deal."

"Not anymore I won't." She pushed from the table and jerked her chin at Kellee.

He rose languidly to his feet, his golden eyes on me, issuing the same challenge as always: *do you think you can fight me and win?*

I didn't understand. Was I supposed to stop him, or was this real?

Kellee watched the fae general approach, and the look in his eyes matched her hunger.

It was the game, wasn't it?

The Harvester, slayer of hundreds of thousands of humans, cupped Kellee's face and ran her smooth fingers across the harsh brush of his unshaven chin. He swayed, reaching for the table, and toppled his cup. Wine sloshed to the floor. I pushed to my feet, but it was too late. He cupped the back of her head and kissed her, not just with his mouth, but with his body, all of him. The way he moved, arching into her as she fell into the embrace, there was a rhythm to it, one she instantly captured and made her own. Heat and magic simmered between them.

It wasn't an act.

Sonia—the invisible saru—brought her wine jug up and

punched the vessel across the back of Sjora's head. Pottery shattered, raining wine and jug fragments around both Kellee and Sjora.

Sjora slammed the girl back against the wall and snatched at her bow. Kellee caught the Harvester's hand, halting the attack on Sonia. He turned, spread his arms, and shielded Sjora *from me.*

Sota whirred. "Who do I shoot?" my drone asked.

"Nobody." I still needed Sjora to free Talen.

Sjora lunged and grabbed Sonia's neck, her hand squeezing the life out of the girl.

Kellee's gaze flickered, and for a moment, as he witnessed what would surely be Sonia's death, sadness doused some of the fire in his eyes.

He wound his hand around Sjora's arm. "Leave her," he said, and then again, more firmly, "Leave her. We have a deal. You have me. You have Kesh's truth. Now free Talen."

Sonia's lips turned blue. She rattled in Sjora's grip like a worthless doll.

Kellee turned toward the general. His hand slipped around her waist, and he whispered into her ear. Sjora's snarl might have been the last thing Sonia heard if Kellee hadn't been there, but the general tossed the girl to the ground. "I will finish you later." She looked at me. "I'll free Talen." Sjora's magic crackled around her. "I'll free your pilot after I've had this vakaru. Stop me and you get nothing." She dared me to speak up, to try something, but Kellee had made it clear this was what he wanted.

"I won't stop you."

She looked the vakaru in his eyes, saw his challenge, and parted her lips, drawing his scent across her tongue.

"Such a noble creature." She saw it too, the sadness, the sacrifice. Despite his effort to hide the truth, he had played the game, was still playing it, and he knew how it would end.

I couldn't let him do this, the stupid, stubborn fool. He'd die a hero if I let him. That wasn't happening. But there was nothing I could do to stop her. Nothing I should do.

She laughed as she made her way to the door. "This will be delicious."

CHAPTER 24

I rushed to Sonia's side and helped the girl into Kellee's empty chair. She wheezed and spluttered, rubbing her throat. I wanted to comfort her, but the words wouldn't come. What she did had taken great courage, courage I wasn't sure I had. The kind of courage it took to keep silent while a fae cut out your tongue.

"Thank you," I said. They were the only words that mattered.

She nodded, coughed, and tried to speak, but the sound she made was more of a groan. She took my hand and tapped my palm.

"I don't understand."

With two fingers, she traced a *c* shape with a line through it and then something like a slanted *f*. She was writing saru symbols. The same symbols we often used when words would be heard as we passed silently down corridors or with our hands poking through our cell bars.

I nodded and let her take my other hand, turning both palms up on her lap. She worked quickly, fingers sweeping.

I hadn't used the language in years, but after a few failed starts, I recognized their meaning.

"They think because no tongue not speak."

I watched her hands move, watched the words form.

"I see I hear I know free pilot."

"You can free Talen?" My heart leaped.

She nodded and smiled.

"Do you know where she took my friend, the vakaru?"

She nodded again and got to her feet. Her little hand closed around mine. "*Come*," she mouthed.

"Wait, why are you helping me?" Despite the abuse, she loved Devere, she didn't have a choice in that, and she had witnessed what I'd done to him. She should be handing me over to Sjora for my crimes, not helping me.

"Change." Her mouth shaped the word while the stump of her tongue tried to make the sound. *"Change coming."*

And I was that change? I saw it in her eyes then. Hope. I could be that hope. No, I already was.

Sonia led me through snaking corridors to where the light faded to throbbing pulses and the ship's monstrous hearts thudded all around us. It seemed to take too long, like hours had passed, and then Sonia stopped outside a draped doorway and pressed a finger to her lips. She parted the drape and pushed through into a decadent bedchamber. Magic and the rich smell of sex scented the air. In the gloom, I saw the bed and the couple intimately embraced chest to chest. Beneath the touch of soft pulsing light, Kellee's skin glistened like honey. Light licked up his back, his flexing shoulders, and over his rapt expression. He gathered Sjora's green hair in one hand and swept it back, exposing a milky white shoulder, and there, he kissed her.

I stepped forward, but Sonia's gentle touch on my arm held me back. She shook her head. *"Wait."*

I wasn't sure I could. The image of them together scorched into my mind like red-hot iron. What was I doing here? He didn't need rescuing. I had Sonia, and she knew how to free Talen. I could leave them. It was what he wanted, wasn't it?

Sjora's hips rocked, curving her spine. She threw her head back. Light poured from her skin, setting her ablaze with power. Kellee's mouth roamed up her neck, and then he stilled to watch the Harvester ride every hard inch of him. Her nails sank into his corded biceps. Her rhythm increased. Kellee's dark lashes fluttered, and his lips parted around quick breaths.

I couldn't watch. But I couldn't tear myself away. That look of pure abandonment on her face—it was bliss. I envied her. I envied her magic, envied her pressed so close to Kellee in a way the Dreamweaver had only permitted me a few times before ripping the fantasy away or making me do things—terrible things, things like I'd done to Devere. I envied the feel of Kellee's hands on her skin, sweeping up to a breast. I envied the way he gathered her hard nipple into his mouth and the way she gasped as his tongue flicked and swirled. Sjora was too lost in her pleasure to see the golden glow in his eyes or the sharp points of his fangs come down. When he plunged his teeth into the flesh of her breast, she bucked and let out a whimpering feminine cry that had everything to do with pain on the right side of pleasure.

I looked away and into Sonia's watching face. She nodded at me to look back, but what was the point? So I could see Kellee give Sjora the best fuck of her life? I could do without that memory.

The press of magic in the room spluttered and jolted back like someone had yanked off a warm quilt. Sjora's tight gasp alerted me to the fact that something wrong. I turned to see her fall backward out of Kellee's grip. She collapsed flat on her back, glassy eyes staring at the ceiling.

What the...?

Kellee braced his arm against the sheets. Shudders trembled down his back and shuddered every breath. His hair had fallen over his face, but I knew what I'd see there: the beast with its near-black eyes rimmed in gold—the wild, hungry thing trying to break free of Kellee's control. Sjora's light magic dripped off him and ran in golden rivulets down his arm and chest.

Sonia moved, but I held her back. There was no knowing how he would react to her presence or whether he was still... hungry.

After a few deep, measured breaths, he dragged his head up and looked me in the eye. "You going to stand there all day or help?" Kellee tried on a smirk, but it slid off him too. The beast was gone. He was just Kellee.

Holy cyn. He had fucked a fae unconscious. He could do that?

"Close your mouth, Kesh," he grumbled, wincing as he shifted position.

I snatched his clothes from the floor and held them out to him, struggling not to look at all the wonderful parts of him coated in dusty glitter.

He crawled to the edge of the bed and planted his feet on the floor, then used the sheet to wipe himself down. I watched that bunched sheet brush across his chest and told myself I was looking for wounds. There were none, but there was a whole lot of male to admire. A male made for long, lazy nights drenched in numbing pleasure.

"Look but don't touch," he said in a gravelly drawl I most definitely wanted to hear from him again at a better time when we weren't trying to free a friend and escape. "Really, don't," he added, holding my gaze. "I've got enough poison on my skin to knock out another five fae."

Poison? "The food?"

"You didn't think I was eating that fairy filth because I liked it?" He raised an eyebrow and took his shirt from my hands. "You were so ready to believe I'd betray you." He stood, swayed, and then managed to step into his pants and pull them up. "I'm not that guy."

I didn't know whether to hug him for being so damn clever or hit him for being so damn clever and not telling me his plan. I'd do neither, given how he was still slippery with poison and untouchable. "You... you... you could have said something—anything!"

"And have Sjora realize I was screwing with her?" He combed his fingers through his hair and pulled it back into its typical ponytail. Passing by me, he made it a few steps before stumbling into the doorframe. He hissed a curse through his teeth.

"You all right?" I reached out but stopped short of touching his skin. It still shimmered with a dusting of color, like the fine colorful dust found on butterfly wings.

He lifted his tired eyes. "I will be. Just need to work through it. Come on, we need to figure out how to get Talen free before she wakes up."

"She's not dead?"

"Who do you think I am, Kesh. You?" His dark eyes flashed, and the smirk was all lawman. I would definitely hit him once his touch was no longer deadly.

The Harvester still lay motionless on the bed, naked and vulnerable. She had killed thousands of people in her long life and swept homes from Halow like they were sticks in her way. "We should kill her," I said.

"That's not your revenge to have," he replied, his gaze settling on Sonia.

The saru gazed at the Harvester who had cut out her tongue for keeping secrets. She caught us watching her and shook her head. *"I am not like them."*

I was. I'd gladly kill Sjora where she lay. Kellee knew it too, which was why he was already leaving, making sure I had to follow or risk losing him in the corridors.

Sota buzzed in low to whisper, "I recorded the entire scene in ultra-high frame rate—for research..."

I patted the drone and felt a smile pulling at my lips when I noticed Sonia's shocked expression. "Research. Right."

"Is it over?" he asked.

"It will be, my friend."

Sonia hurried ahead. If she could free Talen, then not even Sjora could stop us.

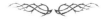

TALEN still hung from the ship's tendrils, dangling above our heads like a macabre puppet. His blood had dried in snaking trails across the floor. Aeon was here too, and judging by his pacing, he'd been here some time. He looked up when we entered and checked for Sjora at the back of the line. When she didn't appear, I said, "She's sitting this one out." Rather than looking pleased, he started pacing again.

The flow of blood from Talen's wounds had slowed to an agonizing *drip-drip* from the ends of his matted hair. The chamber walls were smooth and curved with no way to climb up and reach him. "We have to get him down. Now."

Kellee peered up at his friend's dead eyes. "I can't reach him to cut those veins free. Even if I could, cutting him out might kill him."

"Sonia?"

The saru blinked up at Talen, her eyes big and her face as pale as Faerie's moon. *"Not too late."*

I didn't know if she was hoping or if she knew. She turned to me and pressed a hand over my heart. I flinched as memories of the Dreamweaver's hand pressed over my heart tried to rush in and pluck out my sanity.

"Not too late," the saru said, her eyes pleading.

I covered her hand with mine. "What can I do?"

She pushed against my ribs. *"Inside."*

"I don't understand."

"The bond?" Kellee suggested.

Aeon, Kellee, and Sonia looked at me like I had the answer. "But I don't know anything about it. I can't even feel him. If we were still bonded, I'd feel him. I don't think it's still there..."

"Reach him. Let him know. You are safe. He is safe. Stop fighting."

That all sounded pretty, but how? "But I'm saru, Sonia. I can't do magic."

"Not magic."

"Just close your eyes and..." Kellee grasped at the right words. "I don't know, reach for him like when he gave you the bond. Search for that feeling." He shrugged, clearly guessing, but it was a start. "Just try."

That feeling when Talen had knelt in front of me and tied us together had been an immensely pleasurable and mind-numbing assault on all my senses. Afterward, I'd begged for more and he'd denied me, claiming too much would damage me. How was I supposed to find that feeling here, on an alien ship with the blood-hungry Harvester about to wake and kill us all?

Something deep inside the ship groaned.

Kellee's eyes widened. "Hurry. If she wakes up, we won't get another shot at this."

I looked up into Talen's clouded violet eyes. The same violet eyes that had pulled me from the bad dreams and from the Dreamweaver's grasp. He had pulled me back too many times to count. Now it was my turn to do the same for him.

I closed my eyes and pressed my hands over Sonia's hand on my chest. I remembered seeing Talen bleeding and unresponsive and how I'd lain next to him, holding his hand in mine. I remembered waking up and seeing him on the other side of the screen. I remembered the desire, the need to be close to him. And the kiss, the stolen kiss when he had given me the coat, the kiss that had scorched me inside and out, freeing a wildness I hadn't known I had in me, the same wildness the kelpies had sensed. The same wild magic he had inside him. He was a pilot, rare even for Faerie. A world apart, distant and hauntingly mysterious, he wasn't for the likes of me, but that was all right. I had the bond, and I was here because I'd promised him he wasn't alone—not anymore.

Warmth beat through my chest, igniting my veins and surging through my human DNA. I chased it, sensing the flickering of a life that wasn't mine. It shone like a star, brilliant and all-consuming like it might swell and swallow whole worlds. I wondered if it had once, if this ancient, glorious thing was too big for me to fathom.

"You're nothing."

"You're wrong. She is everything."

I heard Talen's voice somewhere far away and chased that too, until the sensation of being anchored to my body fell away, and I was falling through the darkness, the stars rushing away. Fear snagged me as I fell, turning me over. I lost the light, and all around there was nothing. I fell on and on through the dark with nothing and no one. That wasn't right. This couldn't be Talen's doing. I was doing it all wrong. *I can't do magic. I'm not like them. I'm saru.*

Laughter echoed inside the nothingness. *"Ask his name,"* the Dreamweaver hissed.

No, no! The Dreamweaver could not have me here. I searched the dark for the light, searched for Talen, and sensed the darkness had turned hungry and might close its mouth around me, crushing me into nothing too. The dreams were his domain, and this was a dream. *"How do you know what is real?"* He laughed. *"Come back to me, Wraithmaker. Be mine."*

"I will never be yours!" I screamed into the night.

Twin hearts thudded like drums.

Around and around I tumbled. But I didn't care. He once had my mind, but he would never have the real me. I'd die before I let him win the truth of me.

There. Light. My heart leaped at the sight, and the light blazed. Silver hair rippled to one side, swept by the fingers of silent winds, the same winds that tugged on his silver-lined coat. Talen walked through the dark, trailing droplets of silver from his fingertips. Not blood, but power. So much power. A star in the darkness.

The Dreamweaver fled, snatching his shadows from Talen's path.

I snapped my eyes open.

Above my head, Talen jerked against the ship's tendrils. Some tore free and writhed in the air, searching for their quarry. Talen arched. Air rushed into his lungs. His eyes rolled and flickered.

The floor dropped a few inches beneath me, and a vast shudder rumbled through the walls, through the air, as though the enormous warcruiser was breathing in. Because Talen was breathing in.

A third heartbeat thudded around us, strong and loud, and a monstrous groan rumbled through the floor, walls, and air. Everywhere. The ship *wailed*.

"He's the ship."

The floor rocked again, and Kellee staggered.

A scream sailed through the corridors that splintered into a thousand knives, each one piercing. Sjora was awake.

"Talen!" I reached up to him, still so far away. "Talen, please!"

He blinked, eyes focusing on me, their color now a molten silver swirling around a pinprick of blackness, but still not seeing.

"Please!" Desperation made my voice raw. "You are mine, and I will not let you go!"

The thick rope-like tendrils lowered him closer, jerking and snagging. Another tore free, spraying blood.

Pain tore across my hip, cracking like a whip made of iron blades. I cried out and tried to whirl away from the attack, but there was none. Another slash struck across my chest, sinking in and tearing free. I jerked, blinded by agony. I needed to run, but I was trapped in the mind-shattering agony.

This was *his* pain. Oh, by-cyn, everything I felt was his nightmare. He had kept this from me. Protected me.

Sonia tried to keep me on my feet. Where her hands gripped me, my skin seemed to bubble. My knees hit the floor.

The bond.

I'd opened the bond.

And now I felt it all. Every slash from those vicious tendrils, every hook sinking in, every suckling draw of his magic.

Another crack, this one tearing up my spine as though it sought to split me in two.

"What's happening to her?!" Aeon. He sounded... furious.

I reached out, not knowing who was there, but someone wrapped my hand in theirs. Aeon or Kellee, I wasn't sure.

I couldn't fight this.

No whip, no drone, not even Kellee's claws could stop this.

Another strike slashed down my leg. I jerked away and felt wetness soak through my clothes. Blood. Mine. Talen had protected me, but I'd torn open his barriers, and in saving him, I'd killed myself.

Kellee's growl tumbled through me. It was his chest I was pressed against. "She's mortal." I wasn't sure if he trembled or I did. "She can't take this like he can. She's dying." His hand touched my face, his skin as rough as razor blades. "Kesh... you're not leaving me, you hear me?" I did, but my mouth wouldn't work, and the words stuck like glass in my throat. "I've lost too much. I can't... I can't lose you. It doesn't matter what you are, what you were. Do you hear me? I know you didn't have a choice, and I'm sorry... I'm sorry for leaving you with *him*."

Sjora's sweet voice sailed through the storm of agony. "She must let her fae go or the bond will kill her."

Hot metal poured into my chest, wrapped around my ribs, plunged into my heart, and set me ablaze. I screamed, but nobody heard, because those screams never left my lips.

"Let him go," Sjora ordered. "Let him bond with the ship. He lives. You live. We get our deal."

Let him go. I couldn't. I didn't want to. I was saru, and he was fae, and no saru had ever been equal to a fae. It meant something. Something I didn't understand. But I wasn't ever giving that up.

Kellee's lips brushed my forehead. "You don't die here."

"You won't die in four days." Talen's words. Had he known? Had he seen my death coming?

I opened my eyes. My vision swam with tears. But I saw him above us. The others crowded around me, so they missed the silver crawl through the ship's tendrils, creeping higher and higher, infecting the ship. And Talen's rage blazed with the intensity of a hundred stars. Teeth clenched, he brought his arms up, straining against the ship's hold. A tendril sprang free. Pain slashed across my breast. His pain. Mine. It didn't matter. We were one. Power thrummed its steady beat through my body, stirring to life beneath my skin.

He was killing me, and all I could think of was how I had made my choice, and it seemed like such a waste for me to die without ever having seen it through. What was the point of my surviving the saru harvesting, surviving the arenas, and Mab, and the Dreamweaver if I was to die here, torn apart on a warcruiser floor?

"Her eyes," Aeon said. "They're silver."

Eyes like Talen's.

I didn't need to let him go.

I had to let him in. All of him. I had to stop fighting.

I let my mind clear, let my body fall, and I let go.

Sjora straightened away as though something about my limp state terrified her. Her confident face crumbled. She jerked her head up and saw the brilliance of Talen—saw the shining power beating the air around him, a power too great to be just fae.

He fixed her in his sights and pulled hard against the ship's hold. The entire vessel groaned in agony, and with a thunderous roar, Talen tore himself free of the ship's physical bonds. Fire blazed across my flesh. I screamed, torn open, mind shattered, skin and bone wrecked. I should have been dying, should have been broken, but he was somehow inside me, holding my pieces together. I was dying and living, both at once.

Talen landed in a crouch. When he lifted his head, silver lightning rippled beneath his skin, veining across his cheek before vanishing. I thought I saw something flicker in the air behind him, something take the light and break it apart, but the ghostly shimmer passed in a blink.

"It's you," Sjora gasped. The Harvester, immortal slayer of thousands, ran.

She didn't get far.

Broiling lengths of ship tendrils poured from the ceiling and snatched up the fae general, whipping her legs out from under her. The eel-like appendages twisted her into the air. She screamed and grabbed for her bow. It dropped and clattered to the floor. Talen hissed, jerked his chin, and the entire ceiling came alive with tendrils.

"They'll know!" she screamed. "They'll know you! They'll hunt you to the ends of the three systems. They will find you. They know your name. I know your na—"

Something inside her gave a grisly crack. She stopped talking, stopped moving, and then the ship—Talen—tore the Harvester clean in half. Her blood splashed across the floor like rain.

CHAPTER 25

$\mathcal{I}$ woke slowly, drifting somewhere warm and soft, skin buzzing, and rolled over, reaching for the presence I felt beside me. My fingers splayed across an empty bed sheet. My eyes opened. It took my thoughts a moment to catch up with the sight of Marshal Kellee leaning forward in a chair beside the bed. The intensity in his green eyes had me self-consciously tucking my exposed leg back under the sheet.

"Talen took you deeper into the ship," Kellee said, back in factual lawman mode. The heat in his gaze was fading fast. "To heal you. He didn't say exactly how." He hesitated and glanced down. Whatever I'd missed, it worried him. "How do you feel?"

I did a quick check and stretched beneath the sheets, wincing as my stiff muscles protested. "Good." I felt better than good. I felt like something had been worshipping my body for hours, like warm hands had stroked me, kneading inside me, filling me up with life. But reaching for the memories produced nothing. The last thing I recalled was

279

PIPPA DACOSTA

Talen using the ship's horrible eel-like tendrils to tear Sjora in half.

A cool shiver chased away some of the warmth and scattered gooseflesh across my exposed arms. I pulled the sheet higher, tucking it under my chin, and faced Kellee. "She's gone?"

"Yeah. And we're on our way back to the priso—"

"Where's Talen?"

Kellee leaned forward and brushed his hands together. "He's fine." That wasn't what I'd asked. "He's somewhere in the ship. What he did... What he's *doing*..." He rolled his lips together and shook his head in disbelief. "It's not possible."

"What is he doing?"

"Controlling the ship without a physical connection. He's free and bonded at the same time. I don't know... I'm starting to think I don't know anything about him."

Beneath the sheet, I pressed a hand to my heart and felt the gentle throb of warmth that wasn't me. "Can a fae be bonded to more than one creature at a time?"

"No."

I didn't tell Kellee I could still feel the fae inside me, but the concern in his eyes told me he knew something was different.

Kellee sighed. "He has a royal fuckton of power."

My lips twitched. "Is that a technical term, Marshal?"

His smile came slowly, reluctantly, and it didn't stay long, but it was nice to see it all the same. "We need to be careful. I don't think he's out to hurt us, but... I have no idea what he's capable of."

And Talen was threaded through my heart, maybe even

280

through my saru soul if I still had one. But I wasn't afraid of him. Of what he could do, yes, but not him.

I buried my head deeper into the pillow and sighed, feeling more content than I could ever remember feeling before. "Sota, Aeon, and Sonia?"

"Exploring the ship."

"Is it over?"

"For now. But..." That pause again as he tried to find the words.

"Give it to me straight. I won't break."

His gaze trailed over my shoulder, down to where the sheet rested in the valley of my waist, over my hip and leg, before darting back to my face. He was making the mistake of thinking me vulnerable just because there was nothing but a sheet between us. I wondered what would happen if I accidentally let the sheet slip, but then I remembered the startling image of him and Sjora. Even though it had been an act, all part of the game, it had looked and felt real. He had wanted her. *That* was real. I couldn't blame him. I was saru, and I ached to have Talen as mine. Kellee wasn't so different. We were both vulnerable to the fae. They'd made sure of it.

He sat in the chair, looking back at me, trying to get a read on my thoughts while attempting to appear casual, but he sat too still, and he fought too hard to hide his expressions from that stubborn face of his. He had said a lot while I'd lain dying in his arms. Things he probably wished he could take back.

"I er... I need to be clear—" He cleared his throat and sat back, stretching out a leg. "What happened between me and Sjora, it meant nothing. I had to get her close for the poisons to work. It was just... what it was. What I mean is—"

"It's fine." I smiled and hoped it didn't look wooden. "It's nothing." Curiously, it was fine. More than fine. I would have done the same. I *had* done the same. Kellee likely didn't want to see it, but in many ways, we were the same. The only thing that separated us was a line of morals. He had them. I didn't.

Nodding more to himself than to me, he continued. "Sota picked up some Resistance communications. The fae have abandoned Calicto, but they'll be back for their magic, if nothing else. And they'll return with force. And you..." He almost laughed, but his eyes held a pinch of sorrow. "If you weren't infamous before, you are now. They're calling what you did the *Game of Lies*. And they have a new name for you, *Messenger*. Your name is whispered throughout Halow. Oberon will soon hear of your betrayal, if he hasn't already. The Faerie King can ill afford to ignore you any longer."

I rolled onto my back and blinked up at the dome-like ceiling. "While I'm alive, I'm a threat to the king's rule." I had no wish to go up against Oberon's wrath. He had created the vakaru. He oversaw the gladiators and commanded the fae legions. He had lived and breathed warfare for thousands of years, all while keeping one eye on Faerie's throne. I had always been on the right side of him, always been his secret obsession. I was his saru girl plucked from the starlit arena and sent out into the night to kill for a king. I could almost hear his voice calling me home, where I belonged. The Wraithmaker in me wanted to answer. But I wasn't just her, not anymore. I had survived for a reason. I was the Messenger.

Cool resolve solidified into determination. I didn't need to answer Oberon's call. I made my own choices. "We have this ship." I turned my head and saw that righteous spark in Kellee's dark eyes. Was it mirrored in mine? I hoped so. "We have Talen, and Sota, and Aeon, and you. For the first time since the fae came, we won something. We drove them off Calicto." I pushed up, holding the sheet to my chest. Excitement and something like happiness thrummed inside. "This can be the beginning."

We could fight back.

Humans, saru, and the last vakaru.

We could do this. Together.

Kellee's smile bloomed across his face, brightening it for the first time in weeks. "I was hoping you'd say that." He picked up a bundle of clothes and set them down next to me. On top of the pile was my original whip, coiled like a steel snake. Cleaned of blood, it gleamed. I thought I'd lost it when Kellee and I had fought Sjora's flight. Kellee had found it and brought it back to me.

"Get dressed," he said. "We have work to do." He headed for the door, but I wasn't done with my complicated vakaru.

"Kellee...?"

He half turned, waiting. Something like delight or pride danced in his eyes, and it made my wrecked heart stutter. *My unseelie monster.* What a terrible pair we made.

"You owe me an apology."

His eyebrows jerked. "If I remember correctly, I said I'd apologize any way you wanted *if* you saved me and Talen."

I let the sheet slip and felt the kiss of cool air whisper down my side. "So, where's my apology, Marshal?"

His gaze dipped, but he caught it and smirked, so pleased with himself for not falling into my feminine trap. "Talen and I saved *your* ass, Messenger."

I screwed up my face. "There's no I in team, Marshal." And threw my shirt at him. Kellee had vanished before it fluttered to the floor.

I NEVER WOULD HAVE BELIEVED a barren rock in the middle of nowhere could feel like home, but the prison we had set up camp in had begun to.

While I moved the books I'd borrowed from Talen out of the cage, Aeon examined its tek and glass construction. Sonia had gone off to explore the prison in search of a room to call her own until we found a saru or human colony she might like to stay in.

Kellee was sitting on one of the couches, boots up on the table, legs crossed at the ankles. He had shaved his raggedy beard and almost looked like the same pretty-boy marshal I'd run into in the sinks. Almost. His smile didn't seem as broad, and his eyes had lost some of their sparkle.

"Talen takes scary to a whole new level," he grumbled, apparently still getting over the way Talen had silently guided the enormous ship into the comparatively tiny prison dock by thought alone.

"He would kick your ass in a duel." That was from Sota, who hummed gently in the air above the table, deliberately baiting the marshal.

Kellee scratched his cheek. "I could take him."

"The statistical calculations make that outcome unlikely, Marshal."

Kellee bristled. "Wanna bet, Sparky?"

I pinched my mouth closed and swallowed a laugh.

Sota's motors whirred, thinking it over. "What can we wager?"

Kellee planted his boots on the floor so he could lean in close. The conversation just got serious. "What does a drone want?"

"What I want is impossible."

"Oh? I've heard a lot of impossible talk over the years. Given enough time, impossible turns out to be possible. C'mon, tell me. Just between you and me. It can be our secret."

Talen's presence simmered nearby, leading my thoughts away from Kellee and Sota's wager in the same merry dance the fae once used to lure innocent human children into the forest. I felt it first as a pleasurable all-over warmth and then as a sharp need to be physically close to him.

Something had happened to our bond in the ship. Everything I'd felt before paled compared to what I felt now. Now the bond was wide open, alive, and hungry. I had to know what I'd done and what it meant.

I left the chamber and followed the pulling sensation through the prison until I found Talen in the observation room. The monitors cast him in a soft greenish light, and for a few selfish moments, I admired him from the doorway. My silver fae. The piloting chamber on the warcruiser bore the scars of what he had done. His silver had infected the entire room, making it look... dead.

The connection between us pulled tighter, demanding contact. I had to concentrate to keep from stepping inside the room.

"I warned you the bond could be damaging."

He didn't look up. In his hand, he turned over a glass thimble. Sjora's. Carefully, he set it down among the bank of screens. I shivered at the sight of it and wondered if he'd let me crush it. Or did it mean something to him? I tried to read his face, but like always, his expression was neutral and guarded. Was he angry that the bond had intensified, or saddened, or relieved? I never could read him, and he wasn't making it any easier.

How could he be less than a few strides away and still feel as though he wasn't here at all? I wanted to reach out to him, but I wasn't sure if that was me or his magic inside me trying to return to where it belonged.

Determined to keep my own mind, I folded my arms and casually leaned a shoulder against the doorframe. "You don't have to stay. It would be more comfortable for you on the ship, right? No tek." I hadn't meant for it to sound like I wanted to be rid of him, and I had to bite down to keep from backtracking.

His gaze fell as he considered my words, and then he looked again at the ship displayed on every screen from various angles. "I told her she can go."

For a few moments, I thought he meant Sjora, but that didn't match the gentle scrutiny in his eyes. Or had he meant Sonia? And then it clicked. "The ship?" If we lost the ship, we'd lose an enormous advantage in the war. Kellee would be... furious. "But aren't you bonded to it?"

"No."

"Then how can you control it—*her*?"

"I asked. Nicely." He smiled at the simplicity and touched the screen. The tek all around us must have hurt him, but he showed no sign of that either. "I told her she's free, but she is still there, waiting."

I didn't know much about the warcruiser, but I knew they were in service to the fae their entire lives, and if there was something I was familiar with, it was serving the fae. "Maybe she knows nothing else?" There was a big difference between being offered freedom and being brave enough to take it.

"Perhaps." He pulled his hand back, curling his fingers into a loose fist. "Or perhaps she does not know how to go back."

A ship like her, nobody could stand in the way of what she truly wanted. If she wanted to be free, she would be.

"Perhaps it has been too long," Talen continued, his tone softer, "and she has forgotten what it means to be part of Faerie."

We were no longer talking about the ship. Maybe we hadn't been at all.

He turned his head, and the look he gave me speared through any mental barrier I could have slammed into place. Power blazed and filled the tiny room, making the walls appear to stretch outward, making him shimmer. The screens flickered. I wavered on my feet, drowning in too much Talen, and clutched at the wall to keep myself from falling all the way in. And then he was in front of me, his long, strong fingers gently sweeping through my hair, eyes darting over mine.

"I want to stay," he whispered, but I couldn't tell who he was trying to convince. Me or him?

I had the wall suddenly at my back, hard and real. But in front of me stood something—someone I didn't understand, someone I could barely touch without falling into whatever he had created between us.

His fingers toyed with my hair and tickled my cheek. I lifted my hand and touched his jaw. His lips parted fractionally, and when he didn't pull away, I brushed my thumb over the corner of his mouth, delighting in its softness. The look in his eyes was at odds with his restraint. There, wildness roamed. "What is your name?"

His hands clutched my face. I gasped, wondering if it was too late to fight. He pressed his forehead to mine so that all I saw were his eyes, their color fractured by veins of magic. "My name is not something you can possess." The words came out in a hurried hiss, sounding vicious and hate-filled. It was all I could do not to shove him away and run. But behind the intensity, behind the sudden emotion, I saw the sharp flicker of fear, or perhaps more than fear. Raw terror.

"Because I am saru?" I asked.

His grip eased. "No..." He tilted his head, and his lips brushed the corner of my mouth, but he held me too tightly to let me chase that promise of a kiss. "My name is stardust and shadow and cannot be spoken aloud." His words touched my lips and eased inside, landing sweet-like on my tongue. I wanted to swallow them, but I feared what might happen if I did, because they felt solid and real like seeds that might take root and grow inside me. "It was meant to be an anchor, nothing more... I tried to protect you." His touch softened, one hand lifting to stroke a thumb down my face. The intensity was fading, the magic dissolving. "But you were mortal, and I... I made a mistake." He pulled away.

I was done with mistakes. Done with being afraid. I

had lived my whole life from one day to the next among immortals, never knowing if the next fight would kill me. I *was* mortal, and because of it, I didn't have the luxury of riddles or the time to figure them out—figure him out. How dare he toy with me and turn away. He wasn't escaping so easily. I slipped my hand to the back of his neck and pulled him down into a kiss. I expected hesitation, expected him to stall and freeze, maybe even tear away from my saru boldness. I hadn't expected the fever with which he kissed me back. His lips burned, and his tongue swept in, answering my hunger with a sudden need of his own. So much for resisting. I fell into the taste of him, needing more of him in me. I sought a thin piece of skin at his waist with my free hand, and I clamped the other on his neck, making it clear I had him. His clothes had him wrapped up so tightly I couldn't find what I wanted and settled for gripping his lower back and pulling him close.

Our maddening kiss broke apart, scattering my thoughts and breaths with it. It wasn't enough. His mouth grazed my neck, and his tongue traced my collarbone where a collar had once rubbed me raw. His breaths fluttered cool against my flushed skin, the brush of air like that of whispered things. I had my hand twisted in his hair and the other on his ass when I realized he wasn't moving.

He would deny me this. Of course he was. Whoever he was, he was important, a fae of the high courts, of the old bloodlines, one in a billion, one of two Faerie born every millennium. And what was I? *A nothing girl,* Eledan's haunting voice supplied.

"I'm sorry…" he said and meant it.

I couldn't catch my breaths to reply, and with him

shutting down, I didn't want to speak because he'd hear the pain. I freed my hand from his hair and let the other slip to my side, then I turned my face away. Sorry? Such a little word that meant nothing in the end.

His hip dug into my waist, and his thigh pressed between my legs, shudders riding through him, transferring to me, lighting my vulnerable saru body on fire. I knew he wanted this, and to prove it, I slid my hand down his front, over the too-tight belt, and deliberately pressed hard over the length of his arousal jutting against the inside of his pants. He gasped—to hear him react almost undid me—and I swallowed the sound, chasing his parted lips with a tantalizing tease of my tongue. He leaned in, seeking more, and ground himself against my palm. When it happened, and it would, we would clash like two wild things, and it would be sweet bliss.

"This doesn't have to be wrong." I looked into his eyes and moved my hand, applying just enough pressure to widen his pupils and summon something of a wrangled growl from my reserved fae. Just hearing him react, feeling him push into my hand, made me want to find a blade and cut his clothes from shoulders to ankles. Our connection pulled so tightly it threatened to snap. This was another form of madness, wasn't it? But a good one.

"It's not wrong," he whispered, his usually smooth, seductive voice hoarse. His hand slid to my lower back and then around my hip. If he kept following that path, if he touched me where I pulsed for him to touch me and then pulled away, I would lose my mind or do something I'd later regret. Or not.

"I can't." Those words came from me. Impossibly. Ridiculously. I wanted him so badly it hurt, so why was I shutting down? But Talen was dangerous, more so than any fae I'd met, and they were all terribly treacherous, but Talen... he was different. *Stardust and shadow.* And the bond beating inside me like a second heart made every touch, every glance, every kiss something more, something I wasn't sure I could survive. I'd survived everything, but could I survive him? That was what he had meant. I was mortal, and he was untouchable. I was saru, born of the earth, raised as a tool, fed with reality, and he was magic and myth.

"My saru name is Mylana." I swallowed under the heat of his blazing gaze. "Do you understand the gift I give you?"

Pain racked his face. He knew a saru's real name was sacred. But this name was more, it was the truest part of me, the pearl buried beneath layer upon layer of lies. It was the only thing I truly owned and the only gift I could ever give. "I'm afraid this is madness or a dream. I want so desperately for this, for you to be real. But it can't be. It never will be until you tell me your name."

He cupped my face in one hand, tipped my head back, and kissed me slowly, leisurely, making every touch an agonizing tease. When I tried to kiss him back, he withdrew, and only when I stilled did he tease his mouth over mine. I savored the feel of him, the velvety softness of his lips, the gentleness of his tongue as he pushed in, letting me know exactly what I was turning down. His kiss was slow, and lazy, and painful, because it felt like goodbye, and it was my fault.

He stepped away. Desire, hunger, need, it all showed on his face and in the shudders that racked him and in the breaths he stole. And then, mastering it all, he turned to face the screens and stared at the ship, perhaps reconsidering leaving. He looked exactly as he had when I'd arrived, only I'd messed up his hair and twisted some of his clothes askew, but the expressionless mask was back in place, hiding the great weight of his power and mystery.

He brushed a thumb across his bottom lip. I watched him swallow and knew the separation was killing him too. But when I had Talen in my arms, when I had all of him beneath me, his body in mine, his heart mine, there couldn't be any lies between us. It was the only way I could fully trust him. And he, I.

"Kesh, you need—" Kellee appeared in the doorway, one hand braced on the doorframe. He didn't miss Talen's bedraggled appearance or my startled look. Surprisingly, a warning growl rumbled through Kellee. Talen responded with a cold, unblinking stare, the kind that, had he been Winterborn, could summon winter storms. But he wasn't of the winter. Something else burned behind that gaze. And Kellee glared back, the wild threat of *unseelie* ramping up the tension. I'd never seen them square off, never seen them do more than verbally disagree. Now, violence thrummed between them, raising gooseflesh on my arms. If I had to step between them, blood would spill.

"What do *I need*?" I carefully asked Kellee.

The marshal turned gold-rimmed eyes on me. "It's Aeon."

AEON SAT on the training mat, legs crossed. Out of his scout's leathers and in simple gray sweats, he looked like the boy I remembered, until he looked up, and all the horrors we had witnessed showed in the lines around his eyes and mouth.

On the floor, an inch in front of him, he'd placed the starfruit, stolen from Sjora's feast. The fruit that would take away his memories.

I sat opposite him and folded my legs so I mirrored him. I could probably snatch the starfruit away, but I wouldn't.

I knew why he wanted to eat the fruit. Hadn't I wanted to forget my life and craft myself into Kesh Lasota so I didn't have to be the Wraithmaker anymore? But I was the Wraithmaker. I had to be for Halow. I understood that now. But Aeon, Aeon who had fought so hard to find the right in a world full of wrongs, Aeon with his heroes who had never come for him.

Outside, Kellee had told me to keep Aeon from eating the starfruit, that our memories, as bad as they were, shaped us. Kellee would know. He had several lifetimes' worth. But what if Aeon didn't want to be that person? This wasn't my call or Kellee's.

We sat in silence for a while, with the sounds of the prison clanging and humming around us. "I'm not like you," he finally said. "I didn't take it all and master it. It mastered me. He... *he* mastered me."

He spoke of Dagnu, our overseer, our jailor. Oberon had saved me from a life under Dagnu. Nobody had saved Aeon.

"You once talked to me of dreams," I said carefully. "You told me stories of a world without the fae, where the saru would rise and win their freedom. Do you remember?"

His lips smiled, but it didn't reach his eyes.

"I listened, and I kept those stories close to me, as precious as my slave name, and now... now we have a chance to make your dreams real."

"I'm not that boy anymore." He snarled the words, hating them. I saw what Sjora had seen. Hate surrounded Aeon and consumed him.

I could only imagine what all the fae had done to him, but I'd seen enough to imagine the worst. He was right; he was no longer that boy. He was a man who had survived, and he was here with me. "I need you to help me beat them."

He laughed dryly. "You don't need me."

"The Aeon I remember would have jumped at the chance to fight back. This is our chance. It wasn't the right time back then... but you survived for a reason. Just like me."

"I survived because Dagnu wasn't done with me. After you killed me, he had a lifegiver revive me. And it wasn't the only time he brought me back. That was just the first."

They had killed him and brought him back over and over. I hid my rage at the injustice and kept the guilt deep inside. This was Aeon's moment, not mine. "We'll find Dagnu, and we'll punish him. I promise on my saru name."

When Aeon next looked up, his eyes shone with unshed tears. "You made me a promise before. We planned to kill Oberon that day at the arena. We planned it for years." His voice wobbled. "It would have worked, Mylana. We could have started something then..."

And I'd turned on Aeon for a pat on the head from Oberon. I'd become the Wraithmaker that day.

I hated that part of me, but I needed it too. I would never forget and didn't want to. "A night hasn't gone by where I haven't dreamed of you. You kept me alive, Aeon. It was always you. You taught me never to run from them. I loved you since I met you, since the moment you stood up to them and never let them win. You showed me what I could do. What *we* could do." *I never stopped loving you.*

"But they won." He bowed his head. A single tear fell to the floor.

"No." I reached out, passing my hand over the fruit, and gently eased my fingers beneath his hand resting on his knee. He looked at my touch and let me draw his hand into mine. I never dared to dream I'd get him back, but here he was, his hand warm, his skin rough from the battles he had fought without me. "It's not over. Change is coming. Help me, Aeon. Help me and Kellee and Talen and all the people who are still fighting for those dreams of yours. Help the saru left behind on Faerie." He swallowed and squeezed my hand, but he didn't look up. I was losing him. I didn't deserve to have him back, and I had no right to ask anything of him, but what I felt for my friend was real. For years, loving him had been the only truth of a life made of lies. "I don't want you to go," I whispered.

His mouth twitched into a smile. "It's your turn to tell the stories." He pulled his hand from mine, scooped up the starfruit, placed it on his tongue, tossed his head back, and swallowed.

EPILOGUE

*A*ll around was silent, though Faerie never truly permitted complete quiet. The endless chatter of the court, the protests and demands, had all faded from the throne with the passing of the sidhe lords and their glittering attire. Mirrored walls reflected themselves, sending shards of light dancing into the open spaces between the throne room's proud columns. But not all fae had left. One lone male remained, standing framed inside a vast arched window, a thin rowan crown marking him as different.

A distant sighing sailed on the breeze, bringing with it tiny wisps, each one twinkling like the stars in Faerie's multicolored sky, but so close they could be captured in hand. Oberon, the new Faerie King, snatched a wisp from its flight. He closed his fingers around the barely there creature and brought it close to his chest. His gaze lifted to the sprawl of dwellings crowding the palace walls and farther to the undulating lands glittering in the near dark. Nothing glimmered as brightly as his crystal palace, though the sharp towers and cavernous halls were not really his. Not yet. While doubt remained, none of Faerie was truly his. And doubt was everywhere. The sprawling rose gardens wilted, the ancient oaks cried dry leaves, and the emerald sea withdrew farther and farther from shore. The decline of Faerie was all around him, mortality clawing at the immortal, staining his world with decay. He had hoped that removing Mab and her ineffective rule would spur life back into Faerie's roots, but nothing had changed, and the sidhe were growing restless. Like sand in an hourglass, he felt his reign slipping through his fingers.

"My lord." The guardian approached and bowed low.

Oberon noted the autumnlands reds and earthy browns of Sirius's coloring and how the guardian's clothes were degrading at the seams. His colors had dulled since Oberon had last sent him away. To be absent from Faerie too long, to be separated from her magic, took its toll. But Sirius would never falter. The guardian would follow his every word to the death if necessary, though Oberon hoped it did not come to that.

The king returned his gaze to the lands outside, letting Faerie's forever-song soothe his mind. The wisp, still caged inside his hand, fluttered gently. "You have news, Sirius."

"I do, sire."

Oberon waited. The guardian remained silent. It was unlike him to hesitate. The news was dire, indeed. "Then speak it."

"Calicto is lost."

Calicto. The Halow colony with its lost-and-found-again font of magic. The human city in which his scarred brother had thought himself safe. "Lost?"

Sirius lifted his head and met Oberon's gaze. A muscle

fluttered in the guardian's jaw. "Details are proving difficult to confirm, but we know the Wraithmaker publicly slew over a thousand of our people. The *humans*," he snarled, "have begun calling her..." Sirius wet his lips. "The Messenger, sire."

Oberon's eyebrow jerked, the only outward sign he had heard Sirius's words. Sjora's arena game—the general had forced his hand, and so too that of the Wraithmaker's. He was not surprised his saru gladiator had survived the Harvester. She had a talent for surviving. Of all those he had guided over the centuries, of all the saru, vakaru, and namu he had molded, she was the strongest and most dangerous. He had deliberately crafted her that way. "What of Devere?"

"He and Sjora are missing, along with the ship."

The loss of a ship was yet another devastating blow to his forces. But a saru could not command a warcruiser. A pilot was required for that, and none would work with a saru. "Did the Wraithmaker work alone?"

Sirius hesitated. "She has formed an alliance with a vakaru and a..." He swallowed. "... fae pilot."

"Impossible?" He worded it as a question because it wasn't impossible at all. Oberon had tutored the Wraithmaker in the art of subterfuge, honed her into a weapon of illusion, made her a puppet of lies pulled by his strings. She was collecting weapons of her own: the last vakaru and a pilot. Two mythical creatures, even among Faerie's myths and legends. He couldn't help but be intrigued. She was his finest work and his secret to keep. But her actions at the arena may have sealed her fate. She had killed the queen and delivered to him his brother. It was time for her to come home. "I want her found and brought to me." She had the power to unseat him or strengthen his rule. He could ignore her no longer. "Discreetly, Sirius."

"Of course." The guardian nodded. "And her retinue?"

Oberon turned to the window and slowly tightened his grip on the wisp. Fragile wings collapsed, and warmth seeped from its tiny body into his hand. He felt the creature's power brighten his own—if only for a blink. There was power in death, just like there was power in life. He could not allow the Wraithmaker to discover the truth. Oberon smiled. "Kill them."

"It will be done."

With Sirius gone, the throne room once again fell under the weight of Faerie's simmering quiet and its whispering song. The king lifted his chin and admired his world outside the window. The winds would soon change for him. He would lead the sidhe court to a glory the likes of which they hadn't seen since the unseelie were vanquished. He was sure of it. His mother was dead, his brother was mad, and the sidhe—as fractured as they were —now danced to the tune of his making. Finally, he was Faerie's king.

"Your reign is one of glass, like this palace you hide in, princeling."

A dart of icy fear froze the king's thoughts.

The oily voice wove tendrils around him, sank through his silk robes, seeped into skin, and knotted into his immortal bones, leeching his life away. He dared not turn to face the *thing* that had joined him inside the throne room. It could not be here. The palace was warded, the mirrors protected him... but it was here. The creature's fetid breath whispered through the king's hair, stirring loose strands. He could not look. To look upon their kind invited the darkness, and he had already dealt in too much darkness.

A fluttering sounded, like that of thick drapes or wings. Moments passed, moments in which Oberon's heart stuttered too loudly and sweat glistened from his hairline, seeping beneath the band of his crown. Outside, the sky lightened and Faerie's song drifted once more through the window. Mouth dry, his pulse pounding in his throat, he turned to find the room as empty as the oak throne at its center.

His ragged thoughts fell to the Wraithmaker and her tenacious desire to thrive among chaos, to climb the bones of her fellow saru so she might live. Sacrifices must be made.

Oberon lifted his chin. It was his duty to ensure Faerie's survival. At any cost.

To be continued in *The Nightshade's Touch*, #3 Messenger Chronicles, coming Summer 2018. Read on for a sample.

Sign up to Pippa's mailing list for all the news, free ebooks, and never miss a new release.

Did you enjoy Game of Lies? Click here to leave a review. Just a few words will do and every review counts.

EXCERPT ~ THE NIGHTSHADE'S TOUCH

As a gladiator, there'd been no need for dance in my life, unless I counted the killing dance I'd performed for years in the arena. And so, when Kellee had declared we were visiting a backwater colony to "celebrate," I was too curious to decline. But on arrival, it was all I could do to stand on the periphery of the revelry, wide-eyed and uncertain.

Percussion instruments made of discarded barrels and tins thumped out a beat, instruments stringed from horse-hair rang tricky notes, and pipes whittled from wood sent the revelers into a merry frenzy. The human colony, some two hundred lives from a ravaged farming planet, danced and sang and laughed. I wasn't even sure what for. There seemed to be little cause for celebration in Halow. We had beaten the fae back from Calicto, but warcruisers still swarmed around Halow's old spacefaring channels, watching for survivor ships, and millions were dead. Families, homes, generations snuffed out by the fae who believed it their divine right to cleanse Halow of its human infestation.

Dancing and singing to celebrate one small victory seemed ridiculous. I was about to retire outside, when I caught sight of Arran among the dancing throng. Arran, previously known as Aeon. He had eaten starfruit, wiping his mind clean of his entire past. He danced now like he didn't have a care in the world because he didn't. Arran was the first name that had come to me when he had blinked and asked me who he was. It was fae, but I didn't know his saru name, and Arran sounded a little like Aeon.

I had told him he was saru, that he had been a fighter, but that was all. He didn't know his name for most of his life had been Aeon. He didn't know he was the saru gladiator who had wanted revenge on the Wraithmaker. He didn't know he had spent ten years at the mercy of the jailor Dagnu. I had told him his new name, and he had smiled back at me, shallow and polite, like two strangers bumping into each other on a street.

Aeon was gone.

Arran, on the other hand, was very much here, and he had caught the eye of more than a few young women. I couldn't blame them. He apparently liked to dance, and he looked good doing it. That was something I hadn't known about him and wondered how it had come about. He'd spent ten years in captivity after I'd left him for dead, and Sjora—the fae Talen had torn in two—had implied he had spent some of that time as more than arena entertainment. He wasn't namu, humans bred for pleasure, so to make him behave as one would have been degrading, even to a saru. But all of that was in the past, no matter how much of it I still witnessed in my dreams.

I had loved him as Aeon, but as Arran, I had to let him go.

"Have you seen the buns on that man?"

Hulia appeared at my side, dreadlocks swishing. She took the tankard from my hand, sloshed pink liquid inside it from the cracked bowl, and handed it back. Hulia *was* namu, or so Eledan had told me while she had been locked in his thrall. On waking, she had stabbed him in the back. I considered her a friend, although my past experience with friends had been... rare.

"I mean, dayam honey. He has enough thrust to rival my old shuttle."

Her eyes flashed, and I rolled mine. She had managed The Boot, a mishmash of bar and whorehouse on Calicto. She had also acted as something of a pimp, seeing to it that her girls were looked after and paid well. She could also make music and lull humans into a sense of safety and admiration. If I thought about it, her being namu was obvious, but I'd missed it because I'd been living a life as Kesh Lasota, invisible messenger, and I had wrapped myself in so many lies that I couldn't see the truth even when it was right in front of me.

"What did you say his name was?" She leaned a hip against the table and watched him clamp his hands on his partner's hips while she threw her arms around his neck. The two of them practically got it on right there on the dancefloor for all to see. Nobody cared. Everyone here was lost to the party, celebrating like it might be their last.

"Arran."

She made a face. With his darker skin and fae-like eyes, he didn't much look like an Arran, especially when he rocked his hips in harmony with the girl he danced with.

Hulia watched like she would happily take Arran outside to teach him a few moves of her own. "I could put him to work and make a fortune."

"Don't," I snapped with too much force.

Hulia flinched. "Okay, all right, I didn't realize you and he were a thing—"

"We're not."

Hulia frowned with one eyebrow raised. "Touchy much."

I smiled at my friend. I owed her more, a lot more. "It's all right. It's just… complicated."

"What about that one?" Hulia jerked her chin at the only man in the room wearing a coat. The dark fabric matched his dark hair, currently tied back in a tight ponytail. And all that dark worked to brighten his intense green eyes. He cut through the crowd like an apex predator striding through Faerie's jungles and eyed them like he might arrest half of them for wanton behavior in a time of crisis and the other half for breach of the peace. He wasn't wearing his gold star, but he didn't need to. *Lawman* was written in the way he walked, the way he scanned for threats, and the way he pinned me under his challenging glare. I'd also recently seen everything beneath those layers of lawman. He had a body to match his impressive presence and a physique made for stamina *and* strength. A rare combination, but then, he was the last of his vakaru kind.

Hulia caught my too-long stare in the marshal's direction. "Huh, guess not." She snorted something like a laugh. "I hear you have a fae too. Dayam Kesh, leave some of the sexy for the rest of us." She smirked into her drink. "You know I'm namu?"

I turned my back on the approaching Kellee and pretended to be interested in the colony food. "Sure."

"Well, being namu means I got a few tricks, *Messenger*, like sniffing out when someone really, really wants to f —*Hullo, Marshal Kellee*." She flicked her hair back and straightened, purring his name and making it sound filthy in a good way. I'd known she could flirt, but I figured I'd probably only seen a fraction of what she could do.

"Hulia," Kellee greeted from behind me. I heard the polite smile in his voice. They knew each other. He had helped get her to safety after Eledan had screwed with her head. She likely also knew him from her profession. The Halow law and Hulia had rarely gotten along. Now there was no law, and we were all on the same side.

"You smell delightful," she gushed. "What *is* that cologne?"

I stamped on Hulia's foot. She laughed a bright, tinkling, seductive laughter that turned half the heads in the room and sashayed into the crowd, looping a few unsuspecting males in her arms.

I glanced at Kellee side-on and caught his puzzled frown mixed with that superficial smile. Once Hulia was out of sight, he took up her spot beside me and spotted my drink. "What is it?"

"I have no idea. She keeps refilling this." I showed him the tankard. "And when she's not looking, I dump it back into the bowl." The last time I'd gotten too liberal with my emotions after drinking Faerie wine, I'd had sex with a fae ambassador and strangled him with my whip. Granted, I'd thought he was Eledan. But while I wasn't craving Eledan like before, I still didn't entirely trust myself not to lose control.

Kellee picked up a discarded cup and sniffed. "Smells like cleaning fluid." He set it back down and turned his attention to the room. "Arran's enjoying himself."

I couldn't read his flat tone but knew I didn't want to watch any more of Arran, so I just nodded and made an agreeable sound. Setting down my drink, I picked up a piece of flatbread and picked at it. Kellee was too astute to miss my mood. His gaze warmed my face. He hadn't said much after Aeon had eaten the starfruit. Hadn't said much about anything since we had survived Sjora and her arena games. He knew something was going on between Talen and me. He didn't like what had happened with Aeon/Arran, and then there was the fact I'd watched him fuck a powerful, immortal fae unconscious. There was a lot going on in everything we didn't say.

A violin, or something like it, started up, but the sound held an electronic note. I instantly recognized Hulia's music and stiffened. She had played like this in The Boot. She had magic. Not a lot, but it was enough. There wasn't any harm in it, but it reminded me too much of all the things I'd been hiding from and everything we had lost.

Kellee's hand boldly found my waist, and then he was there, leaning close to my side so that when he spoke, I heard him clearly despite the music. "Do you dance?"

"No, I..." He pulled back a little, but the electric flutters he'd sparked to life in me felt too good to lose so soon. I dropped my bread and covered his hand on my waist with my own, trapping his fingers against me. "I don't know how," I admitted, expecting him to laugh. I had never danced in my life. It seemed silly here, surrounded by dancing people, but these weren't my people. Saru didn't dance.

His fingers closed around mine, and he wordlessly led me to the edge of the crowd. There, he stepped in front of me, took my hand, placed it neatly on his waist, and clasped my other hand in his. He rested his other hand on my hip, where it might as well have scorched a hole in my clothes. I stared at the laces tying his shirt closed. It seemed like the safest place to look.

"Feel the movement and let yourself drift with me."

My face was hot. I could kill a thousand fae, lie to the Faerie Queen's face for years, and cut out a prince's heart, but this... this wasn't me. Half of me wanted to run, the other half was too stubborn to let Kellee see me weak. And so I stomped on the spot, with no idea where to put my feet. My heart raced as if I were being stalked in the arena, like I was preparing to fight.

Kellee's hand slipped to the dip at my lower back and his fingers spread there, and to make it worse, he pulled me close so my lower belly grazed his belt and my chest brushed his. I had been close to him before, mostly while trying to kill him. This was different. What was the point in dancing anyway? Was I supposed to enjoy being this close to Kellee without an endgame?

"Just tell me if you want to stop." His words tickled my hair against my forehead.

He swayed to the music. I focused on my feet and the feel of him moving, and soon, everything else fell away.

"I didn't know you could dance." I sounded okay, not like the high-strung mess inside my head.

"There's a lot you don't know."

Of course there was. He was the last of a race the fae had all but wiped out centuries ago, and somehow, he'd survived. He looked young, my age, but he wasn't. He looked human, but he wasn't that either. He had a hunger inside him, one that had once looked at me like I was prey. Marshal Kellee had teeth, literally and figuratively. And beneath all that rugged prettiness lurked something *unseelie*. Something forbidden. My footing stumbled. Kellee caught me. The music quickened, and so did our pace.

Kellee's rhythm swept me with him, his body strong in ways that had nothing to do with attacking. "We've fought often enough that this should be second nature to you."

"Give me a weapon and I'll know how to dance with you." My hand had moved to his back, inside his coat, so I felt the warmth through his shirt. I didn't remember moving it there, but it felt good to feel the smooth shift of muscle, feel him move beneath my touch. I wondered what it would feel like to feel the heat and softness of his skin under my hands. I had dreamed it over and over and over, and Eledan had ripped those dreams away. I wanted the real Kellee in my memories. Always had since I'd first seen him. But in many ways, the marshal, like Talen, was untouchable. I'd seen him with Sjora. He hadn't killed her, but he could have. I was sure of it. Their lovemaking was one memory I could have done without. The two of them rocking together, her fae skin glistening magic, his mouth on her shoulder, her breast, his sharp teeth sinking in—

"Then dance like that," he said, bringing me back into the room. "Use your emotion."

If I did that, I'd probably kill him. I laughed at my dark thoughts.

His fingers touched my chin, tilting my head up. "You don't laugh enough."

I looked in his dark eyes, flecked with green. Sometimes they were black, sometimes rimmed in gold, sometimes red. He had so many facets, all of them dangerous. But I hadn't feared him until I'd seen the truth at his center. The unseelie. Did he know he had the darkest part of Faerie inside him?

The music still played, and bodies moved around us, caught up in Hulia's spell, but Kellee and I stood motionless. He looked down at me, seeing... I wasn't sure. But he seemed puzzled, like I was the mysterious one. He knew more about me than I did about him. I wanted to know more, but getting answers out of him had never been easy. Getting a kiss was even harder. If I rose onto my tiptoes, I could kiss him... and ruin this tentative truce we'd built up over the past few weeks. I wouldn't force him. There were more lies than truths between us. I'd betrayed him. I wouldn't make this decision for him. It had to be his, even if I ached all over for him to lower his mouth, to sweep his tongue in and claim me the way the rest of him wanted. I knew what he was, both sides of him. And the only thing that frightened me was never having him know me in return.

The violin sang, its vivid notes weaving a spell through the crowd.

I brought my hands up between Kellee and me, creating space and room to think, but as I did, I noticed the crowd no longer moved. "Something's wrong."

Hulia played, but the rest of her band members gazed slack-jawed like all the others. She swept the bow across the violin, her body locked in its own dance, and the crowd watched her with glassy, unblinking eyes.

Kellee's eyes narrowed, golden edges glowing. "Stop

Hulia's song." He cocked his head, listening to something I couldn't hear. "Go."

I shoved through the bodies. "Hulia!" Her eyes had glazed over too.

I heard Kellee's growl and glanced back in time to see him pitch the bowl of pink water off the table, splashing the entire contents across the floor. Poison.

"We're not alone." Kellee ran from the room, his swirl of coat the only part of him I recognized in the blur.

A trembling shook the floor and swung the strings of lights overhead. Thunder followed, but it rolled on and on. A ship. And Kellee was out there alone.

He'd be fine. He was always fine.

"Hulia." I scrambled onto the makeshift stage made of rows of tables. She continued to dip and sway, her body one with the music and the magic. And it was magic she wove. I could taste it, the sweetness of Faerie sprinkled in the air. This wasn't Hulia's doing. Something mixed with the drink had left an entire people susceptible, including Arran. He stared up at the stage just like all the others.

This trance was fae made. It had to be.

I placed a hand on Hulia's shoulder, moving with her. "Hulia, snap out of it."

She didn't respond, just played her hauntingly beautiful music.

I slapped her, putting weight behind it. Her grip on her bow slipped, and the violin jolted in her hands. Silence.

She blinked and touched her face.

"Fae." Kellee was back. He grabbed a table, upended it like it was as light as paper, and wedged it against the door.

"How many?"

Hulia fluttered her lashes and frowned at her audience. "I've never done *that* before."

"Too many," Kellee replied. He turned and frowned at the nonresponsive crowd. "Can you play them back to life?"

"I don't even know how I did... this..." She dropped the violin. It clattered to the stage at her feet. "My music doesn't hurt people. I don't hurt people."

Until now, I thought.

We couldn't move them all, not in time.

I watched my friend's face crumble. "It's not you, Hulia. It's Faerie. Something in the wine must have left them susceptible to your song—more than usual." I jumped down, wove through the crowd to Arran, and gave him a gentle shake. He didn't wake.

"Why not just kill them?" Hulia asked. "Why do... this?" She lifted her hands, and I knew what was going through her head. Had they gotten to her too? Made her play at the right time?

"They want them alive," Kellee growled. "Unharmed."

They're harvesting them. My eyes met Kellee's. We couldn't save them. Talen might be able to with the ship. If he saw the fae approach, there was a chance he was on his way, but we couldn't wait for that chance.

"You have to leave," Hulia said. "There's a basement exit. Hurry."

Kellee scooped Arran over his shoulder, and we made it to the basement in time to hear the door above explode open. Hulia lifted a hatch in the floor.

I remembered another time, just like this one, when she had saved Kesh Lasota, who'd been on the run from Calicto authorities a lifetime ago.

Kellee carried Arran into the tunnel. I dropped down after him and reached up for Hulia.

"I did this," she said, her eyes remorseful. She glanced behind her.

"No, Hulia, don't go back. They'll take you too."

When she looked down, her face had hardened with determination. "I can't leave these people alone at their mercy."

I should have been the one saving them. I was their Messenger, wasn't I? But I didn't see how we could survive hundreds of fae, and if their ship was a warcruiser, we didn't stand a chance. But Hulia was surrendering.

"This isn't the time to take a stand," Kellee said from behind me. "We run today and fight tomorrow."

He was right, but it didn't change the fact that I should be taking Hulia's place. Wasn't that what good people did?

"I'll be all right." She smiled for my benefit. "I'm namu. There's nothing they can do to me that they haven't already done." She began lowering the hatch.

"Wait—"

"Go, friend." Her eyes flashed. "I'll see you again soon."

The hatch closed, shutting her and the rest of the colony away and plunging me and Kellee into darkness. Kellee's warm hand found mine, and he led me into the dark.

The tunnel twisted and turned, eventually spitting us out high up on a hillside a long way from the huddled colony buildings. A hot wind, spiced with magic, blasted over us the second we stepped outside. We hunkered down behind a mound of rocks, shielded from sight. Above the colony, a fae warship hung low in the churning sky. Colored light flashed along its undercarriage, washing the entire area in an eerie green hue.

Kellee propped Arran up against a boulder and peered into the saru's unseeing eyes. "Benrin's Spite."

I'd heard of it. It was among the fae's many magical poisons, used to steal their victim's will.

"He should come around soon." Kellee shifted position and crouched beside me. The greenish light from the ship reflected in his eyes as he scanned the scene below.

My attention lingered on Arran. When he came around, would he demand to go back down there? Aeon's fight had been taken out of him, but Arran had a reckless wildness, like he thought he had something to prove. He wouldn't react well to us abandoning the colony. I'd deal with it once he was awake. Or Kellee would. Arran didn't dare cross the lawman.

"There's some activity," Kellee said.

A flight of soldiers had formed a line leading from the ship's ramp to the building we had been dancing in. How quickly things changed.

A single fae marched toward the colony building where a string of people had started filing out one by one like mindless puppets.

Kellee crouched lower. "Sidhe lord," he said.

Sidhe was a collective name the higher families gave to themselves, separating them from the fae riffraff and granting them godlike status among fae-kind. Most made up the court, but others kept out of courtly politics. Some vanished altogether. Either way, the only time I'd known one to leave Faerie was Mab when she'd forged the now-dissolved human treaty thousands of years ago.

I squinted into the wind to get a clear view of the lord.

"Can you describe him?" Kellee's eyesight was better than mine in low light.

"Red hair. He's wearing dark earth-colored clothing."

"Autumnlands." Unlike winterlands, they weren't quick to anger and didn't make rash decisions. Their strength and determination made them excellent allies and devastating foes. I only knew of a handful who regularly attended Mab's court. Most stayed away from the ruling families.

"I don't see any markings, but he's well covered beneath a hood. He's armed." Kellee's eyes narrowed. "With... steel?"

Only four fae were permitted metal weapons at court: the guardians.

Kellee must have caught the hitch in my breath. He glanced my way, suspicion knotting his brow. "You know him?"

I tried to get a better look, but all I saw was a tall fae dressed in dark clothing. "Not all fae are averse to metal. To tek, yes. But some wield forged steel. I know of only four who do, and all are Oberon's personal guards." In antiquity, the guardians had been in service to the queen, but Oberon had made them his long before my birth. It was one of the reasons Mab had agreed to let me stand beside her when Oberon so kindly suggested I become her guardian. She had argued that a true Faerie queen should not need a personal guard, but she'd taken me on, to humor her son.

"A royal guardian? What, by-cyn, is he doing out here?" Kellee asked.

"If he is a guardian, he's not here for the people."

"He's here for us."

316

EXCERPT ~ THE NIGHTSHADE'S TOUCH

More specifically, me. It was no mistake that Oberon had sent that particular guardian here. The red hair, the sword —he had to be Sirius. Sirius and I had a... history.

I might have looked away if Hulia hadn't walked out of the colony building with enough sass in her stride to have the flight of soldiers uncomfortably shifting their aims.

Kellee mumbled, "They'll kill her," followed by, "Where the fuck is Talen?"

They wouldn't kill Hulia. Namu were sought after. She had worth. They would make her sing, and dance, and love. Some of the best namu were priceless possessions. My gut told me Hulia was one of those.

She strode up to Sirius, so much smaller than him but carrying enough confidence that she looked as though she was the one in control. Maybe she didn't know who he was because, had she known, she would have dropped to her knees. Instead, they seemed to be having a conversation, though they could equally be just staring at each other. I couldn't tell from this distance, but Kellee watched them keenly, either reading their lips or listening. While they faced off, the colonists shuffled up the ramp and out of sight.

"She's insane," Kellee murmured.

I was about to ask why, when Sirius's hand shot out and clamped around Hulia's neck. The guardian lifted the namu clean off her feet. She kicked uselessly at the air.

Kellee's warning growl sparked my internal rage. Not long ago, I wouldn't have cared. I would have blamed her for speaking out, for defying them, but things were different. I was different. Hulia had only ever tried to help people. The Boot had been a sanctuary in a part of Halow all but forgotten by the rest of the system. But more than that, she was my friend, and I'd learned there were few things worth more than friendship in these dark days.

All I had to do was walk down there and trade myself in for her. Maybe, if I did that, they would all be safe. The people too. And I saved people now. I was the Messenger.

"Don't."

I ignored Kellee and gripped the rock, ready to push to my feet.

"Kesh."

"I have to."

Sirius threw Hulia to the ground.

I shot to my feet but somehow got turned around, and before I could right myself, I had my back against the rock and all of Marshal Kellee in my face. "Use your sense. I know you have some. You can't save her."

He had his hand fisted in my coat, pinning me down. I grabbed his wrist and tried to shove him back, but it was like pushing against a wall. "Get your hands off me, Marshal."

Frustration flashed in Kellee's green eyes. "This is exactly what he wants. He knows Hulia's connected to us. He probably knows we're watching. He wants you to do something stupid, exactly like this. Stop being their tool and think for yourself."

His words stung. "I'm not their tool."

"Prove it." He shoved off me and went back to watching over the rock.

I twisted and saw the flick of Sirius's cloak as he disappeared inside the warship. Hulia was nowhere in sight. The people had all filed inside, and now the flights were spreading out, investigating the abandoned buildings. My chance to do something, anything, had passed. The fae had captured the colony and Hulia, and I'd watched it happen.

"That anger you feel," Kellee said, "shape it into a weapon worthy of the people's Messenger."

My insides squirmed like the time I'd been caught pickpocketing a fae lord. I'd been whipped for that. But here, now, Hulia had paid the price.

Kellee had to be right. Every. Damn. Time. Part of me hated him for that, but a larger part of me reluctantly thanked the know-it-all marshal for stopping me from rushing in with no real plan—besides throwing myself at their mercy like a martyr.

"We can't stay here." He scooped up Arran and plunged into the brush.

I lingered a few moments, watching the fae pour through the colony, in search of stragglers and us. I was getting Hulia back. I would save those people. And Sirius would feel the bite of my whip. Because Kellee was right. I was the people's Messenger. And this was war.

The Nightshade's Touch, coming Summer 2018. Sign up to Pippa's mailing list for al the news and release dates direct to your inbox.

Add to Goodreads here.

Serpent's Game (#5)

Edge of Forever (#6)

The 1000 Revolution

#1: Betrayal

#2: Escape

#3: Trapped

#4: Trust

New Adult Urban Fantasy

City Of Fae, London Fae #1

City of Shadows, London Fae #2

Printed in Poland
by Amazon Fulfillment
Poland Sp. z o.o., Wrocław

50572800R00193